Praise for the
New York Times Bestseller

Love, Honor, and Betray

"Lively, action-packed, and full of sassy sensuality...
Roby once again has created a story that grabs the reader's attention and holds it in her grip until the very end."
—*Las Vegas Review Journal*

"Lawdy, lawdy, lawdy! You need a scorecard to keep up
with all the infidelities and drama...This is a book that
should not be missed. One can only wonder: What will
Roby come up with next?"   —*Philly.com*

"Like her previous fiction, LOVE, HONOR, AND BETRAY
provides an unflinching examination of the human condition while keeping the reader engaged and entertained at
the same time."   —*Examiner.com*

"Much of Kimberla Lawson Roby's bestselling success
is due to her irresistibly complex character Rev. Curtis
Black. In LOVE, HONOR, AND BETRAY, her fifteenth
book and eighth about the self-justifying, greedy, womanizing minister, she tackles one of the most challenging
situations facing the explosion of blended families today."
—*Heart & Soul*

"Full of drama and splashed with plenty of suspense and
love triangles."   —*Upscale*

"An entertaining read and remains true to Roby's style of
creatively telling a story."   —*New York Amsterdam News*

Love, Honor, and Betray

Kimberla Lawson Roby

GRAND CENTRAL
PUBLISHING

NEW YORK   BOSTON

Copyright © 2011 by Kimberla Lawson Roby
Excerpt from *The Prodigal Son* copyright © 2014 by Kimberla Lawson Roby

Grand Central Publishing
Hachette Book Group
237 Park Avenue
New York, NY 10017
www.HachetteBookGroup.com

Grand Central Publishing is a division of Hachette Book Group, Inc.
The Grand Central Publishing name and logo is a trademark of Hachette Book Group, Inc.

The Hachette Speakers Bureau provides a wide range of authors for speaking events. To find out more, go to www.hachettespeakersbureau.com or call (866) 376-6591.

The publisher is not responsible for websites (or their content) that are not owned by the publisher.

Printed in the United States of America

Originally published in hardcover by Hachette Book Group
First mass market edition: April 2014

10 9 8 7 6 5 4 3 2 1
OPM

For my dearest, Will.
Thank you for twenty fabulous years of marriage.
You are the absolute best husband and have always been
such a tremendous blessing in my life.
I love you with all my heart, and I certainly
look forward to another twenty years and beyond.

Acknowledgments

As always, I thank God for guiding my direction and for protecting my family, friends, and me every day of our lives. Without You and Your countless blessings, nothing would be possible.

To the man I love with all my heart and all my soul: Will Roby, Jr. Thank you for absolutely everything and, of course, for just being you.

To my wonderful and very loving family: my brothers, Willie, Jr., and Michael Stapleton; my mother-in-law, Lillie; my stepson and daughter-in-law, Trenod and LaTasha Vines; my step-grandsons, Lamont, Trenod, Jr., and Troy; my brothers-in-law and sisters-in-law, and all my aunts, uncles, and cousins. I love all of you so very much and thank you for always supporting me.

To the women who genuinely love me like a sister and who have encouraged me to do what I do as a writer for over fifteen years: Kelli, Lori, and Janell. I wish everyone on earth knew what it was like to have friends like each of you.

Then, to the best literary agent ever, Elaine Koster (1940–2010). You took me completely under your wing, you took such great care of my career and represented me for twelve fabulous years, and I still can't believe you are gone. You were such an amazing friend and confidante, and Will and I will never forget all the wonderful times we shared with you and Bill whenever we visited New York. We had such great times, and I will love you and miss you always, Elaine.

To Dr. Betty Price at Crenshaw Christian Center—there are no words fitting enough to describe how kind, caring, and encouraging you are, so I'll just say thank you for everything, and that I love you so, so much.

To my brand-new publishing family, Grand Central Publishing! Words cannot express how excited I am and how grateful I am to have joined such a warm and very talented group of people. So, from the bottom of my heart, thank you, thank you, thank you, Karen Thomas (my editor), Jamie Raab (my publisher), Deb Futter (my editor-in-chief), Emi Battaglia (my associate publisher), Linda Duggins (my publicity director), Elizabeth Connor (my art director), Latoya C. Smith (assistant editor and Karen's assistant), Dorothea Halliday (my production editor), the entire sales force and marketing team, and everyone else at Hachette/GCP.

Then, to the most efficient and kindest assistant I know, my assistant, Connie Dettman; the most efficient and kindest freelance publicist I know, Shandra Hill Smith; and the most efficient and kindest website and e-blast designer I know, Luke LeFevre. Thank you for all your amazing talent and for doing all that you can to make things run as smoothly and competently as possible.

To Janet Salter and Jaymee Robinson for working around my sporadic schedule and to Scinetra Martin in Florida for all your encouragement and support!

To all my wonderful writer friends, including Patricia Haley (my cousin), Victoria Christopher Murray, Eric Jerome Dickey, Trisha R. Thomas, Eric Pete, Mary B. Morrison, Curtis Bunn, Trice Hickman, ReShonda Tate-Billingsley, and so many others.

To all the book clubs that choose my work as their monthly selection year after year and to all the wonderful bookstores and libraries that carry it. I will always be indebted.

To all the local, regional, and national media folks and outlets, including newspapers, magazines, TV, and radio, who promote my work to the masses. It certainly means everything.

Last but most important, to the people who make my writing career possible: my fabulous and very dedicated readers. Your loyal support over the years has made all the difference for me as a writer, and I will forever love and appreciate all of you.

Much love and God bless you always,
Kimberla Lawson Roby

Love, Honor, and Betray

Prologue

The verdict had sort of been in for months now. But at this very moment, Charlotte's feelings were crystal clear: She hated Curtina. She despised this tiny, little two-year-old with a passion and wanted her out. She wanted her gone because it wasn't fair that Charlotte had to stomach Curtis's illegitimate daughter on a daily basis. Curtina was there all the time, what with her tramp of a mother going in and out of the hospital on the regular. Of course, it was true that Tabitha had been stricken with the AIDS virus and hadn't been able to care for Curtina the way any mother would want, but that wasn't Charlotte's fault. As a matter of fact, it was Tabitha's *own* fault a thousand times over, thanks to all the whoring around she'd done.

But since today was Christmas and Curtis and Matthew were so elated to have Curtina there with them, Charlotte was going to plaster on the best fake smile she could and pretend to be happy. She would act as though she loved Curtina and was overjoyed about being her stepmother. She would do this even though she couldn't stand that little heifer.

"Wow, Dad, thank you!" Matthew yelled out when he

opened yet another one of his gifts and then went over and hugged his father. Then, he reached down, all six foot two inches of him, and hugged Charlotte. "This is exactly what I wanted, so thank you, too, Mom. And just wait until Elijah and Jonathan hear about this!" He was already pulling out his iPhone to text his two childhood best friends.

Charlotte looked at Curtis and they both smiled. Of all the presents they'd gotten Matthew, they knew this two-thousand-dollar gift card would be the one he loved most, since he would now be able to purchase that set of chrome rims he'd been begging for over the last three months. Never mind that a perfectly nice set of rims had come standard with the brand-new ragtop BMW they'd bought him shortly after he'd finished driver's school, Matthew had still decided he wanted something different. But since he continued getting straight A's at the college preparatory school he'd attended for years now, and as a junior he had already aced both the ACT and SAT exams in the fall, they didn't see why he shouldn't have the one thing he wanted most. It was also hard to deprive any child who'd already received early interest from Harvard.

"We thought you'd be pretty excited," Charlotte told him.

"Excited isn't even the word," he said, keying in the last of his message. "I'm ecstatic and thrilled out of my mind."

Curtis laughed. "We're glad, son. You're a good kid, and you deserve it."

"So, can we go get them tomorrow?" Matthew asked his dad.

"Yeah, I suppose we could. Although, I have to say,

that day-after-Christmas shopping traffic is going to be a monster."

"Maybe, but I doubt the auto shops are going to be crowded," Matthew said.

"I doubt it, too. So yes, we'll head there first thing in the morning."

Matthew smiled and then scooped up his baby sister, who squealed with total joy, the same as she always did whenever her big brother gave her his undivided attention.

It was enough to make Charlotte ill. She hated the fact that Matthew loved Curtina as much as he did, and what she loathed even more was the brightness she saw in Curtis's eyes as he watched both of his children. He seemed so relieved and so at peace seeing them together and living as what appeared to be the perfect American family. But what he didn't know was that Charlotte hoped, wished, and prayed every chance she got that Tabitha would be healed. She prayed that, if nothing else, Tabitha would live at least for the next sixteen years, so she could raise her own child and keep primary custody of her until she graduated high school. Charlotte wanted this so desperately that she asked God for this very thing every night before going to bed and then again each morning as soon as she woke up. It was the first thought in her mind, once she opened her eyes and realized her nightmare was reality.

But no matter how much she prayed, for some reason God just didn't seem to be hearing her because instead of Curtina spending less time in their household, her visits had only become more frequent. So much so that she was making Charlotte's life unbearable. This little girl that Curtis loved with his entire being was ruining the wonderful life Charlotte had worked so hard to create for herself and Matthew. Curtina was destroying everything, but Charlotte could tell Curtis had no idea how strongly she felt about this. Not to mention, she did feel somewhat guilty—not much, but somewhat guilty—about once having an affair herself and then having a child by her lover. Needless to say, this was the real reason Charlotte couldn't be as verbally outraged as she wanted to be when it came to Curtina and the reason she had at least *tried* to love her and forget that she was a product of Curtis's extramarital philandering. But the truth was, she couldn't forget. She didn't want to, and instead she longed for the opportunity to speak her mind, loudly and forcefully. However, she knew Curtis would quickly remind her of her own sins. He would toss all her past mistakes right back in her face, and she wouldn't have any ground to stand on.

Charlotte lifted a cup of the hot cinnamon apple tea she'd made earlier, sipped some of it, and admired the beautiful twelve-foot Christmas tree. It was stunningly adorned with velvet bows as well as crystal and gold ornaments, and the woman she'd been hiring to decorate for the last two years had completely outdone herself. One year ago, the main color scheme had been purple and white, but this year she'd chosen the traditional red and green and it was fabulous. Even the wreaths layered across the fireplace mantel and those circling all three levels of the staircase couldn't have been more striking, and Charlotte was going to make sure to call Lettie before the day was over to thank her.

Charlotte looked up when she saw Curtis walking toward her with a tiny little turquoise bag swinging from his hand.

"Oh my God," she said, thinking how she'd already opened five other very expensive gifts from him. "You got me something else?"

"That I did," he said, leaning down and kissing her.

Matthew walked over with his little sister in tow. "We both know what that is, don't we, Curtina?"

Curtina clapped her hands, acting as though she fully understood that Charlotte was obviously in for a pleasant surprise.

"Now I'm almost afraid to open it," Charlotte said.

Curtis reached his hand out. "Okay, then, I'll just take it back."

"No," Charlotte said, quickly pulling out the container, unwrapping the white satin bow, and pulling out the jewelry box. When she opened it, her heart skipped a beat, and all she could do was place her hand over her mouth. What she saw was at minimum a six-carat diamond, with the center diamond alone being no less than three carats.

"Wow, Dad, that ring looks even bigger than when we saw it at the store. I mean, talk about bling-bling, Mom."

They all laughed, and Charlotte stood up and hugged her husband. "I don't believe you did this."

"Why not? Because it's not like you don't deserve it, and I just wanted you to know how much I love you and how much I appreciate the way you've supported me and stood by my side, no matter what."

"I love you, too, baby," she said as Curtis slipped the monstrous rock on her finger. Then, the two of them held each other and gazed into each other's eyes. This was by far one of the best moments they'd shared together in recent months, and Charlotte didn't want it to end. She wanted them to be happy and content, and after what

Curtis had just done for her, she was going to work harder on her feelings toward Curtina. She would never accept her, but what she would do is learn to tolerate her more than she had and focus more on the bond she and Curtis shared as man and wife.

After a few minutes passed, Charlotte realized what time it was, and since their housekeeper, Agnes, had the day off to be with her own family, Charlotte went into the kitchen to start breakfast. Thankfully, she didn't have much to do when it came to Christmas dinner because her aunt Emma had invited everyone to her house. Aunt Emma was an extremely wonderful cook, so even Charlotte's parents were driving over from the Chicago area, and Charlotte's best friend, Janine Wilson, and her husband and daughter were joining them as well.

But just as Charlotte opened the refrigerator to pull out a carton of eggs, the phone rang and she walked toward it. She could already see the words Mitchell Memorial displayed on the caller ID screen, and she immediately thought back to the day Curtina had been born and how Tabitha had called Curtis to inform him of it. Charlotte knew this was her calling now, too, and she hoped Tabitha hadn't been admitted, because this would mean she'd had yet another setback and they would have to keep Curtina well beyond the holiday weekend.

Charlotte hesitated but finally answered. "Hello?"

"Charlotte?" Tabitha's best friend, Connie, said in tears.

"Yes?"

"I just wanted to let you know that Tabitha was rushed back to the hospital early this morning...and she's gone. She passed away about a half hour ago."

Charlotte heard what the woman was saying but couldn't respond. She just stood there thinking how she could never love Curtina the way she loved Matthew and how she could never be a mother to her. Then, as more seconds passed, fast and furiously, she thought how none of this drama would be happening if Curtis hadn't slept with that witch, Tabitha, in the first place.

This was all his fault, and she hated him for it. She hated what he was putting her through, and this sprawling mansion they lived in wasn't going to be big enough for both her and Curtina. One of them would clearly have to go, and it wasn't going to be Charlotte.

She decided that Curtis would either get rid of that little brat or find himself in divorce court.

Chapter 1

One Month Later

It was Sunday morning, bright and early, and almost time for Charlotte and Curtis to start getting ready for church. Right now, though, they were lying in bed, snuggling close and reflecting on the beautiful love they'd made last night as well as the steamy hot bath they'd taken together right afterward in their whirlpool tub.

"I wish we could stay in bed all day and skip service altogether," Charlotte commented.

"That would be nice."

"Then, let's do it. Let one of the associate ministers preach today's sermon."

Curtis chuckled. "You're serious, aren't you?"

"Very."

"Maybe another time. And when I've given one of the other ministers ample time to prepare."

Charlotte nestled closer to Curtis and groaned playfully. But right when she did, Curtina burst into their room, climbed on top of the bed, and giggled.

Charlotte moved away from Curtis and got up, wanting

to strangle her. This little girl may have only been two, but she seemed to have a knack for bad timing and always knew how to interrupt what was otherwise an enjoyable moment. There was ten thousand square feet of space— ten whole thousand—for her to walk around in and play in, but she always wanted to stay stuck under her father.

Curtis snatched her up, rocked her back and forth like she was on some amusement park ride, and they both laughed out loud. Charlotte looked on in a despising manner and wished to God someone else could have taken Curtina away from them. But to Charlotte's great disappointment, Curtis had made it clear that Curtina was *his* daughter and *his* responsibility, and her going to live with any of Tabitha's relatives was out of the question. Charlotte had objected profusely, trying to make her case, but Curtis had told her his decision was final. He had also reminded her for the umpteenth time about Marissa, her illegitimate child, and how he'd accepted her with no problem, even though he'd known all along she wasn't his. So Charlotte hadn't had any choice but to go along with Curtis's wishes. Still, though, she wholeheartedly didn't want Curtina there with them, and while one month ago she'd prayed at night and then again in the morning for things to go back to the way they used to be, she now prayed every waking moment—she prayed that only she, Curtis, and Matthew lived in their house and that Curtina had never been born.

"You're the most beautiful girl in the whole world, and Daddy loves you," Curtis told his daughter.

"I love Daddy," she said.

Curtis held Curtina tightly, and Charlotte went into the bathroom and turned on the shower. She had taken all she could, witnessing this pathetic little Kodak moment, and refused to watch any more of it.

When she finished drying off, she put on her robe, opened the bathroom door, and walked back out into the bedroom. Curtina was still sitting in their bed, now watching the Disney Channel, and Curtis stepped out of the walk-in closet when he heard Charlotte strolling past. "Hey, baby, can you do me a favor?" he asked.

"What is it?"

"Get the little one dressed for church?"

Charlotte cringed inside but smiled as genuinely as she knew how. Getting Curtina dressed was the absolute last thing she wanted to do, but she also wanted to keep peace between her and Curtis. The only problem was, she didn't know how much longer she'd be able to continue this façade because ever since Tabitha's funeral, which Charlotte had flat out refused to attend, her disdain toward Curtina had only gotten worse. There were times when she did feel guilty and wished she could feel differently about her, but those particular moments were very rare, and Charlotte couldn't seem to help herself.

"Come on, Curtina," she said in a chipper voice, and they headed down the hallway and into her bedroom. Once there, Curtina rushed toward her play area, but Charlotte became even more disgusted because this room of hers looked as though it had been stolen from the pages of some well-known fairy tale. It was beyond beautiful with all the hot pink, purple, and white accents, and what angered Charlotte the most was that Curtis had even gone as far as hiring a specialist to decorate it. He'd acted as though his precious little Curtina was nothing short of royalty and that she deserved anything and everything his money could buy her. Which was interesting, because had Charlotte been the one making Curtina's decorating decisions, she'd have found her some cheap little cot to sleep on and maybe some small inexpensive dresser to dump her clothes into. She certainly wouldn't have ordered her this classy armoire and canopy set she was looking at. But that was neither here nor there, because Curtis had done what he wanted to and hadn't bothered asking her opinion.

Charlotte searched through the first few items inside Curtina's closet and pulled out a black and white velvet dress and black patent-leather shoes. Then, she went over to her dresser and pulled out a pair of white cotton panties and a pair of white tights. Thankfully, though certainly against her wishes, Charlotte had already given Curtina a bath last night right before Curtis had put her to bed, and she needed to give her only a washup this morning.

When they finished in the bathroom, they came back into the bedroom and Charlotte kneeled onto the floor. "Come here so you can get your underwear on, Curtina," she said. Curtina rushed toward her with open arms and wrapped them around Charlotte's neck.

"I love Mommy," she said and Charlotte wished she'd stop calling her that. She did understand that Curtina was just a small toddler and was only calling her that because this was what she always heard Matthew calling her, but she still didn't like it. Although, since Matthew called her Mom, she wasn't sure why Curtina didn't just stick to that and drop this whole "Mommy" business.

The other thing that unnerved Charlotte was that Curtina was so happy all the time. The first couple of weeks after Tabitha's death, she had spent most of it saying she wanted her *mommy*, but now she was adjusting very well to her new home and seemed to love it. Although, maybe it was because she'd already been spending quite a bit of time there, anyway, over the last year, and nothing was really all that new to her. She was comfortable, didn't ask for Tabitha much at all anymore, and acted as though she belonged where she was.

Curtina held on to Charlotte and wouldn't let go. Then, she started singing the way children tend to sing when they're content and having a good time.

"Just stop it, Curtina!" Charlotte said through gritted teeth, grabbing both of Curtina's arms, moving them away from her and slightly shaking her. "Stop playing, so I can get you dressed and then get you out of my face."

Curtina gazed at her with teary eyes, but thankfully her tears didn't fall, because the last thing Charlotte needed was for Curtis to walk in and see how upset she was. He would have a fit if he knew Charlotte wasn't showing Curtina the kind of love he thought she deserved, and she didn't feel like dealing with that right now. Although the more she thought about the way Curtis had slept with Tabitha behind her back, and had even allowed her to travel with him to many of his speaking engagements, the angrier she got. She was steaming and knew it was only a matter of time before she and Curtis had the blowup of a lifetime. She'd tried her best to avoid it, but she now knew it was inevitable.

Chapter 2

The choir sang its second selection, and Curtis sat at the far side of the pulpit thinking about his household situation. He knew Charlotte was trying to hang in there, but whether she realized it or not, he wasn't oblivious to what she was feeling. She smiled when she was supposed to and laughed when something was funny, but deep down he knew she was miserable. They'd been together for just over ten years now, and if he didn't know anything else, he knew his wife and who she was. He knew she wanted Curtina out of their lives for good.

Only thing was, though, sending Curtina away wasn't an option, and he wished there was some way Charlotte could learn to love her. He wished she could let bygones be bygones, and that she would soon accept Curtina as her daughter. Curtis had been praying for exactly that for more than a year but even more so over the last month since Tabitha's passing. Part of him understood why Charlotte wasn't happy about them taking full custody of Curtina, but part of him didn't because there was no denying that Charlotte had slept with his best friend, Aaron Malone, conceived a child with him, and then tried to pass her off as Curtis's. She'd lied and schemed, and while Curtis had learned the truth about Marissa's paternity, shortly after she was born, he'd never said a word to Charlotte. Charlotte had allowed a terrible thing to happen, and though Curtis had sometimes played this humiliating scenario over and over in his head, more often than Charlotte realized, he'd still forgiven her and continued loving her with all his heart. The reason: he always thought about his own previous misgivings and outside affairs, and that always humbled him. He thought about all the women he'd bedded, not to mention all the pain he'd caused his two eldest children, Alicia and Matthew. Even worse, he thought about the fact that he hadn't actually met Matthew, his own biological son, for the first time or become a father to him until Matthew was seven—partly because Matthew had been conceived while Curtis had still been married to his first wife, Tanya (Alicia's mother), and partly because Charlotte's father had demanded that Curtis stay away from his daughter and grandson or else. Yes, Curtis thought about all that and so much more, but as far as he was concerned, he'd done his thing, Charlotte had clearly done hers, and it was high time for both of them to move beyond it.

Curtis listened as the choir continued singing and scanned the audience. Every seat had been taken, and the folding chairs that had been placed throughout the vestibule and down the center aisle were also occupied. God had truly blessed Deliverance Outreach and Curtis's overall ministry. When Curtis had first started out as a new pastor down in Atlanta, he'd only had maybe three hundred members. Then he'd taken a position at Faith Missionary Baptist Church in Chicago, which had a membership of three thousand. After that, he'd become the

pastor of Truth Missionary Baptist Church, and they'd
had a large membership, too. But after being ousted from
both the latter two congregations, Curtis had made the
decision to found his own church out here in Mitchell, a
smaller city about ninety miles northwest of Chicago. He
and Charlotte had worked diligently toward gaining the
trust of every Mitchellite they could, and from the looks
of the crowd they had clearly succeeded. They had a huge
following, and once they moved into a larger facility, Curtis had no doubt their membership would grow tenfold.
He knew this because folks regularly came up to him in
public, saying how they just couldn't deal with struggling
to find a parking spot and then fighting to get a seat inside
the sanctuary. But then they would go on to say how they
couldn't wait for the new building to be completed so they
could finally start attending service, and in some cases,
people couldn't wait to join.

The choir finished singing and took their seats, and
Curtis went to the podium.

"This is the day the Lord hath made, so let us rejoice
and be glad in it."

"Amen," everyone said.

"You know, for the last few minutes, I sat here scanning every single pew and couldn't help but give God a
lot of praise and much thanks. I know we're overcrowded,
and that it's not the most comfortable situation for any of
us to be in, but if you can just hold on for another four
months, we'll finally be moving into the new building
Memorial Day weekend."

Applause echoed from every direction, and Curtis
smiled.

"It's been a long journey, but one I believe has been

very well worth traveling. As a congregation, we've had a number of ups and downs, mainly because of some very selfish mistakes I made in my personal life, so I just want you to know how much I love and appreciate all of you. I want you to know how indebted I am to each of you for remaining by my side and not giving up on me."

There was more applause.

"I also want to remind everyone about the business meeting two days from now, as we'll be giving an update on the final stages of the building process. We'll share what our overall sanctuary capacity will be, which thankfully is a bit more than we'd originally talked about, and we'll also discuss a few surprises and answer any questions you might have. Elder Jamison has put together a wonderful agenda, so I hope you will all plan on being here."

"What surprises?" he heard a woman say and many other members chattering.

"Oh, did I say 'surprise'?" he said teasingly, and everyone laughed. "Well, since we were planning to tell you on Tuesday anyway, you may as well know that we've added on a full café, an amazing coffee shop, and a Christian bookstore."

The congregation was thrilled and spoke among themselves accordingly, but what saddened Curtis was the nonchalant look on his wife's face. She looked as though she couldn't care less about the news he'd just announced, or anything else for that matter, and now Curtis knew it was time—time they had a heart-to-heart conversation about Curtina. Time they got everything completely out in the open and dealt with this troubling dilemma. It was time they both stopped pretending that all was well inside the Black family household—when it clearly wasn't.

Chapter 3

As soon as they'd left the church, they'd driven straight over to Aunt Emma's to have Sunday dinner, but now they were home and Charlotte was stuffed. Aunt Emma, of course, had done her usual and cooked way too much food, but everything had tasted wonderful. The corn bread and turkey dressing, candied yams, green beans, macaroni and cheese, and a to-die-for banana pudding.

"See you later, Mom," Matthew said, rushing into the bedroom and kissing her good-bye, the same as he did every Sunday afternoon. "See you later, Dad," he said, bumping fists with him. "I'm out."

"You be careful, Matt," Charlotte said. "Because you know how nervous you make me whenever you're out driving around."

"Aw, Mom. I'm not a baby, and I'm only going over to Elijah's."

"Still, you be safe out there. And absolutely no texting when you're behind the wheel."

"Listen to your mother," Curtis said, smiling, and Charlotte knew it was because he thought she was a bit too overprotective. He did agree with her about the "no texting" policy, but he was a lot more lax about every-thing else. He didn't worry nearly as much as she did, but he was a man and couldn't be expected to.

"I hear you, Mom, and I will," Matthew yelled from downstairs.

"He'll be fine," Curtis said.

"I know, but it's just that he's my baby, and teenagers never take enough precautions. He's a good driver, but I still worry about him."

Charlotte unbuttoned the jacket to her gold-buttoned knit suit and slipped off her skirt. Then, she removed her pantyhose and put on a velour sweat suit. When she'd taken her church clothing inside the closet, she came back into the bedroom, preparing to go down to the family room, but Curtis stopped her.

"Hey, we need to talk. We need to do it today, and that's why I asked Aunt Emma if she could keep Curtina for a couple of hours."

Charlotte wasn't sure what this was about exactly, but she sat down on the side of the bed. Curtis sat down next to her.

"First of all, I know you're still not happy about Cur-tina having to move in with us, and I'm really sorry about that. So what I want to know is how I can make things better for you. All you have to do is tell me, and I'll do whatever I can."

At first Charlotte just looked at him, debating what she should or shouldn't say, but then she said, "I didn't ask for this, Curtis."

"Baby, I know you didn't, and I will never be able to apologize to you enough. But at the same time, I can't turn my back on my daughter."

"But it's not like Curtina didn't have anywhere else to go, because both Tabitha's sister and one of her cousins each offered to take her. And I didn't see what was so wrong with that. Especially since you'd still be able to visit her whenever you want."

"But it's like I told you before, giving her to someone else isn't an option, because I'm Curtina's father, and she needs me."

Charlotte locked eyes with Curtis but didn't say anything. So he continued:

"You know, part of the problem is that you still haven't forgiven me."

"Yes, I have."

"No. You haven't. Because if you had you wouldn't still feel so much animosity about all of this."

"I can't help all the anger I keep feeling, and I have to be honest with you—I don't know that I will ever feel any different."

"Maybe if you could just be a little more open, things would get better. Plus, I know you can tell how much Curtina loves you."

This time, Charlotte looked away from him.

However, Curtis gently turned her face back toward him. "Baby, I'll never be able to say this enough times, but I'm so, so sorry for having that affair with Tabitha. I'm more sorry than you could possibly ever imagine, and there's not a day that goes by that I don't think about the horrible mistake I made."

Charlotte heard all that he was trying to say, but for some reason his apologies were starting to piss her off.

"Baby, you have to believe me when I say how bad I feel about what happened, but more than anything, I need you to know that I never stopped loving you, and that you mean everything to me. I love you so much that my heart is literally aching right now, even as I sit here next to you."

Charlotte stood abruptly, rage overtaking her. "Look, Curtis, I've tried to be nice and quiet about all of this, but enough is enough. I don't want to be a mother to Curtina," she yelled. "I never did, and I never will. And you had no right moving her in here when you knew I didn't want that."

"But I didn't have a choice."

"Of course you had a choice. But you chose to do what you wanted to. You slept with that trick, and you never even cared how it would affect me one way or another."

"So what you're saying is that you've not made any mistakes? Because you and I both know that you haven't been some perfect little angel yourself. And another thing. How would you have felt had I totally disowned Marissa and then told you she couldn't live with us?"

"What? Curtis, please! I am so tired of you bringing up that same old tired crap. I'm tired because Marissa is completely beside the point. That's all in the past, and she's dead. She's dead and gone forever, Curtis," Charlotte screamed. "And I wish you would stop trying to compare my little girl to yours."

"I can't believe you. I can't believe all your double standards."

"What double standards?"

"You know exactly what I mean. You thought it was okay to sleep around and get pregnant by some lunatic, but when the tables turned, you decided you had a huge problem with it. You wanted me to forgive you and accept a child that wasn't mine, but now you want nothing to do with Curtina."

"That's different."

Curtis frowned. "Different how?"

"Just different."

"No, it's not. It's exactly the same and you know it."

"What I know is that when we got married, we took sacred vows and promised to keep each other first. And right now, with this whole Curtina business, you're not doing that."

Curtis laughed out loud. "Funny how you so conveniently forgot those *sacred vows* the whole time you were whoring around with Aaron."

Charlotte wanted to slap the mess out of Curtis. He was making her sound like a common tramp, and now it was time she put an end to this conversation.

"You know what, Curtis, the bottom line is this: I want Curtina out of here."

Curtis raised his eyebrows, clearly stunned by her words. "Oh yeah? Well, let me make myself clear. Curtina isn't going anywhere, and you might as well get used to it."

Charlotte looked shocked. "So then, what you're saying is that this little girl is more important than I am? More important than your own wife?"

"No. What I'm saying is that Curtina isn't going anywhere, and you might as well get used to it."

Charlotte laughed, her tone sarcastic. "Well, then, if that's the case, you'd better start looking for a nanny as soon as possible, because I'm done playing mommy to your mistress's daughter."

"You mean *my* daughter."

"Fine. Then, I'm done playing mommy to *your* daughter," she said and left the room.

Chapter 4

*C*harlotte drove out of the driveway as fast as she could and then out of the subdivision. She needed to get away from Curtis before she did something bad to him...or to Curtina the next time she saw her. Charlotte was so incensed over the way he'd spoken to her, and the idea that Curtina "wasn't going anywhere" was enough to make her consider murdering somebody. She hated this insane situation she was in and would now have to think long and hard about her next move. Curtis seemed so set on his decision, and this was what bothered her the most. In the past, he'd always made things right and gone out of his way to make her happy, but not with this. No, with this whole Curtina drama, he was acting like some crazy man she didn't even know.

Charlotte drove a few more miles and then turned into Janine's driveway. She'd phoned her right before leaving and since Janine's husband, Carl, had gone to visit his brother, she'd told Janine she really needed to come talk to her.

She parked, turned off the ignition, and stepped outside her vehicle, then closed the door, and strolled up the walkway. She rang the doorbell, watched the beautiful wooden door open, and then burst into tears.

"Sweetie, oh my goodness," Janine said, pulling her inside and hugging her. "What's wrong?"

"Everything." Charlotte sobbed. "Just everything."

"Honey, let's go sit down," Janine said and then she went into the powder room. Charlotte took a seat on the family room sofa. When Janine returned with a few pieces of tissue, she sat down next to her.

"Thanks, girl," Charlotte said. "And I'm so sorry for coming over here like this."

"No need to apologize at all. I'm glad you called me."

"I hate burdening you with my problems, but I really needed to talk to someone. I really have to figure out what to do about this."

"Well, what is it exactly?"

Charlotte wiped more tears and sniffled. "It's Curtina."

"Is she okay?"

"Huh!" Charlotte said, suddenly no longer feeling quite as sad or like she wanted to cry. "That little brat couldn't be better."

Janine looked at Charlotte, and Charlotte could tell how taken aback she was. She was astonished to hear Charlotte speaking so negatively about her stepdaughter.

"J, I just can't do this anymore. I can't pretend like I love that child when I hate the ground she walks on. I hate the fact that she was ever born, I hate that ugly name her mother gave her, I hate everything about her."

Janine looked baffled.

"I know this all comes as a surprise, but, J, I have felt like this from day one. And it's never gotten better."

"Gosh, girl. I guess I don't even know what to say."

"I'm sure. Especially since I led you and everyone else around me to believe that I was fine with Curtina. But the only reason I did that was because I knew if I didn't pretend to be okay with her, it would cause serious problems between Curtis and me. And I didn't want that."

"I'm so sorry" was all Janine said.

"Not more than I am. And what I can't get over is the fact that Curtis is choosing that child over me. He told me she's not going anywhere, and I'm so disappointed in him."

"Maybe you just need more time."

"No, I've had all the time I need. She's been around for a little over two years now, and if anything, I dislike her more than ever. So what I need Curtis to do is wake up. What I need is for him to realize that we will never be happy again until this issue is resolved."

Janine sighed.

"And I'll tell you something else, J. I'm so tired of having all these problems with Curtis. I mean, every time we try and work past one thing, there's always the next thing staring us straight in our faces. And I just don't want to keep living like that. We've now been together for ten years, but very few of those years have been completely happy and peaceful. I know I've caused some of our problems, too, but this thing with Curtina is the worst because Curtis has basically told me to take it or leave it. And he's not backing down."

"Regardless, I still believe you guys can work this out. Especially since I know how much Curtis really loves you and how much you really love him. And that's what's important."

"That's what used to be important, but now I'm not so sure."

"Maybe as more time passes, you won't feel so betrayed and upset about this."

"No, I'll never be okay with having that child around me. And while there was a time when I thought maybe I had forgiven Curtis, now I know for sure that I haven't. I can't forgive him because Curtina is a constant, daily reminder of Tabitha and the affair Curtis had with her."

Janine rested both her hands on top of Charlotte's. "I just hate hearing this, girl. I hate seeing you so upset."

"I hate it, too, but it is what it is." Charlotte took a deep breath. "But enough about me and my craziness. What's going on with you? And where's my precious little Bethany?" Bethany was Charlotte and Curtis's baby goddaughter, who was now approaching her first birthday.

"She's fine and sleeping away. You wanna look in on her?"

"Yes, definitely," she said, and they both started toward the stairway.

Janine and Carl's home was breathtaking. Very few people knew how to put together furniture and accessories the way Janine did. The dining room was elegant and spacious, and the living room was just as lovely. Charlotte had always admired how beautifully decorated all four bedrooms were, too, which they were now passing on the upper level. When they arrived in front of Bethany's nursery, Janine eased open the door and they tiptoed in.

Charlotte smiled at how gorgeous and innocent her goddaughter looked. Bethany was a pure doll, and with all that Charlotte was going through and with as much as she missed her little Marissa, she wanted to scoop Bethany up and take her home with her. She wanted to keep her for days, weeks, and possibly even months, just so some of her pain would go away. She wanted her own little girl to love, nurture, and care for. So, actually, maybe that was it. Maybe it was time she considered the idea of getting pregnant again.

After Charlotte leaned into the crib and kissed Bethany on the cheek, she and Janine went back downstairs.

"Can I get you something?" Janine asked.

"No, I'm fine. We ate over at Aunt Emma's," Charlotte said, sitting back down.

"We went out because Carl is sort of on this new trip about me doing too much around the house and not taking out enough time for myself."

"You are so lucky to have a man like Carl. Someone who loves and respects you and who always seems to put your needs before his."

"Carl really is wonderful, and I thank God for him all the time, but so is Curtis. I know the two of you have been through a lot, but you do mean the world to Curtis. That much I'm sure of."

"I used to think that, too, but now I really don't know."

"What you guys need is a nice long weekend away at some resort. Some time with just the two of you."

"Maybe."

"You do."

"We'll see," Charlotte said, feeling somewhat better than she had earlier, although it was mostly because she hadn't stopped thinking about Bethany and how having her own baby might be the answer to saving her marriage. She was only in her thirties and certainly still young enough to conceive and bear a child, so her mind was made up. She would tell Curtis what she wanted, he would quickly agree, and life would soon be better for them. She wouldn't give up on the idea of trying to get rid of Curtina. No sirree. But at least she'd have something happy to think about in the meantime. She'd be able to focus on something good and positive, and she could pretend Curtina didn't even exist. She'd be able to ignore her even more than she had been.

Chapter 5

So much for big ideas, Charlotte thought as she sat at the kitchen island, watching Agnes serve breakfast to the entire family. She'd hurried back home yesterday evening and told Curtis how much she wanted to have another child but all he'd said was, "Baby, I don't think this would be good for us, because you know you wouldn't be doing this for the right reasons." He'd allowed her to say her piece but had basically dismissed her and went on with the rest of his evening. He'd acted as though this conversation about her possibly getting pregnant hadn't even come up. Which was the reason she hadn't said a word to him since, and as she'd promised herself, she was officially through when it came to doing anything for Curtina. She hadn't gotten her dressed this morning and had barely glanced at her.

"Mommy, Mommy, look," she heard Curtina say but ignored her. "Mommy, Mommy, look."

Charlotte picked up the *Sun-Times*, opened the front section as widely as possible, and Curtis and Matthew continued their small talk.

"So, Dad, you *know* the Saints are going to be the new Super Bowl champs, right?"

"As Mister said in *The Color Purple*, 'Could be, could be not.'"

"Yeah, right. You know they're gonna win. Easily."

"We'll see. And it's not like I have anything against New Orleans anyway, but since the Indy coach is from Beloit, Wisconsin, barely a half hour from here, I gotta go with the Colts. I gotta root for my homeboy."

"Please," Matthew said, cracking up. "You don't even know that man."

"Still, he's from the area, and I believe in supporting all homeboys. Whether I know them or not."

"How sad. And pitiful, too, when you know they're gonna lose."

"Like I said, we'll see."

"We sure will. We'll see those Saints go marching home with that trophy."

Charlotte set down the paper she was reading, but as soon as she did, Curtina started up again. "Mommy, look."

Charlotte still paid her no attention and had no idea what she was trying to show her. To be honest, she didn't care what it was.

"Mom, what's wrong?" Matthew asked, catching Charlotte off guard.

"Nothing, sweetie. I'm fine."

"Then why are you so quiet?"

"No reason. No reason at all."

She could tell Matthew didn't believe her because the next thing he did was look at his sister, who was sitting next to him, and then he said, "Let me see, Curtina." Then he pulled her arm closer to him. "Wow, that's a pretty little bracelet you have on. Now, that's what's up, little girl."

Curtina giggled, and Matthew ran his finger down

her nose. Curtina giggled more, and Charlotte sat there, stone-faced.

"Oh, well, I guess I better get out of here," Matthew said, glancing at the clock on the microwave and picking up Curtina. He kissed her good-bye, kissed Charlotte, and then did his usual fist bumping with his dad.

As he gathered his book bag and keys and headed out to his car, Charlotte yelled, "Be careful, Matt."

When he was gone, Curtis put down the sports section of the newspaper and turned to their housekeeper. "Agnes, if you don't mind, would you please take Curtina upstairs to get her ready? I'm taking her shopping today."

"Of course, Mr. Curtis."

Mondays had always been Curtis's day off, so Charlotte had wondered why he'd gotten dressed so early. This upcoming father-daughter excursion he'd just spoken about explained it.

"So, you wanna go with us?" Curtis asked.

Charlotte looked at him like he was nuts. He must have been out of his ever-loving mind if he thought she was going anywhere with the two of them.

She didn't say anything, though. But seconds later, Curtis got up and walked over to where she was sitting. He smoothed the side of her face with his hand and lifted her chin upward. "I'm sorry that I don't agree with you about having another baby, but no matter what, I do love you. And who knows? Maybe if we can work through our current situation and come to terms with that, we can talk about this again. It's not that I don't want another child. It's just that if we have a baby, I want it to be conceived with love and no heartache."

Charlotte wasn't sure what it was, maybe her hormones,

but suddenly all she could do was close her eyes, cry, and rest her hand on top of Curtis's. He continued caressing her face, and chills eased through her bloodstream. She loved him, too, and thought it interesting how after all the years they'd been together, he still had such a mesmerizing effect on her.

Curtis pulled her up from her chair, and Charlotte opened her teary eyes. She gazed into his and couldn't stop thinking that no matter how much time had passed, Curtis was still the most handsome man she knew. Actually, the more she analyzed his face, she would swear he looked even better than when she'd first met him, if that were even possible.

They stood holding each other, and then Curtis kissed her in a way that told her he did love her, that he still had extreme passion for her, and that he didn't want to be without her.

But from there, things went downhill.

"Look, baby, I know you're unhappy with the idea of Curtina being here and that you're also sad about Marissa being gone. But if you could just try to see that regardless of the mistake I made with Tabitha, Curtina is simply an innocent child. If you could just try to see that maybe Curtina is God's way of replacing Marissa. Maybe Curtina is God's gift to both of us."

Charlotte shoved Curtis away from her. "God's gift? You can't be serious!"

"Okay, baby, maybe that didn't come out right. But you know what I mean. I—"

"I just don't get you, Curtis," she shouted, interrupting him. "I don't get any of this."

"Baby, look, I'm sorry. And why don't you please try to calm down."

"Don't tell me to calm down! Hell, why don't *you* calm down? Or better yet, why don't you tell that little bastard child of yours to calm down?"

Curtis stared at Charlotte in a way she'd never seen him stare before, and she knew she'd gone too far. She would even take it back if she could, but her pride wouldn't let her.

Curtis finally shook his head and then left the kitchen.

When he was out of sight, Charlotte tried settling her nerves and regaining her composure. Things were spiraling steadily out of control, and she was getting scared. She'd been telling herself for a while that she didn't think things would get better, but deep down there had been this part of her that wanted to believe she and Curtis would eventually be fine. Now, she wasn't so sure. They were playing a very dangerous game of tug-of-war, and she didn't see how anyone had a chance at winning it.

Charlotte sat for another twenty minutes, then went upstairs. When she entered their bedroom, she saw Curtis putting on his shoes, though he wouldn't look up at her. So she went into the bathroom and turned on the shower. However, to her surprise, when she came back out, Curtis had already left. She wanted desperately to go find him, but at the same time she was still too angry about that whole Curtina-replacing-Marissa comment he'd made. She could just kill him for being so thoughtless.

Finally, she walked closer to the doorway and heard Curtina singing in her bedroom. This infuriated Charlotte even more, and she wished Curtina's little jovial behind would just shut up. For good.

Charlotte returned to the bathroom, took her shower, and then stepped back out into the bedroom. This time, she looked out of the window and saw Curtis backing his shiny, black SUV out of the garage and the wrought-iron gate closing. As he drove away from the house, Charlotte saw Curtina sitting in her car seat, clapping her hands. Probably to one of those irritating DVDs she loved so much.

Charlotte watched until her husband and stepdaughter drove completely out of the subdivision and knew she had to do something. She still didn't know what exactly, but something. Anything. Anything at all as long as it had to do with eliminating Curtina from their lives. Maybe not literally—although literally doing away with her would solve everything.

Chapter 6

"Mom, things really couldn't be worse between Curtis and me right now," Charlotte told her mother as she curled her legs up on the chaise. She'd browsed the Internet for a while and then decided to call her mom at work.

"Why? What's wrong?"

"Curtina is what's wrong. I can't stand her, Mom, and I want Curtis to send her to live with one of Tabitha's relatives. My husband just won't hear of it, though, and he's acting as if I don't even matter to him anymore."

"Sweetheart, I'm so sorry. I had no idea. And why have you kept this whole thing from me? I mean, I knew when Curtina was born you didn't want Curtis having a relationship with her, but once she started coming around I just assumed you'd accepted her. I thought you and Curtis were very happy now."

"Yeah, I'm sure everybody thinks that. But so much for appearances."

"You do think the two of you can work through this, though, don't you?"

"I don't know because, Mom, I can't deal with being around Curtina every day. It's enough to drive me insane."

"Well, I do have to admit, I can't imagine that you would be happy living with your husband's outside child. I don't think any woman would."

"I know, so I'm not sure why Curtis can't seem to understand that."

"Maybe he'll soon come to his senses and will realize that keeping Curtina isn't good for your marriage."

"I don't think so. Not when he's already said Curtina isn't going anywhere. He loves that child, and she thinks the world of him. As a matter of fact, even Matthew thinks the sun doesn't shine the right way unless it's shining directly on his baby sister. She's got them both wrapped around her little finger, and it's sickening."

"Then, what we're going to have to do is pray over this one. And you should also talk to Curtis again. Get him to see why having Curtina there with all of you isn't a good thing."

"I'll try. But I doubt it'll change his mind because whenever the subject comes up, he always brings up Marissa and yada, yada, yada. He keeps harping on what I did to him."

"I'm sure he does. But you just hang in there. Curtis is a wonderful man who loves you, and in the end, that's what'll count."

"I hope you're right, Mom."

Charlotte chatted with her mother for a few more minutes and then hung up. Soon after, she flipped through channels on their mounted flat-screen but stopped when she heard a show host on TBN talking about forgiveness.

"No matter how much another individual has wronged you or betrayed you, God still wants you to forgive, forget, and move on. He wants you to forgive others the same as He has forgiven you for all your misdeeds," the bearded man explained.

Charlotte wished forgiveness was truly that easy. She wished she could somehow accept Curtina and go on with her life, business as usual. But she couldn't.

She flipped through more channels; however, when she didn't see anything interesting, she decided to change out of her loungewear and take herself to lunch. At first, she considered calling Janine at the university to see if she already had plans, but then realized she just wanted to spend some time alone, enjoying a nice meal. She searched through her closet for an outfit and hoped getting out of the house would make her feel better.

ta ta ta

Charlotte sashayed inside The Tuxon, told the hostess she needed a table for one, and the sixtyish maître d' escorted her into the dining area. As they strolled further along, though, Charlotte thought her eyes were playing tricks on her. Had to be, unless it really was Curtis and Curtina sitting only a few feet away. Charlotte moaned silently and wondered why she couldn't get away from them. Not even at a restaurant.

As they stepped closer, Charlotte knew this was going to make for an awkward situation because while she did love her husband and would have loved nothing more than to make up with him, she wasn't about to sit with him and his daughter. If she could have had things her way, she would speak and pass on by them. But so much for that.

"Hey, baby, I didn't know you were coming here for lunch," Curtis said, smiling. "So, why don't you join us?"

"Mommy!" Curtina sang with excitement. "Yeaaahhhh, Mommy."

Charlotte wanted to vanish. Literally.

"Is that what you'd like to do, ma'am?" the maître d' asked. "Would you like to sit here with your husband and beautiful little daughter?"

"Of course she does," Curtis said.

"That'll be fine," the man said, patting Curtina on the head and then pulling the chair out for Charlotte.

Charlotte gave the man a half smile. "Thank you."

"No problem, and enjoy."

"Baby, I'm really sorry about the argument we had this morning, and I'm really glad to see you."

Charlotte didn't know what to say or how she should have felt, but there was one thing she did know. No matter how hard Curtina kept trying to get her attention, which was what she was trying her best to do at this very moment, Charlotte refused to make eye contact with her.

Curtis picked up his menu. "I was just about to order, but I'll wait until you decide what you want, too."

"I'm really not that hungry anymore."

Curtis slightly frowned, confused. "Then why did you come?"

"Because I wanted to spend some time with just myself."

Curtis didn't comment, but she could tell his feelings were hurt. His eyes conveyed much disappointment.

So they sat in silence until the waitress came to take their orders.

"What can I get for you, ma'am?"

"Actually, my water is fine for now. I may order something later, though," Charlotte said, but she knew she wouldn't.

"For you, sir?"

"I'll have the Chilean sea bass," he said, then looked at Curtina. "And what about you, my beautiful little princess?"

Everything was so hunky-dory with the two of them, and Charlotte was irritated.

"I'll tell you what. She'll have the gourmet cheese pizza."

"She'll love that," the waitress added. "All the kids do."

"Wonderful."

The waitress turned to Charlotte again. "Are you sure I can't get you anything? Maybe an appetizer or a salad?"

"No, I'm good. Really."

As soon as she left the table, Curtis leaned back in his chair. "So, what do you have planned for the rest of the afternoon?"

"I haven't really decided on anything specific."

"Do you wanna go with Curtina and me to the movies? There's some kiddie movie playing, so I figured I would take her."

Charlotte shook her head no, becoming more and more uncomfortable by the minute.

"Mommy, look," Curtina said, but Charlotte looked away from the table. "Mommy, look," she repeated.

Charlotte still ignored her, but she could see Curtis through her peripheral vision, eyeing her and waiting to see if she was planning to say anything. When she didn't, he spoke up.

"Yes, sweetheart, Daddy sees it. You did an amazing job, and Daddy is very proud of you."

"No, want Mommy."

Curtis looked at Charlotte. "Baby, do you hear her talking to you?"

Charlotte finally looked at Curtina, but only quick enough to see the sheet of paper she was holding up, the one she'd been coloring on.

"That's nice, Curtina," she forced herself to say. Thankfully, that seemed to satisfy Curtina, and she went back to drawing. When Charlotte had first sat down, she hadn't even noticed any crayons or a coloring sheet, but it was probably because she'd made it a point not to look in Curtina's direction.

Charlotte drank more of her water and set the glass back down. There was more awkward silence, but Curtis tried to make conversation with her again.

"So you are planning to be at the business meeting tomorrow night, aren't you?"

"I'm not sure."

"Why not?"

"I don't know. I guess it depends on how I feel."

Curtis didn't say anything else, and before long, the waitress brought out his and Curtina's food. Charlotte looked on as they began eating, for all of thirty seconds, and then said, "I just remembered. I have some errands to run, so I'll see you when you get home."

"Baby, please don't do this," Curtis said.

But she stood up anyway, told him she was sorry, and then made her way to the entrance. She left the building and decided to do something she hadn't done in years— drive over to one of her favorite jazz clubs in Chicago to have a few drinks.

Chapter 7

Interestingly enough, Jazzy's, a quaint little establishment out in Covington Park, one of the South suburbs, still looked exactly the same, and Charlotte was excited. So much so, she couldn't wait to go inside and enjoy herself, and she was glad she'd gone home to change into a very tight-fitting, above-the-knee, sleeveless dress. It was barely above twenty degrees, but since she had on one of the five full-length furs she owned, she didn't feel a thing.

When she turned off the new silver Mercedes Curtis had purchased for her birthday last year, she was sort of hesitant about getting out and going in because she knew Curtis wouldn't approve of her being at a place like this. But then she quickly thought, *Why should I care how Curtis feels when he's made it perfectly clear that my feelings don't mean anything?*

Charlotte locked her doors, headed toward the building, and entered it. She scanned the seating area, spotted a vacant booth, and then removed her coat and took a seat. She was starting to relax already.

"Welcome to Jazzy's," the fifty-something woman said. "What can I get for you?"

"Well, since I'm practically starving, I think I'll have your specialty. The Jazzy Burger, medium, and the homemade fries. But before that, I'll have a glass of Zinfandel."

"Coming right up."

The Jazzy Burger was by far the juiciest burger Charlotte had ever tasted, and to this day she'd never eaten an order of fries that could compare to those they made here. Actually, ever since she'd married Curtis and had begun frequenting mainly upscale restaurants for dinner, she never really got a chance to eat like this very often. She never had much opportunity to eat badly, but tonight was going to be different. Tonight was her night to do whatever she wanted, and she felt relieved.

The jazz band played magnificently, and Charlotte leaned forward onto her elbows and exhaled. It just didn't get much better than this, and until now she'd had no idea how much she missed going out from time to time. She missed having the kind of fun she'd once had pretty regularly before agreeing to marry Curtis.

When her dinner arrived, Charlotte ate and watched all the people who were still coming in, as well as those who were already dancing, eating, and having a great time. She was truly enjoying herself, and this wouldn't be the last time she came here.

The waitress stopped at her table again. "So how was it?"

"Excellent. The best burger ever."

"That it is. Can I get you anything else?"

"Yes. Another glass of wine, please."

Charlotte swayed to the music but looked up when a man at least in his seventies stopped in front of her.

"Good God Almighty. Girl, you look good enough

to eat, and back in my prime I woulda showed you somethin'."

Charlotte couldn't help laughing.

"You think it's funny, but shoot. Back in the day, a woman who looked as good as you coulda had all my money and anything else she wanted. Even now, I feel like gettin' down on the ground and barkin' like a dog. Especially if I thought I had a chance with your fine self."

"I'm very flattered, and thank you for the compliment. But as you can see," she said, flashing her wedding ring, "I'm married."

"I can respect that, and your husband's a lucky man. I'm still disappointed, though."

"Sorry," Charlotte said, smiling.

The man looked her up and down. "Mm, mm, mm. Girl, girl, girl," he said and then walked out of the club.

Charlotte laughed again because it was this kind of thing that made her feel right at home. Years ago, older men had always tried to come at her. She loved older men, which was the reason she'd always been so attracted to Curtis, but not graveyard old. Ten to fifteen years was enough for her.

She drank her second glass of wine, but it wasn't long before another man stopped at her table. This one, though, was maybe in his late forties and looked good.

"So, how are you this evening?" he said.

"I'm well. And you?"

"I'm good. And if you don't mind my saying so, you're absolutely beautiful."

"Why thank you. You're very kind."

"I've been watching you from afar all night, so I figured I'd come see if you wanted to dance."

Charlotte knew she shouldn't, but then she replayed that whole restaurant scene with Curtis and Curtina and then pictured Curtis in bed with Tabitha, and she said yes before she realized it.

The man led her out to the dance floor. However, it wasn't until he took her into his arms that she noticed what kind of song the band was playing. It was a slow one, the kind she should dance to only with her husband. It was too late, though, to do anything about it now, so she followed his steps and relaxed.

That is, until the man whispered in her ear. "You know, I have to say I'm a little shocked to see such a well-known pastor's wife hanging out in a place like this."

Charlotte's stomach churned fiercely. She was stunned.

"I mean, you're bold, and I really like that."

Charlotte was speechless and the most she could do was swallow the huge lump in her throat.

The man pulled slightly back and looked at her. "Oh, come on now. Don't tell me you thought no one would recognize you."

"As a matter of fact, I didn't. I grew up not far from here, but I haven't lived in this area since I was twenty years old and was out on my own."

"Well, I can guarantee you that I'm not the only one who spotted you because I heard two women over at the bar saying they were pretty sure you were Curtis Black's wife."

Charlotte fell silent again.

"But don't feel bad," the man said. "Because as far as I'm concerned, you should be able to go anywhere you please."

"It's not that simple when you're talking about the

church. If this gets back to our congregation, they'll have a field day with it."

The man laughed. "Well, if you want, we could get out of here and go somewhere private."

"No, I don't think so," she said, but what scared her was the idea that she had to think for a few seconds before finally turning him down. Maybe, though, it was the alcohol she'd been drinking.

"Are you sure?"

"I'm positive."

The song ended, and the man walked her back to her booth. "Thanks for the dance."

"You're welcome."

Charlotte leaned her head back, wondered if she'd made a mistake in coming here, and then beckoned for her waitress.

"Having a good time?"

"I really am. And I'll have another glass of wine, too."

"Coming right up."

Charlotte couldn't remember the last time she'd ordered three glasses of anything in one evening, but it felt good. So good that when she remembered what a shambles her life was in and how miserable it had been making her, she took her drinking choice to another level. Zinfandel was nice but soon she ordered a glass of Long Island iced tea and felt like she was on top of the world. She felt a little dizzy, but right now she wouldn't trade this euphoric feeling for anything. She loved it and didn't want it to end.

Another hour passed, and Charlotte decided it was time to head home. She still felt a little light-headed, but not so much that she couldn't drive back to Mitchell. After all, it was only ninety miles, and at this time of night there wouldn't be any traffic to complain about. On the other hand, since she'd been drinking a lot more than normal, maybe it was best to just crash at her parents' house, as they lived maybe ten minutes away. She didn't want them seeing her in an intoxicated state, but she also didn't want to be caught driving under the influence, nor did she want to hurt anyone.

So, yes, spending the night with her parents was a much better idea. Curtis wouldn't be happy about her absence, especially since he had no idea where she was anyway, but he would just have to deal with it. If he couldn't, well, then it was just too bad.

Chapter 8

*C*urtis was completely beside himself. Last night, when it had gotten to be pretty close to midnight, he'd become worried and had begun calling Charlotte's cell phone. He'd called several times. She'd never answered, though, so he'd then called Janine, and Charlotte's aunt Emma. They hadn't heard from her either, so finally, he'd called her parents around three a.m. Her mother, Noreen, had summoned her to the phone, and after the first few words she'd spoken he'd known for sure that she'd been drinking. Not once had he imagined that this issue with Curtina would cause Charlotte to resort to doing such a thing, but now he knew this matter was serious and that she wasn't planning to get over it. Worse, while very short, their conversation hadn't gone very well and Charlotte had hung up without even saying good-bye.

Now, as he sat in his office at the church, he decided to try her again.

"Hello," Noreen answered.

"Hey, how are you? Is Charlotte still there?"

"She is. Let me get her for you."

Curtis waited maybe a minute before Charlotte picked up on another extension.

"Hello?"

"Where were you last night?"

Charlotte sighed loudly, already irritated with him. "I was out."

"Out where?"

"Just out."

"Out drinking?"

"Curtis, please. I'm really not in the mood for all these questions, so if you don't mind, I'm going back to bed."

"Why are you doing this?"

"Doing what?"

"Hanging out and getting drunk?"

"You know what? If I were you, I wouldn't worry about it. What I would do is continue focusing solely on your precious little Curtina the same as you've been doing for weeks now."

"I just don't understand you. I don't get your attitude at all."

"And I don't get yours either."

"Well, let me tell you this," he said. "I'm not about to be okay with you staying out to the wee hours of the morning whenever you feel like it. I won't stand for it, Charlotte, so I suggest you make last night your final night hanging out like some street person."

"Excuse me? Because I just *know* you're not trying to play daddy to me. You can play daddy to that little heifer you call your daughter, but sweetheart, I'm a grown woman. A full-grown woman who will do whatever she pleases whenever she gets ready to."

" 'Heifer'?"

"Well, it's not like I whispered it, so I know you heard me."

"The only heifer I can think of right now is your little ignorant drunk behind."

"Ignorant?"

"Like you just said, it's not like I whispered it, so I know you heard me."

"Jackass," Charlotte said and slammed the phone down.

Curtis pressed the Off button on his phone, leaned back in his leather chair, and rubbed both his hands from the top of his head to his neck. He was so livid with Charlotte, but he was also devastated because reality had finally set in. He wasn't sure how they'd ever be able to work out their differences, especially since there was no way he could ever stop being a father to his daughter and wasn't planning to. He even hated having to leave Curtina this morning when he'd had to come to the church, and he would always be indebted to Aunt Emma for agreeing to keep her. He'd finally explained to Aunt Emma how bad things were between him and Charlotte, and Aunt Emma had told him she would keep Curtina whenever he needed her to. She'd retired a couple of years back and said she was glad to have the company.

Curtis heard a knock at his door and looked up. "Come in."

"Hey, Pastor," Lana, his longtime executive assistant, said. She was also the woman Curtis looked to for motherly advice, as she treated him more like a son than her boss. "Here are the revisions to the agenda that Elder Jamison wanted me to give you. We had one of the other girls make the changes and print all-new copies, so we should be all set for this evening."

"Good. And Lana, if you don't mind, can you shut the door and have a seat for a few minutes?"

"Sure, Pastor." Lana did as he'd asked and then sat in front of Curtis's desk.

"I really need to talk to you about Charlotte." Lana nodded. "Okay."

"Long story short, she hates Curtina and is demanding that I send her to live somewhere else."

"Well, as much as I hate to say it, I'm not surprised."

"Really? Why?"

"Because whenever I see Charlotte and Curtina in the same room, I can always tell Charlotte isn't very happy. Oh, she always does a very good job of pretending, but I've always seen right through it. Although, I'm not sure I thought she hated her. Just disliked her and didn't want her around."

"Well, she does hate her, and she now treats Curtina pretty badly. Even in front of Matthew and me."

"Goodness gracious. So, what are you going to do?"

"I don't know. Because Lana, as much as I love my wife, I'm not going to neglect my daughter. It's bad enough that she's already lost her mother, so sending her elsewhere is simply out of the question."

"I don't blame you. Curtina isn't responsible for the selfish decisions her mother made, and let's be honest— because you know I'm always very honest—she also didn't ask for the selfish decisions you made either. No child asks to come here, but in the end, it is the parents' responsibility to take care of them."

"I agree, and you're right. I've done a lot of wrong throughout the years, but I'll never turn my back on any of my children. I never have, and I'm not going to start now."

"What about counseling? Have you considered that?"

"I have, and actually, I'm going to suggest that to

Charlotte. Because with the exception of God's help, I'm not sure what other chance we have of fixing this."

"I'm really sorry that you're going through this, and of course I'll keep all of you in my prayers."

"I appreciate that, Lana, and thanks so much for listening."

"Anytime. And Pastor, you keep your head up. You do what you know is right, and I'm just going to believe that everything else will take care of itself."

"I'll remember that."

Next, Curtis prepared for a short meeting with his two lead officers, Elder Jamison and Elder Dixon. They now sat in his office discussing the new building.

"It's been a lengthy process, but when I say the new church is going to be out of this world, I really mean that," Elder Jamison said.

"I agree," Curtis added.

"Yeah, it is somethin'," Elder Dixon commented. "One of the nicest churches I've ever seen and certainly the best-lookin' one here in Mitchell."

"And it's so high-tech." Elder Jamison said. "The computer system, media system, and sound system are all top of the line, and we'll be able to do wonders during Sunday morning service. Not to mention when we begin broadcasting."

Curtis smiled. "I think I'm excited about that part the most, and it was all I could do not to mention the radio studio we've included. And I was dying to tell them that we're planning to begin televising one year from now."

"The whole project is such a huge blessin' from God, I tell you," Elder Dixon said. "Just huge."

"That it is," Curtis said. "We have a lot to be thankful for."

Elder Jamison and Elder Dixon continued speaking to each other, and without realizing it Curtis slipped into deep thought. He still couldn't get over Charlotte and the way she was acting. The way she was treating him, the man she claimed to love so much. He also thought about how after all these years he was still reaping every bit of what he had sown. He had been doing the right thing for a few years now and working hard to obey God's Word, but he was still suffering the consequences of his prior actions.

"Pastor?" he finally heard Elder Jamison say. "Pastor, is everything okay?"

"Oh, I'm fine."

"You don't seem fine," Elder Dixon said matter-of-factly. "And boy, after all we've been through with you over the years, I know when somethin' ain't quite right. So, what is it?"

"Nothing I can't handle." Curtis wasn't shocked at how forthcoming Elder Dixon was. He was a good man, and he treated Curtis like a son the same as Lana did, but he didn't have much tact.

"All right now. Don't try to deal with somethin' all by yourself when you've got people around here who care about you."

"I appreciate that, Brother Dixon, but I'm good."

Elder Dixon widened his eyes, clearly not believing a word Curtis was saying, but he left the conversation alone just the same.

"Just know we're here for you, Pastor," Elder Jamison offered.

"I know that, and I depend on it."

There was another knock at the door, and Curtis looked at his watch. "That's probably Raven. She has some information for me," he told the elders and then said, "Come in."

Raven Jones opened the door and entered.

"Hey, Raven," Elder Jamison said.

"Whatchu know good, Miss Finance Lady?" Elder Dixon said, teasing her.

"How are you, Elder Dixon? Elder Jamison?"

"I think that's all we have, anyway," Elder Jamison said to Curtis. "And we'll just see you tonight at the meeting."

"Yep," Elder Dixon said. "See you then."

Both men left the office, and Raven sat where Elder Jamison had been sitting.

"So, were you able to find someone highly recommended but not here in the area?" Curtis asked.

"Yes, an attorney by the name of Richard Cacciatore. He's a founding partner at one of the top downtown law firms, and he's one of the best in the business when it comes to wills, probate, and estate planning." She passed him a sheet with Richard's contact information on it.

"Good."

Curtis hadn't wanted anyone to know he was looking for a new lawyer, and it was the reason he hadn't told Raven, his CFO, why he wanted the information nor why he needed her to keep his request confidential. It was also the reason he hadn't elaborated to the two elders about Raven's visit to his office. She was the church's chief financial officer, so it wasn't like they would suspect her to be advising him on anything law related. He was keeping his intentions to himself because he didn't want anyone wondering why he was getting ready to move a good portion of his money around, making sure Alicia,

Matthew, and Curtina received as much money as Charlotte did. When he'd first asked Raven to locate him a reputable attorney, his only desire was to get Curtina added more prominently into his will. He had already included her, but after her mother had passed he'd decided to make sure she received just as much as his other two children if something happened to him. Actually, he'd wanted to give Curtina equal shares from the very beginning, but Charlotte had thrown such a fit about the possibility of Tabitha being the true recipient that he'd left the idea alone.

That was then, though. But now that his relationship with Charlotte had taken an unsettling turn and she'd proven how much she hated Curtina, he felt he needed to look out for his children even more. He knew Matthew would always be fine because Charlotte would always take care of her own son. She would probably even make sure Alicia received a few extra benefits as well, since they'd had a wonderful stepmother-stepdaughter relationship for years now. But he knew she wouldn't do a single thing for Curtina. So what he would do now was sit back for a few more days or weeks, waiting to see how things panned out between him and Charlotte. Then, he would determine how to proceed.

"Pastor?" Raven said. "Helllllooo?"

"Oh, I'm sorry," he said. "I guess I just have a lot on my mind. Please accept my apologies."

"Is everything okay?"

"Nothing for you to worry about."

"Still, even though I've only been working here for just under a year, I can still tell when something isn't quite right with you. I can tell when you're not happy."

Curtis wondered why everyone seemed so able to read

him, but he was sure both worry and concern were written all over his face. He was trying to act normal, but now he knew it wasn't working.

"It's nothing that can't be worked out," he said.

"I really hope so, but either way, I'm always available if you ever need someone to talk to."

"Thank you for that, Raven. It really means a lot."

"Anytime," she said, smiling, and then stood up. "See you tonight."

She turned and looked at Curtis one last time before exiting his office. Interestingly enough, this was the first time Curtis realized how attractive Raven was. It was true that she always seemed to be about business, always dressed in professional attire, and was extremely talented and knowledgeable when it came to handling the church's finances. But until now, he guessed he'd never bothered paying much attention to just how good-looking she was—he hadn't bothered focusing on the fact that she was the kind of woman any man in his right mind would have taken a second look at.

Curtis knew, though, why he hadn't noticed her flowing hair, flawless cocoa skin, or well-formed silhouette in the past. It was because he'd been completely happy with Charlotte. He loved her more than ever, and he had decided point-blank that other women no longer mattered to him. Of course, Charlotte hadn't been as happy as he'd been with their marriage, not since Curtina had been born, but he'd still been totally committed to her and their vows. It was the reason he was working doubly hard, trying to tolerate the very selfish and blatantly cruel way she was treating Curtina, not to mention how callously she was treating him.

What worried him now, however, was a popular saying he'd heard so many older people say throughout the years: even iron eventually wears thin. Meaning even the strongest and most dedicated person could take only so much and ultimately had their breaking point.

He hoped he wasn't slipping into that particular category.

He prayed his sinful ways and struggle with temptation were a thing of the past.

For his sake as well as for Charlotte's.

Chapter 9

Charlotte drove into the far right lane on I-90 West as she prepared to take the Genoa exit. She was only fifteen minutes from their house, and she couldn't wait to crawl into bed. Her head still pounded from her hangover, her stomach still didn't feel the greatest, and she was utterly wiped out. Thankfully, however, her parents hadn't pressured her about where she'd been until well after two in the morning or about the way she'd thrown up all over one of their bathrooms. They hadn't even questioned her about why she'd needed to spend the night with them. She could tell her father hadn't been too happy about her condition, though, so she was glad he'd gone on about his day and hadn't said anything.

Then, this morning, she'd called Matthew, letting him know she'd been visiting a few friends in Chicago and when it had gotten too late, she'd realized she was too tired to drive back. She hated lying to her son, but it wasn't like she could tell him the truth either. From the sound of his voice, though, he hadn't seemed bothered or worried, so she was very happy about that.

But the worst part of her morning thus far had been that annoying call from Curtis. He'd kept pushing and interrogating her like he had a right, and it was the reason she'd hung up on him. It was the reason she didn't care what he thought or what he had to say—the reason she was going to be her own woman, making her own decisions from now on. She would do whatever it took to keep her mind totally occupied and completely off Curtina, and there wasn't a thing Curtis could do about it.

It was the reason she didn't feel the slightest bit of guilt about last night, her sleeping with another man behind Curtis's back—the man she'd danced with at the club, the man who'd finally told her his name was Tom, the man who had followed her out to her car and convinced her to go to a motel with him. In fact, when she thought about how special and awesome he'd made her feel, she felt liberated. Felt like she was getting some much-needed payback for all the pain Curtis was causing her. Plus, it wasn't like she'd ever have to see or hear from Tom again, so as far as she was concerned, her one-night fling had been fun and well worth her time but was now simply a thing of the past.

When Charlotte arrived home, Agnes greeted her but didn't say much else. She seemed almost embarrassed and like she was afraid to look at her. But Charlotte knew it was because Agnes wasn't used to her staying out all night without telling her. She also wasn't used to seeing Charlotte wearing the same clothes from the day before or walking around with her hair looking a mess. Plus, she had to know things were bad between her and Curtis, because they now argued like animals.

"Can I fix you something to eat, Miss Charlotte?" she finally asked.

"No. But thanks for asking, Agnes."

"You're welcome, and just let me know if there's anything I can do for you."

"I will. But right now, all I want to do is head upstairs to lie down."

After closing the bedroom door, shedding her clothing, slipping on a pair of flannel pajamas, and turning on the fireplace, Charlotte climbed into bed.

"Finally," she said, pulling the comforter up just past her waist, turning on her side, and curling into a ball. But to her unfortunate dismay, only minutes later Curtis waltzed into the room and slammed the door, ranting and raving.

Charlotte frowned. "What in the world are you doing here?"

"I figured you'd be home this afternoon, and I wanna talk to you."

"Well, I don't wanna talk to you. I'm tired, I'm sleepy, and I wanna be left alone."

"No, we're going to deal with this before things stretch too far out of hand."

Charlotte looked at him and then closed her eyes. "Curtis, why don't you get out of here?"

"Where were you? And why were you out drinking?"

Her eyes were still shut but she said, "I don't wanna talk about it."

"Why?"

"Because I don't, and because it's not important."

"It is important."

"No. It's not."

"Look, Charlotte, I'm really trying here, but I'm also starting to lose my patience."

Now she opened her eyes and sat straight up. "Oh

yeah? Well, I've got news for you, Curtis. I started losing my patience the moment you started bringing that daughter of yours here to our house. Then I lost it completely the day Tabitha died and left Curtina behind for someone else to take care of."

"No, not someone. Us. She left Curtina with her father and stepmother."

"No, she left her for you because I've already made it clear that I'm not playing mommy on Tabitha's behalf."

"You hate Curtina that much?"

Charlotte glared at him.

"So you're not going to answer me?"

"Like I said, Curtis, I'm really tired, so will you please just leave me alone?"

"No, not until you answer my question."

"Okay, fine. Yes, I hate her. I hate every inch of her, and I wish like hell that something bad would happen to her. Is that answer enough for you?"

Curtis stared back at her with no emotion. He seemed almost shell-shocked and like he couldn't believe what he was hearing. She waited for him to lash back at her, but to her surprise, all he did was leave.

Good, Charlotte thought. Then she repositioned herself in the bed, laid her head back onto the pillow, and closed her eyes. She was so glad Curtis was no longer bothering her and glad she could finally get some rest. She lay there in total comfort, like she had not a care in the world.

Chapter 10

I love you so, so much, Curtina," Curtis said, holding his daughter in his arms and squeezing her tightly.

"I love Daddy."

Curtis didn't want to put her down, but he knew he had to if he didn't want to be late for the church business meeting.

"You'd better get going," Aunt Emma said.

"I know. And thanks a million for having me over for dinner and for taking care of my little princess. I have no idea what I would do without you."

"It's no problem at all, and I've already told you I'm glad to do it. You just worry about Charlotte and that marriage of yours. My niece is as wrong as the day is long, but I know she loves you."

"Well, she sure has a strange way of showing it."

"She's spoiled, stubborn, and full of herself, but you knew that when you married her," Aunt Emma said, laughing.

Curtis chuckled, but even Aunt Emma's humor wasn't enough to brighten his spirits or offer him any hope about his personal future. Things were bad. Worse than he'd

thought, and now he wished he hadn't gone home this afternoon. If he hadn't, he wouldn't have had to hear her say
how much she hated Curtina, and worse, how she wanted
something bad to happen to her. Curtis knew Charlotte was
upset, but he wasn't sure he'd ever be able to look at her the
same. Not after hearing her wish tragedy on an innocent
child. Specifically a child whose father was the man she
was married to. He couldn't imagine anyone being so evil,
regardless of what the situation might be, and he couldn't
push Charlotte's words out of his mind. He'd played them
over and over on his way back to the church. Then again,
while he was trying to work on next Sunday's sermon, and
again while he was having dinner with Aunt Emma and
Curtina. He couldn't stop thinking about any of what was
happening, and his faith in both Charlotte and their marriage had weakened. He was tired, hurt, and, God help
him, thinking of various ways to make himself feel better.
The kind of ways that wouldn't be very Christian-like.

A couple of hours passed, and while Curtis felt worse
than he had earlier, the business meeting was now being
called to order. Everyone was there. A large portion of the
general congregation, the elders, the associate pastors, all
other church officers, the administrative staff, the finance
committee, Raven, and of course, all the building committee members.

"Thank you all for coming out this evening," Curtis
said. "This is an exciting time for Deliverance Outreach,
and I can't tell you how excited I am about the progress
we've made as a church and also with the planning of our
future. I'm sad to say, though, I'm not feeling the best this
evening, so I'm going to turn everything over to Elder
Jamison and Anise Miller." Anise was Charlotte's first

cousin and one of the original coordinators when the new church project was first being planned. "Elder Jamison?" Curtis continued, offering him the floor.

Elder Jamison went through the agenda point by point, Anise made a few important announcements, and the entire building committee took questions from the congregation. Curtis sat listening, but also spent most of the hour zoning in and out and thinking about his home life. He thought about how far he and Charlotte had come, how well they'd finally been doing, and then he thought about where they were now.

"Well, if there are no more questions," Elder Jamison said, after another hour had passed, "then I think we can adjourn."

Soon after, everyone slid out of the pews, shook hands with each other, and headed out of the sanctuary.

"Pastor, are you feeling any better?" Anise asked him. She normally called him Curtis, but whenever they were at church and around other members, she used his given title.

"I'll be fine."

"Well, if you're not feeling well, maybe you should call Mom and just ask her to keep Curtina overnight for you."

"No, I'm good."

"Okay, but I know Mom would be fine with doing it."

"I know she would. But by the time I pick Curtina up and get her home, she'll be ready for bed, anyway."

"All right, well, I'm heading out, and you take care of yourself," she said, hugging him.

"I will, and you, too."

Curtis watched as Anise walked away and couldn't help wondering how she and Charlotte could be first cousins yet be so very different. He wondered why Charlotte didn't have the same kind of heart Anise had or care about others the way Anise did.

"Pastor, I know you're not feeling well," Raven said, now standing before him, "and I'm really sorry to have to bother you with this. But if you don't mind, I need you to sign a couple of documents."

"Sure, let's head up to my study now."

"I'll stop by my office to get the file and will be right in."

Curtis shook a few more hands, said a few more good-byes, and then met Raven in his office.

"These aren't anything major," she said. "Just the normal monthly authorizations for a few special items a couple of the departments are in need of."

Curtis skimmed the sheets in front of him, and she was right. They weren't anything out of the ordinary or overly important, so he wondered why his signature couldn't wait until tomorrow. Still, he went ahead and signed them.

"Here you go," he said, closing the folder and passing it back to her.

"Thanks. And if you don't mind, I'd like to talk to you about something personal. I know you're not feeling well, so this won't take very long."

"Sure. Go ahead."

Raven inhaled and exhaled audibly. "Okay, the deal is this. For some time now, I've tried my best to ignore my attraction to you, but it's now to the point where it's unbearable."

Curtis leaned back in his chair. He was shocked, to say the least, but he let her continue.

"I know you're married and that you're a wonderful man of God, but I can't help the way I feel."

"You're right," Curtis said. "I'm married, and I want to remain that way."

"I understand that, but I just couldn't keep this to myself any longer. I've been struggling with the idea of whether I should tell you, but today after I left your office, I decided I had to. Especially when everything in me says that you're not happy at home. I don't know what's going on, but I just have this feeling that you deserve someone so much better than a woman like Charlotte."

Curtis wanted to tell her that she was out of line, but the sad thing about her comments was that he had to agree with her. He said nothing, though, and his silence must have made Raven uncomfortable because she quickly stood up.

"I'm really sorry, Pastor. I'm so sorry, and I hope you'll somehow be able to forgive me."

She backed away from his desk and then left altogether.

Curtis watched her every move and finally had to admit something to himself. He was attracted to her, too. He'd known it ever since this morning when she'd come into his office, but he'd thought about her even more ever since that big blowup between him and Charlotte this afternoon. He'd had all kinds of thoughts. Sinful thoughts and the kind he wasn't very proud of.

Thing was, though, he really did love his wife and wanted to remain faithful to her. He wanted them to be happy and enjoy their life to the fullest, and he wasn't ready to give up on that happening. He'd been more upset with Charlotte today than he'd been in a long time, but during the business meeting he'd reminisced on all the good times they'd shared. He'd thought about all the laughs, all the fun, and all the joy they'd given each other, and while she'd said some pretty harsh things to him earlier, he still wanted to keep trying. He told himself that Charlotte loved him as much as he loved her, and that she *would* come around. Eventually, anyway. His prayer was that she would suddenly wake up one day, that she would realize how wrong she'd been about Curtina, that she would learn to love her, and that their problems as a whole would be solved. Curtis believed all of this and more—because if he didn't, he knew they were doomed.

Chapter 11

*I*t was shortly after eight p.m., and Charlotte was glad she no longer felt hung over. She'd taken a very long nap, and now she was signed onto Facebook and loving every moment of it. She'd made the decision to join this particular social network not even two months ago, but she was certainly very glad she had. For a long time, she hadn't seen what all the raves were about, not until her stepdaughter, Alicia, had insisted it was the best thing since the introduction of the Internet. She'd told her how wonderful it was reconnecting with childhood friends and school-mates, and how convenient it was being able to communicate with anyone you wanted to on a regular basis.

Still, for a matter of months Charlotte hadn't thought it was for her, but as of late, she'd found she could barely do without it. She wasn't addicted per se, but she was on for at least sixty minutes or so every single day—and this evening she'd already been on for nearly four hours. She'd been making and accepting friend requests, commenting on a number of different status updates, and searching for other family and friends who might be members as well.

Charlotte continued browsing for folks she knew,

including mere acquaintances, but smiled when she came across her cousin Dooney's name. Of all people. Drug-dealing, hustling Dooney. She was actually pleasantly surprised, because even though Dooney lived a life she would never live, he was one of her favorite family members, and she loved him. He was loyal, too. And she would always be indebted to him for vandalizing Tabitha's house. He'd risked being caught and arrested, all because he wanted to help save Charlotte's marriage to Curtis, and Charlotte didn't know many people who would be willing to do that. Charlotte clicked on the Friend Request link on Dooney's page, but then she couldn't help searching for Michael Porter, a guy she'd dated just before getting back together with Curtis. At the time, Matthew had only been seven, so she hadn't spent nearly as much time with Michael as she would have liked, but she'd never forgotten about him.

She wondered how he was doing these days, so when the search engine listed a number of members with his exact same name, she scrolled through all the photos until she found his. The man still looked just as good as ever, and it only took her seconds to remember how intense their lovemaking had been. She remembered how they hadn't been able to get enough of each other whenever they'd been together. The only problem was, he'd been married and unwilling to get a divorce; thus she'd moved on with Curtis without any regrets.

Now, though, she could barely click on the link to his Facebook page fast enough. She wanted to see if he had his privacy options set in a way where only his current Facebook friends could read his wall postings or if basic-ally anyone could view them. She smiled when she saw that she could in fact read some of his most recent updates, then clicked on his Info tab to see what personal information she could find out. Interestingly enough, not much had changed. He still resided in the Chicago area, still worked in investment brokering; he loved watching old movies, loved golfing, and, yes, he was still very married.

Charlotte read as much as she could about him, but when she could no longer fight her desire to contact him directly, she clicked on the link that would allow her to send him a private message—a *behind the wall* sort of way of communicating with Facebook members when you didn't want anyone else seeing what you had to say.

When the window opened, Charlotte began typing her note.

> Hey Michael,
>   How are you? I'm sure my contacting you will come as a huge surprise, but I do hope you are doing well. It's been a long time, but since I came across your name here on Facebook, I thought I'd send you a quick hello.
>   Take care and hope to hear back from you soon.
>   Charlotte

Charlotte reread her message, checking for any typos, and hit the Send button. Then she returned to her home page and browsed the comments of friends who had also posted new statuses. She immediately saw one from Alicia that said, "God has given me a second chance with the best man in the whole wide world, so life truly doesn't get any better than this." Charlotte smiled because she knew Alicia was talking about her first husband, Phillip, and the fact that they'd been seeing each other again exclusively. They'd had a very painful breakup, which had all

been because Alicia had started sleeping with a successful drug dealer named Levi Cunningham. But now she
and Phillip were working on a brand-new relationship
with each other. After her divorce from Phillip, however, things had only gotten worse because she'd quickly
married that horrible JT. The man had been the biggest
whoremonger on this side of hell, even worse than Curtis
had been at one time. So everyone had been thrilled when
Alicia's marriage to him had only lasted a few months,
and she'd been able to walk away without children or any
other JT Valentine connection.

Charlotte clicked on the Comment button and typed a
response:

> You couldn't have said it better, Alicia, and I'm so happy
> for you and Phillip!

Alicia answered right away, thanking her. Just then,
though, Charlotte saw that she had a new message in her
inbox, so she clicked on the icon. It was from Michael, and
she couldn't believe he'd responded so quickly. Strangely,
she felt a little nervous but opened his note so she could
see what he had to say.

> Hey you,
>   This really is a very pleasant surprise, and I'm so glad
> you made the effort to contact me. I still think about you
> from time to time, and I've always wondered how things
> were going with you.

Charlotte knew Michael was only trying to be kind,
because there was no doubt that, like most other people,

he surely knew about the many public scandals she and
Curtis had found themselves involved in.

Well, I won't keep you, but I do hope we can catch up
and try to stay in touch. I mean, isn't Facebook amazing?
Michael

Charlotte hit the Reply button and typed another note.

Yes, Facebook is wonderful, and I really would like to stay
in touch with you, Michael.

**A minute or so passed, and Charlotte saw yet another
message from him.**

So if you don't mind my asking, how's married life treating
you? And yes, before you ask, I am still married to Sybil
but we're basically only going through the motions.

**Charlotte wasn't sure how to respond to his question. Part
of her wanted to bare her soul and tell him how miserable
she'd been lately with Curtis, but instead, all she said was:**

I'm sorry to hear that and hope things get better for the two
of you.

She waited for Michael's response.

I appreciate your well wishes, but you still haven't
answered my question.

Charlotte hesitated but knew she had to type something.

You know how it is. Marriage can be great on certain days and not so great on others.

She thought about how much easier this would have been had she sent him a friend request right from the start, because then they'd simply be able to chat in real time by instant message.

Michael's next note said:

I'm sorry to hear that, and I may as well admit that I have heard rumors and know things haven't always gone so well between you and your husband. But I was hoping maybe you were happy now.

Charlotte heard Curtis's truck entering the garage and knew it was time to end her conversation.

Thanks so much. But hey, it was really great chatting with you, however, I have to get going now. We'll connect again soon, though, okay?

Michael told her yes in another message and to have a good evening.

Charlotte signed off of Facebook altogether but then sat wondering how her life might have turned out had she continued dating Michael and not married Curtis. She wondered if maybe Michael would have eventually left his wife. Probably not, at least not back then, anyway, but she couldn't help wondering if he would have the courage to leave her now. Charlotte wondered if maybe he'd had enough and couldn't wait to get away from her.

More than that, though, she wondered what it would

feel like seeing him again. She knew it was wrong for her to even consider the idea of getting together with any of her ex-boyfriends, but she needed someone to talk to besides her best friend, Janine, or her mom. She needed to talk to someone she felt comfortable with. Not someone like that guy Tom from last night, but someone like Michael. Someone who knew her from back in the day. At least as far back as eleven years ago, anyway.

And she would see him, too—that was, if Curtis didn't do something about this Curtina situation. Charlotte would live like a single woman if Curtis didn't man up and do the right thing.

He would man up or deal with the consequences.

Chapter 12

Curtis unlocked the door and carried Curtina into the house, and Matthew walked into the kitchen, greeting them.

"Maaattt," Curtina said, smiling.

Matthew took her into his arms. "Hey, little girl. So how was your day today?"

Curtina spoke in her own little language, and while she probably knew what she was saying, Curtis certainly didn't and he knew Matthew didn't either.

"Is that right? Well, good for you," Matthew told her, pretending that he understood every word she'd just said. Then he put her down, unzipped her hot pink coat, removed it, and picked her back up.

"So how was school?" Curtis asked him.

"Good. I had a really hard chemistry test, but I'm pretty sure I got an A. I did some mad studying for it, though."

"I'm sure you did fine, and having good study habits is why you've always gotten such excellent grades. Those study habits are also going to be of great help to you when you're at Harvard a year and a half from now."

"I hope so. I also have this English project that I have to turn in on Friday, so I need to work on that every night until then. Oh and there is something else, Dad. There's a rumor going around about one of the history teachers and one of his female students. Kids were saying that they've been sleeping together, and that Mr. Rush is going to be suspended until further notice. There were detectives inside the building and everything."

"That's really too bad, Matt. But if the rumor is true, Mr. Rush deserves to lose his job and get jail time. The whole idea of a grown man doing something like that is beyond my understanding, and it's just plain perverse."

"I don't know why any girl would even take a second look at him, anyway. He's always been a very nice man, but he's pretty decrepit-looking."

"Nonetheless, that man has no business being with a minor. Period. And chances are, he probably figured out some way to manipulate her. It could have been something as easy as him threatening to give her a failing grade if she wouldn't be with him. Men like that are sly and conniving, and there are women out there like that, too. There have been a good number of stories about female teachers and teenage boys as well."

"I know. Mom was telling me the same thing when I told her earlier. I just hope it's not true about Mr. Rush, but if it is then you're right, Dad, he should go straight to jail. And for a long time."

"Mommy up," Curtina chimed in, pointing toward the ceiling.

Matthew looked at her. "What? You wanna go up to see Mom?"

Curtina nodded, so Matthew started upstairs, and Curtis followed behind them. He loved the way Matthew treated his sister, but he could only imagine the drama that was about to ensue once Charlotte saw her. Especially since Curtis and Charlotte had argued so intensely this afternoon about her mysterious night out drinking.

When they entered the room, Matthew called out to his mother.

"I'm in here, Matt," she said from the bathroom.

Curtis shed his suit jacket and tie. Matthew walked around the corner and past their closets, and Curtis could see Charlotte washing her face.

"Mommyyyy!" Curtina said.

She called out to Charlotte over and over, but Charlotte acted as though she didn't see her.

Curtina wiggled to get down, so Matthew lowered her onto the floor, and Curtina ran as fast as she could to Curtis—with a pitiful look on her face.

Curtis grabbed her up. "It's okay. Daddy loves you," he said, but it was all he could do not to go off on Charlotte. To his surprise, though, when Matthew and Charlotte moved closer to where they were standing, Curtina made another sad attempt at trying to get Charlotte to notice her. Still, Charlotte ignored her again.

This time, however, Matthew called her on it. "Mom, why do you keep acting like you don't hear Curtina?"

"No reason," she said, barely able to look at Matthew.

"But Mom, she keeps trying to talk to you, and I think you're hurting her feelings."

"That's exactly what she's doing," Curtis couldn't resist saying, but Charlotte never as much as looked in his direction.

"I don't understand, Mom," Matthew said, looking at her in amazement. He then took Curtina from his dad.

"Thanks, son," Curtis told him. "And if you don't

mind, can you maybe read your sister a bedtime story, and then I'll be in to get her ready for bed in a few minutes."

"Okay, Dad."

Curtis watched them leave and then went and shut the door. "You know, I'm really, really getting fed up, Charlotte."

"Whatever," she said.

"Is this ever going to stop? Are you ever going to grow up and stop acting like some self-absorbed child?"

"Not tonight, Curtis, okay? As a matter of fact, I don't want to discuss any of this Curtina business again. That is, unless you've finally made up your mind to move her out of here."

"You're sick."

"No, you're the sick one. And pretty naïve if you think I'm ever going to change my mind about this."

Curtis walked away from her. Had to, before he said or did something he would regret.

"Did you hear me, Curtis?" Charlotte asked, strolling behind him as he entered the walk-in closet. "Because I'm not playing with you."

Curtis turned abruptly, facing her. "And I'm not playing with *you*. Curtina stays, and this is the last time I'm going to repeat that."

"So what you're basically saying is to hell with what I want or how I feel. Am I right?"

"Exactly." Curtis brushed past her, wearing just his underwear and carrying a plush robe over his arm, and headed toward the bathroom. If Charlotte knew what was good for her, she'd leave him alone and go on about her business.

"Then, to hell with you, too, and to hell with that pathetic little brat you're so obsessed with."

Curtis glanced over his shoulder at her and then slammed the door in her face. He couldn't remember ever being so unnerved or outraged, not since that day a few years ago, when he'd learned about Charlotte sleeping with Aaron. He'd been beside himself, and right now, it was best for him to calm down, take a hot shower, and then go tuck Curtina in as planned. After that, he would retire in one of their guest bedrooms. He would settle into the one farthest away from his crazy wife.

He would do this before things turned even uglier. If he didn't, someone would be sorry, and the potential outcome would be disastrous.

Chapter 13

Zero. That was the number of times Charlotte and Curtis had spoken to each other this morning before he'd gotten dressed and left the house with Curtina—taking her over to Benedict Arnold's house. Aunt Emma was currently babysitting that brat every day now, and Charlotte couldn't understand why she would agree to do something like this. For God's sake, Aunt Emma was her own flesh and blood.

Then, Matthew had left before them, and Agnes had run out to the grocery store, so Charlotte was all alone. However, as she stood looking across their backyard at some of the snow that still hadn't melted, she made a decision. She was going on one of the biggest shopping sprees she'd ever been on. Curtis owed her that and then some, and today she was going to treat herself like never before. She would do what always cheered her up and made her happy. She would make Alicia's former shopping obsession seem like mere child's play.

After getting dressed and into the car, she called Janine. She was headed to Oakbrook Center, which was about an hour-and-fifteen-minute drive, so she figured this was a good time to chat for a few minutes. Especially since this was usually the hour Janine didn't have a class to teach, and Charlotte hoped there weren't any students in her office, trying to get help.

"Can you talk?" Charlotte asked.

"Yes," Janine said. "How are you?"

"Not too good, but I'm going to be fabulous by this afternoon."

"And why is that?"

"I'm going *shopping*."

Janine laughed. "Uh-oh. That sounds pretty scary."

"Maybe for Curtis, but not for me."

"So things still aren't better with you guys?"

"Nope. They're worse."

"I'm sorry."

"Don't be. It's not your fault Curtis is being a jerk."

"What about a marriage counselor?"

"Girl, please. I'm not even going to think about wasting my time with some overrated psychology major."

Janine didn't say anything, so Charlotte knew she wasn't happy about her response.

"I'm not going to any counselor because there's only one thing that can fix things between Curtis and me: giving Curtina to one of Tabitha's relatives. But anyway, what I mainly wanted to call you about is a spa day. I thought it would be good for the two of us to get something scheduled."

"Sounds good to me. Remember I was just telling you how Carl really wants me to get out more, so just let me know when you're ready."

"I'll check tomorrow for openings, but just so you know, I'm going to schedule the entire works. Hot stone massages, full facials, pedicures, and manicures. Oh, and the entire day is all on me."

"You know you don't have to do that."

"I know. But I want to," Charlotte said, thinking how Curtis would really be the one footing the bill anyhow. Then, she drove onto I-90 East. "Okay, well, I know your break is almost up, so I won't hold you."

"Yeah, I'd better get going, but Charlotte, please think about what I said. You know . . . about the counseling. I'm begging you."

"I'll talk to you later, J."

"Take care."

Charlotte ended the call. She knew Janine only wanted the best for her, and she loved her for that. But the whole idea of disclosing her personal business to a stranger wasn't an option. It wasn't going to happen.

Charlotte drove a few more miles until her phone rang. It was her mother.

"Hey, Mom, how are you?"

"I'm good. And you?"

"Okay, I guess."

"I called the house, but when I didn't get an answer, I decided to call your cell."

"Yeah, I decided to spend the day at the mall."

"Are you there now?"

"No, not yet."

"Oh, okay. Well, since I hadn't heard from you since you left here yesterday morning, I just wanted to check on you."

"I'm fine, Mom."

"Are you sure? Because you didn't seem fine when you were here. You seemed not yourself, and you know your father is very worried."

"Why? What did he say?"

"You really wanna know?"

"I do."

"He's worried that you might be messing around on Curtis."

Charlotte raised her eyebrows. She'd known her father had looked at her a bit suspiciously, but she hadn't thought he was thinking anything like this. It *was* true that she had messed around, but still...

She tried sounding appalled. "What?! Messing around? Did he really say that?"

"You know your father. He's never gotten over that affair I had on him years ago and never will. He's also never going to forget the time you were with that Aaron guy."

"Well, you can just tell Daddy that he's dead wrong, and that having an affair is the least of my worries," she hurried to say. "I would never do that to Curtis again. I would never deceive him that way. Regardless of how bad things are between us."

"I know, sweetheart, and I'm really glad to hear that."

There was a second or two of silence and then her mother said, "So have you had a chance to sit down and talk to Curtis more about your situation?"

"Not really. I mean, we've argued a couple of times but that's pretty much it. Oh, and before I forget, Mom, can you believe Aunt Emma is now Curtina's full-time baby-sitter? Can you believe Aunt Emma would betray me this way, knowing how much I don't like that child?"

"I can believe it. I've never truly understood my sister, and this just proves she doesn't have an ounce of family loyalty. She and I have had our differences for years now, but Emma is definitely a different bird. Always trying to do the right thing, even if it hurts someone else. I'm really sorry that she's doing this, sweetie."

"All I know is that I'm through with her. She's my aunt, and I love her, but after this, I won't be speaking to her for a good while."

"I don't blame you."

With there still being this sisterly rift between Charlotte's mom and Aunt Emma, Charlotte knew her mother would quickly take her side. It was the reason Charlotte had brought the whole babysitting story up. She'd been planning to tell her mom about it anyway, but she decided to do it now as a means to get her off of that your-dad-thinks-you-might-be-messing-around topic.

"But back to you and Curtis. What are you going to do?"

"I don't know, Mom. I honestly don't. At first, I thought there was a chance, but now I really don't see it."

"So that's it?" Her mother sounded a little upset. "You're just going to give up on being married to a good man like Curtis? Without even putting up a real fight?"

Noreen had always been very proud of the kind of lifestyle Charlotte and Curtis lived, and she also took pride in telling everyone who was anyone that *the* Reverend Curtis Black was her beloved son-in-law. So Charlotte knew her mother didn't want to consider the possibility of divorce. Not to mention, she knew Noreen enjoyed all the monetary gifts Curtis regularly blessed his mother-in-law and father-in-law with. Charlotte knew her mother wanted her to be happy, but she also loved the perks as well.

"Mom, my hands are tied, so unless you know what I can do, then ..."

"There has to be something. Something that will make this problem of yours go away. And maybe your only choice is to give Curtis an ultimatum. Maybe the only chance you have is forcing him to choose between you and Curtina, once and for all."

"I've already done that to a certain extent."

"No, I mean letting him know, nicely and calmly and not in an angry rage, that if Curtina stays then you're going to leave him for good. Because if Curtis really thinks you're serious about leaving him, I think he'll choose you. He'll choose his wife and be fine with visiting his daughter whenever he can."

Charlotte wanted to believe her, but she didn't see it. "I don't know, Mom."

"I know it's a gamble, but what other options do you really have?"

Charlotte sighed with frustration. "I guess you're right. Although, it's not like I really want to move out of our house or be without Curtis, so what if he calls my bluff?"

"It's possible, and if he does, then you might have to leave to really get his attention."

"I don't know. I'll have to think long and hard before I confront him with this."

"I understand that. I will say this, though. You and Curtis have dealt with so much marital strife and public humiliation that I don't think he would want to risk having any of you go through that again. He wouldn't want that for either of you, and he certainly wouldn't want to embarrass Alicia and Matthew again."

Charlotte changed lanes and drove through the I-Pass toll area. "Maybe."

"Well, either way, you can't keep going on the way you are because I know you're miserable."

"I'll figure out something," Charlotte said.

"I hope so. I really do."

Charlotte and her mother chatted for a few more minutes and then hung up. She pondered all that her mother had just said. But it wasn't long before she tossed Curtis and his daughter out of her mind. She wasn't about to let either of them ruin the rest of her day or the wonderful time she was going to have in Oakbrook. She was going to enjoy herself and worry about them later.

Chapter 14

There was no place like Neiman Marcus, and Charlotte felt better already. Just the idea of stepping foot inside their department store was enough for her. She didn't even have to buy anything and would still be happy. But she *was* going to buy something, starting with the three Armani pantsuits she'd just finished trying on and was now ready to pay for. Gilda, her assigned shopping consultant, had taken them from the dressing room and was now ringing them up.

"Such beautiful choices," Gilda told her. "All of them are so very much you."

"Why thank you."

"You're quite welcome. Okay, then, that'll be thirty-six seventy-eight."

Charlotte pulled out her American Express card and passed it across the counter. The total had come to just under four thousand dollars, so now she wished she'd tried on a skirt suit. She still had some more shopping to do in both the jewelry and shoe departments, though, not to mention a couple of other stores she was planning to go in before leaving, so she would just shop for skirt suits another time.

She signed for her purchases and waited for the consultant to place her suits under plastic.

"Also, just so you know," Gilda said, "we're going to begin carrying a couple of new designers next month, so I hope you'll stop back in."

"I definitely will, and thanks for letting me know."

"Of course."

Gilda finished bagging Charlotte's items and handed them to her. "As always, we really appreciate your business, and I'll see you next month."

"Take care."

"You, too."

Charlotte browsed a couple of dress racks, looked at some blouses, and then went on to the jewelry section. She loved, loved, loved David Yurman and went straight to his collection. She loved his style and was due for a new bracelet and a pair of matching earrings.

"Good afternoon," the distinguished-looking salesman said. "May I help you find something?"

"Yes, could I see the bracelet toward the middle?" she told him, pointing at it through the glass.

"This one?"

"Yes."

"The Pave Diamond Waverly is absolutely divine. It's one of my favorites."

Charlotte removed the diamond bracelet she had on and held out her arm. The salesman placed the David Yurman piece around her wrist.

"This is perfect," she said. "I love it."

"We do have matching earrings, if you're interested."

"Really?"

"Yes, and by the way, I'm Bartholomew, but you can call me Bart."

"Nice to meet you, Bart. I'm Charlotte."

Bart pulled the earrings from the case, and Charlotte said, "You can just go ahead and ring those up with the bracelet. No need for me to try them on when I already know how wonderful they're going to look."

"Are you sure?"

"Yep."

"Okay, then, what else can I get you?"

"Mmm," she said, scanning a couple more jewelry lines. She saw some cultured pearls that she sort of liked but told him, "I think that might be it for now."

"Sounds good."

Bart took both pieces over to the counter behind him, boxed them up, and then entered the purchases into the system. At first, Charlotte had thought about asking him the price, but if she wasn't mistaken, she'd already seen both the bracelet and the earrings online. If so, the bracelet was twenty-five hundred, and the earrings were just over a thousand.

"With tax, your total is three thousand six dollars."

How ironic that the amount wasn't much different than what she'd just spent upstairs, Charlotte thought, and then gave him her card. Once the charges were approved, she signed her name. Bart gave her the jewelry and she placed the bag in her tote.

Another three hours passed, and by the time Charlotte had finished up in Neiman's she'd bought herself a whole new set of expensive underwear, two pairs of jeans, and two pairs of three-inch, pointed-toe leather boots, one pair black and the other brown. She'd easily spent ten thousand dollars in there, and had spent another fifteen thousand in Tiffany's, which was what her new diamond necklace and diamond earrings had cost her. Today was by far one of the best days she'd had in a while, and she was glad about it. Glad she'd gotten away from Mitchell and the life she was no longer content with.

Charlotte took her purchases to the car, locked them inside her trunk, and then walked back over to The Clubhouse. This was one of her favorite restaurants, and she rarely came to Oakbrook without eating here. Before she opened the door to go in, however, she scanned a row of less expensive specialty stores. She hadn't had to shop at any of them for so long, she could barely remember what kind of merchandise they carried. This was another reason she didn't want to separate from Curtis. Although, if he pushed her, she would sue him for as much alimony as the court system would allow her. She would sue him for half of everything, the same as any other intelligent wife who had been wronged by her husband—she would do it on purpose and then consider her huge settlement as just punishment for Curtis's sleeping around on her in the first place.

As Charlotte sat waiting on her Caesar salad with no croutons, she pulled out her BlackBerry and signed onto Facebook. She scrolled through her wall postings but then got excited when she checked her inbox and saw a message from Michael Porter.

Hey,
    Look, I know I'm probably completely out of line, and since it won't do me any good at all to beat around the bush, I'm just going to say what's on my mind. Ever since

we communicated last night, I haven't thought about anything else. I've even thought about the wonderful times we once spent together, and I can't deny that all these amazing memories have now stirred up a lot of old feelings. Feelings that really don't seem all that old anymore. Yes, I know you're married, and yes, I'm married, too, but...Anyway, if this note somehow offends you or you never want to speak to me again after reading this, I will totally understand. And I apologize. Still, I couldn't help being honest with you.

Hope you are well.

Michael

Charlotte's hand shook. Worse, she felt the kind of intimate sensations married women should feel only with their husbands. She took a deep breath and reread the note, then set her BlackBerry down on the table. She examined each area of the restaurant, almost as if she were afraid someone might be able to read her mind or peep at the note on her little mobile device. She didn't know how or if she should respond to her ex's message. Deep down, she knew she shouldn't and that she should end all contact with him immediately. But there was also this aching part of her being, the kind that desperately craved individual attention from a strong, smart, gorgeous-looking man. What she needed was the kind of attention Curtis had once given her, right before Curtina had been dumped smack-dab into their lives.

The waitress brought Charlotte her salad and told her to enjoy. But Charlotte was much too flustered to eat anything. She couldn't stop thinking about Michael or the offer he'd made about them seeing each other. At the same time, however, she couldn't forget about Curtis and the love they'd shared for so many years, regardless of all the ups and downs they'd had to deal with.

So, at this point, she didn't know what to do. As she weighed her options, she thought about the affair she'd had with Aaron, and how she'd nearly ruined her and Curtis's marriage for good. She was also reminded of the fact that Aaron had turned schizo on her as soon as she'd told him their little fling was over with. He'd set their house on fire while she was still in it. He'd tried to kill her.

She would never forget what a nightmare that had been and how her mistake had caused a mountain of pain, not just for Curtis but also for Matthew. It had taken a while for them to overcome the entire fiasco, and if that hadn't been enough, Curtis had started up his multiyear fling with Tabitha, gotten her pregnant, and then learned that Tabitha was HIV positive. Worse, a former interim pastor filling in for Curtis, Reverend Tolson, had tipped off the top national media, and it had taken them weeks and months to overcome all the scrutiny and gossip. The whole thing had just about killed Matthew, and Charlotte never wanted to see her child go through such agony again.

So, no, she decided. It was best to ignore Michael's message and pretend she'd never read it. It was best to pretend she'd never searched for him on Facebook in the first place.

Better to just enjoy her meal there at The Clubhouse, head back to Mitchell with her brand-new clothing and accessories, and do what her mother had suggested: give Curtis an ultimatum and then wait for him to send his precious little girl as far away from all of them as possible.

Chapter 15

$\mathcal{M}$ ichael maneuvered his body to Charlotte's side, panting frantically, and Charlotte thought her entire being was going to explode. It had been forever since she'd felt so exhilarated, young, and like she just couldn't get enough of a man. This was how it had always been with Michael in the past, and it was amazing how, even though it was more than a decade later and he was in his forties, nothing had changed. The man still offered the kind of sex that made you want to broadcast it across the country. He gave her what Curtis had always given her, too, before she and Curtis had found themselves at odds over this Curtina issue.

Charlotte lay there, catching her breath, and thought about how easy it had been for Michael to change her mind—when she'd told him she couldn't meet him at his friend's house. She'd sat at the restaurant, debating back and forth, but when she'd checked her Facebook inbox again, this time, Michael had gone as far as sending her his cell number. He'd asked her to call him, and without much hesitation she had done so. Not because she wanted to have sex with him, but because she'd wanted to explain to him why they couldn't get together. Against her better judgment, however, she'd allowed him to convince her that all they would do was talk about old times, and that there was nothing wrong with old friends hooking up for good conversation. But when she'd arrived, one thing had soon led to another, and their lying next to each other right now was the result.

Michael turned toward her. "Girl, I'm completely speechless. I mean, there's a lot I could say, but I honestly don't know where to begin."

"So it was that bad, huh?" she said, teasing him.

"No. It was just that good. It was the best and just as mind-blowing as it was when I first met you."

Charlotte wanted to tell him how much she agreed with him, but out of nowhere, guilt crept in. She'd actually slept with yet a second man behind Curtis's back, and she'd done it in less than forty-eight hours. That Tom guy had pleasured her pretty nicely, but she'd pretty much already forgotten about him. But this, what she'd just experienced with Michael, was something different. They'd made passionate love, but there was also an emotional connection. She'd felt a strong sense of chemistry as soon as she'd laid eyes on him, and it was as if no time had passed at all. It was as if they'd never missed a beat, and it was obvious how comfortable they still were with each other.

"And you're still as beautiful as ever, I see," he said.

"Thank you. You don't look too bad yourself."

"I guess I'll take that as a compliment. It *is* a compliment, right?"

They both laughed. "I'm just messing with you. You are just as handsome as I remember."

"I've really missed you, Charlotte. I didn't realize how much until you arrived here this afternoon, but even yesterday when I saw your note, I don't remember feeling so uplifted about anything in a long time. You really made my day."

"I'm glad we connected, too," she said, but she thought about Curtis again. Her conscience was trying to get the best of her, but she wouldn't let it.

Michael gently stroked Charlotte's hair, over and over. "I think the reason I was so excited to hear from you is because my marriage is a real drag. I can barely stand to look at Sybil anymore, but she won't give me a divorce. Not without my practically going broke, anyway. But I'm to the point where I don't even care about the money, because what I want is to be free of her."

"I'm sorry things are so bad. They're not good for me and Curtis either."

"And why is that? I mean, for Sybil and me, we simply outgrew each other many years ago, and we've never had a thing in common."

"Well, Curtis and I have had our problems, but right now our struggle has to do with his daughter. The one he conceived with his dead mistress. Curtis decided without my consent to move her in with us permanently, and I want her gone."

"Wow, that's a tough one."

"Very. It's a hard situation, and I'm not sure we're ever going to come to terms with it. Curtis isn't budging, and I'm not backing down either. Not about this."

"I hear you."

Charlotte turned on her side so that she faced him. "So what else has been going on? I see you're still working in the financial world."

"You know I've always loved being a broker, and even

with the economy being in such dire straits right now, I still love what I do, and people are steadily beginning to warm back up to the stock market."

"Well, at least you have your work to focus on. I don't even have that."

"No? I just assumed you held some position at your church."

"I sit on the elder board, but with the exception of that, I don't have a daily, full-time position. Until now, though, I didn't mind that because not having a career has allowed me the opportunity to be there for my son the way he's needed me to be, and to also travel with Curtis when he did frequent speaking engagements. But now, Matthew is seventeen and getting ready to be a senior next year, so it's not like he really needs me the way he used to."

"Sounds like you're experiencing empty-nest blues a whole year early."

"Yeah, I guess I am."

"Well, you knew Sybil and I only had the one child, and she's now a sophomore at Yale."

"That's great, Michael. Good for her. Matthew is gearing up for an Ivy League school as well. Curtis practically has him enrolled and already living on campus at Harvard, but if Matthew had it his way, he'd probably go to one of the top football schools. He's very good at football, but he'll never disappoint his father, though."

"I have to say I tend to agree with your husband on the Harvard tip. If you have a child who gets exceptional grades and you can afford to send him or her to Harvard, Yale, Princeton, Stanford, et cetera, et cetera, et cetera, then you definitely should. They may not lead in sports, but they do turn out some of the smartest young men and women in

America. Most of whom go on to earn well into the six fig-
ures with their first job."

"True. And I think Matthew understands that, so that's
why he doesn't complain."

Michael stroked Charlotte's hair some more, and she
finally closed her eyes. She was so relaxed and relieved
of tension.

"So, hey. You know I wanna see you again, right?"

Charlotte wasn't sure how she should answer, but
before she could, his phone rang. Michael reached over
on the floor and pulled it out of his pants pocket. "Hello?"
he said, covering his face with his free hand and laying
his head back on the pillow. He seemed irritated, and
Charlotte knew it was Sybil. She knew because he had the
same look of annoyance he'd had a full decade ago, whenever he heard from her.

"What is it? No. No. I don't know what time I'll be
home. I have a lot to finish up here at the office. I didn't
answer my office phone because I don't want to be dis-
tracted by any business calls. I'm working on something
for a client that requires my full concentration. I already
told you. I don't know what time I'll be home exactly, but
I'll see you when I get there. Goodbye, Sybil. Because I
need to get back to work. Geez," he said and hung up the
phone.

Charlotte watched his body language and facial
expressions and wondered why he didn't just tell her the
truth. But then it wasn't like she was rearing to tell Curtis
about the man she'd slept with two nights ago or about
Michael. She hadn't voluntarily told him about Aaron
either, so who was she to judge anyone?

"So when can I see you again?" he said.

Charlotte thought about Matthew and Curtis. "I don't know."

"I really want to see you again as soon as possible, and I'll do whatever I have to to make it happen. My friend is over in China working for the next three months, so his house is all mine the whole time he's gone."

"Really? So who else have you brought here?"

"I won't lie. Last year, I was seeing someone, and I did bring her here a few times. But I swear, I haven't done that since. The only reason I have a key is because my friend—Gerald is his name—wanted me to check on the place from time to time. So when?"

"Well, aren't we persistent?" Charlotte said, teasing him.

"I am. And on purpose, too," he said, easing on top of her. "I'm persistent about a lot of things, and I work very hard for whatever it is I want."

"Is that right?"

Michael kissed her. "It is. I guarantee it."

"Then, in that case, do what you will to me. Do whatever you want."

Chapter 16

Curtis didn't know what was wrong with him. Last night, before dropping off to sleep in one of the guest bedrooms, the one closest to Curtina, he'd told himself he was finished arguing with Charlotte and was prepared to move on without her if need be. But now, here he was sitting in his office on a Wednesday evening, preparing for Bible study, trying to call Charlotte for the third time. He was almost ashamed of himself because of the way he basically had been kissing her behind, and he didn't like it. He felt like a wimp. Though what kept him making one attempt after another was the love he still had for his wife, regardless of how terribly she was treating him. He'd had the same thoughts only days ago, and he was still trying to hang on. He was still hoping for some sort of miracle.

Curtis read Scripture and jotted down some notes. Bible study would be starting in a couple of hours, but before then he had a meeting with Anise, Charlotte's cousin, the one she still wasn't on the best terms with. Anise hadn't gotten past the idea that Charlotte had slept with her husband when Anise had still been married to him, although the good news was that, as of late, she at least chatted with Charlotte whenever they were in the same room—something she hadn't started doing regularly until maybe a year ago.

As he continued outlining the lesson he was about to teach, he heard a knock at his door.

"Come in."

"Hey, I know I'm a little early, so just let me know if you want me to come back in an hour," Anise said.

"No, no. You're fine. I was just reviewing a few items, so have a seat."

Anise removed her brown, elbow-length leather gloves and then her camel-colored, burnt-wool swing coat with three-quarter sleeves. "It's really cold out there."

"I know. Supposed to get down into the single digits before the night is over."

"Well, I'm ready for spring. It's only February, but I'm praying for May already."

They both laughed.

"I think we all are," Curtis agreed.

Anise pulled a file from her briefcase, but Curtis said, "I know we need to discuss a list of to-do items for the ribbon-cutting ceremony and all the other grand opening activities you're planning, but if you're okay with it, I want to discuss something else with you."

"Definitely. Go ahead."

"Well, I don't know how much your mom has told you, but Charlotte and I haven't been doing too well."

"Yeah, Mom kind of filled me in the other day, and I really don't know what to say about my cousin."

"Neither do I, really, but this whole disagreement is taking a major toll on our marriage. It's affecting every aspect of our lives."

"I'm sure it is," she said. "But as much as I hate telling you this, I don't see Charlotte budging on this. Charlotte has always wanted what she wants when she wants it, and that's just the way it is."

"Don't I know it. But I still never expected her to act so cruelly toward Curtina. Not when she brought a child into our home that wasn't mine."

"Charlotte is the queen of hypocrisy, though, and you can't win with someone like that."

"Well, somethin's gotta give because we can't go on like this forever."

"No, I don't see where you can. And for whatever it's worth, Curtis, you're a wonderful man. Yes, you made some mistakes in the past, but how many of us haven't? So regardless of what happens, I hope you won't forget that. I also hope you won't stop being a good father to Curtina, the same as you've always been to Matthew and Alicia."

Curtis nodded but thought back to the time he'd learned Matthew wasn't his son. For a while this was what everyone else had believed, too, until another DNA test had been administered, proving he was. Curtis had been devastated by the news and had stopped by Anise's house for comfort and encouragement. But then, they'd spontaneously shared a kiss, which had caught them both off guard, and thankfully, they had been saved by Anise's doorbell. Her best friend had come for a visit, and while Curtis had left in a hurry, he'd often wondered how far he and Anise might have gone. He hadn't thought about this in years, though, so he was a little bothered by the fact that he was thinking of it now. He didn't like it, because, slowly but surely, his old desires and his attraction to other women were trying to ambush his psyche. He was now having to battle some very lustful demons, those he'd thought he was rid of, and he was worried.

"So, tell me," Curtis said. "How are things with that guy...what's his name? William, right?" He knew he shouldn't have cared one way or the other, but he couldn't seem to stop himself from asking.

"It's not the greatest, and to be honest, we barely even talk on the phone anymore. He just wasn't my type, and I think he could tell I wasn't as interested in him as he wanted me to be."

"I'm sorry to hear that. You're too good of a person not to be in a happy relationship," Curtis said and then looked over at his cell phone when he heard it ringing. Charlotte was finally calling him back. "Hey," he said.

"Hey. Can we talk tonight after you finish up with Bible study?"

"So you're not coming, I take it?"

"No. But I really don't want to take a chance on Matthew overhearing our conversation, so I'll just come there when I think Bible study is over with. I'll just wait in your office for you, if that's okay."

"That's fine."

"Then I'll see you soon."

Curtis hung up, a little shocked by the calm in Charlotte's voice. She sounded pleasant and not angry, the way she had been for days now. Maybe Curtis's prayers had been answered. Either that or her calm nature was the beginning of a new storm.

Chapter 17

*Y*ou taught a wonderful lesson, Pastor," Mother Johnson, one of the appointed mothers of the church, said to Curtis.

"I'm glad you enjoyed it, Mother."

"Even at seventy-eight and with all that I've learned from the Bible over the years, I still always learn something new because of you."

"Now, that's what I call a real compliment," Curtis said, smiling and hugging her.

"It's the truth. Now, you take care, son, and God willing, I'll see you on Sunday."

Mother Johnson walked away and Curtis shook the hands of more parishioners. Then Elder Jamison walked over.

"Well, Pastor, I'm going to head home, but I'll see you on Sunday morning here at church and then that evening at my house ... you know ... when your Colts take a beatdown from those Saints."

"Yeah, right. I see you got jokes just like Matthew does," he said, and they both laughed.

"Matthew is a smart kid, and like me he knows a winning team when he sees one."

"If you say so."

"I do."

Elder Jamison left the sanctuary, and Curtis shook a few more hands. But as he prepared to head up to his study, a tall, shapely woman with beautiful, wavy brown hair walked up to him and gave him an envelope. "I really enjoyed the lesson, Pastor."

"I'm glad."

The woman smiled and left as quickly as she'd approached him. He wondered what she'd given him, but from time to time, some of the members would bless him with a love offering or submit a special prayer request, so he knew it was one or the other.

Finally, Curtis greeted the last member and went up to his office. As promised, Charlotte was sitting in front of his desk, waiting for him.

"Hey," he said, walking in. "Why don't you come over here?"

"All right," she said.

When she sat down on the sofa, she turned her body toward him, but there was still ample space between them.

"So, what is it that you want to talk about?" he asked.

"Us. We've been at each other's throats and arguing daily, and I don't want us to go on this way, Curtis."

"Baby, I don't want that either. I never did."

"This entire situation has caused me to feel more animosity and rage than I've ever felt in my life, but what I've tried holding on to is the fact that I do love you, Curtis. I have loved you with all my heart for years, and I don't want to lose you. I don't want to break our family up if it can be helped."

"I feel the same way. I love you, and the thought of not being with you literally kills me."

"But even with as much as I love you," Charlotte said, "I can't continue with the existing conditions. So, you need to make a choice. It's either Curtina or me."

Curtis's heart dropped. He was astounded by Charlotte's ultimatum. When she'd called him earlier, saying they'd needed to talk, he'd thought it was because she had decided to work on accepting Curtina.

"I'm sorry," she continued. "But if you won't send your daughter away, then I'll have to begin making arrangements to move out."

"You're not serious?"

"I am."

Curtis leaned his head back and looked toward the ceiling. A thousand thoughts circulated in his mind. His first reaction was sadness and great disappointment, but now he thought about all the dirt Charlotte had done and how she was suddenly trying to play the role of an innocent victim. She had a lot of nerve coming there with some so-called final demand, but he had news for her. He wasn't going for it.

"You know," he said, "I'm not sure how many other ways I can say what I've been telling you for weeks now. But let me say it again: Curtina isn't going anywhere."

"But I can't live in the same house with her, Curtis. Not right now, anyway. Maybe a year or two from now, once I've had some time to digest this whole idea of being a mother to her. Maybe once I've had some time to completely forgive you. I know I said I had, but you were right when you said I hadn't. I just need time, Curtis."

"Fine. Take all the time you want, but my daughter is here to stay. I'm her father, and her home is wherever mine is."

"So you'd rather live there with her instead of me?"

"No, what I want is for both of you to be there. I love you as my wife, and I love my children. All of them."

Charlotte shook her head at him. "So that's it then. You choose your daughter over me."

"I choose both of you, but if you can't handle living in the house with Curtina, then that's your decision."

Charlotte grabbed her handbag and stood up. She never spoke another word before leaving, and Curtis felt numb. He didn't know if she was serious about walking out on him or not, but he was going to start planning for the worst.

Curtis went over to his desk, then remembered the envelope the woman had given him just before he'd come upstairs. He pulled it out of the inside pocket of his suit jacket and opened it.

Dear Pastor Black,

I have been attending Deliverance Outreach for a little over three months now, and I must say, I have never wanted any man as badly as I want you. I'd heard you speak a year ago over at a women's conference in Chicago, and I was drawn to you immediately. I'm totally captivated by your amazingly good looks, your charisma, your encouraging words, and even your mannerisms. So, when I saw that the company I work for had an opening here in Mitchell, I decided to apply for the transfer just so I'd be closer to you. And Pastor Black, I certainly don't regret it. Seeing and listening to you on Sundays and Wednesday nights give me such comfort and such joy that when you allow one of your associate pastors to deliver the sermon or teach the Bible study lesson, I'm ashamed to say I feel very disappointed.

But my reason for writing you this letter is to ask that you please pray for me and these lustful feelings I have for you. I need prayer because my feelings for you have now gotten so out of control that I'm now having vivid dreams of you and me in bed. I know my feelings are wrong, but my struggle is that I also believe I'd be able to satisfy you in a way like you've never been satisfied before. I'd be able to show you the kind of happiness and pleasure most men can only dream about but will never experience. So, please, I ask again, that you will pray for me.

                                        Sharon

Curtis saw that she'd also included her phone number and knew he was dealing with a deliberately bold woman. She was the kind of woman who went after what she wanted with great zeal and never worried about possible consequences. Women like Sharon were the most dangerous kind of women for a man like Curtis because they were willing to do whatever they had to in order to be with him. They were willing to sneak around behind closed doors and then show up for Sunday morning service, acting holier than thou. They were even willing to smile face-to-face with the wife of the man they were sleeping with and didn't see where there was anything wrong with it. Women like Sharon didn't *think* they could satisfy a married man better than his wife, they *knew* it.

Curtis looked at the letter again. Just one month ago he would have been completely offended by it, would have put the woman in her place and then told Charlotte about it. He didn't feel that way today, though. He felt a whole lot differently, thanks to his wife's ridiculous ultimatum and the way she'd been acting toward him. As a matter of fact, he felt so different he was going to hold on to this unexpected piece of correspondence. Not that he'd made the decision to contact the woman or take her up on her offer, but he would file her information for safekeeping, just in case.

He would keep her name and number because one never knew what the future might have in store, and there was nothing wrong with being prepared. He'd been out of the game for a long time now, but not so long that he'd forgotten how to play it. He didn't want to fall back into the rut he'd once found himself in, God knows he didn't, but Charlotte was making things very difficult for him. She was distant and unloving, and truth was, Curtis had never been the kind of man who could be okay with that. Yes, he'd turned his life completely around, but he had needs—the kind of needs that had to be met regularly, and he hoped Charlotte soon remembered that. Before it was too late.

Chapter 18

*H*e actually chose that little heifer over me. Charlotte didn't want to believe it, but now knew that Curtis would never change his mind. She'd gone back and forth, thinking that maybe he would and then thinking that maybe he wouldn't, but now she knew for sure. When she'd left Michael earlier this evening, she'd had a lot of time to think during her drive home, and she'd come to the conclusion that maybe her mother had been right about her needing to present Curtis with an ultimatum, once and for all. She'd decided that she would put forth a very serious effort and would even plead with him if she had to. But it hadn't worked. She'd called him in good faith, spoke to him with a nice, quiet tone of voice, and then told him her position. She'd even asked him to consider sending Curtina away on a temporary basis, just to give her more time to accept things. But he'd quickly dismissed her and made it clear that her attempt at trying to work things out this evening hadn't meant a thing to him. He'd acted as though her visit to his office had been a total waste of time.

So now that he'd called her bluff, which was what she'd told her mother she'd been afraid of, she didn't know what to do. She didn't know whether to pack her bags and leave the way she'd threatened or stay put and continue seeing Michael as well as doing whatever else she pleased. Charlotte weighed the advantages and disadvantages, but for some reason the disadvantages of leaving seemed to carry more weight. If she moved out, she'd have to find a much smaller house than what she was used to, file for a legal separation, fight Curtis about who Matthew was going to live with, and then deal with all the talk around town once word got out that she and Curtis had split. She knew she shouldn't care what anyone thought of her or what they had to say, but she did care. She always had and always would whether she wanted to or not.

So, no, she couldn't leave Curtis. Not right now, anyway. Not until she put more thought into her future and how she wanted to proceed. She would think about her marriage to Curtis and a possible divorce more carefully. She would be smart about the way she handled things; she wouldn't act too hastily and then be sorry for it.

After entering the house, Charlotte set her bag down on the granite kitchen counter and pulled a bottle of Fiji water from the refrigerator. She was also starting to feel a little hungry, but since it was already going on ten, she pulled out a cup of light vanilla yogurt and ate that. Actually, the calcium in it tended to help her sleep a little better whenever she had a cup of it right before bedtime, so she pulled out a second one as well.

"Hey, Mom." Matthew walked into the room, bobbing his head to whatever song was playing in his iPod. Then he turned it off and pulled his earbuds out.

"Hey, sweetie," she said. "So, how was your day?"

"Same ole, same ole. But it was good. I also filled out a couple more online applications not too long ago."

"Just can't help yourself, can you?"

Matthew smiled. "Nope. I just want to see how many of the really good schools, both academically and those that excel in football, I can get accepted to."

"You're funny. Because anyone who's already been contacted by Harvard will more than likely be accepted just about anywhere in the country."

"I know, but I just like filling out the information and reading about all the different schools and majors available."

"Well, just know that I am very, very proud of you, Matthew, and I don't know what I'll do without you when you leave."

"I'll miss you, too, Mom, but I'll still be home during the summer and for all the holidays. And you, Dad, and Curtina can come visit me, too."

Charlotte forced a smile on her face, but it must not have been very convincing because Matthew said, "Mom, why is it that whenever Curtina is around or someone mentions her name, you seem upset?"

"Because it's very hard for me."

"But you're so mean to her all the time."

Charlotte wasn't sure how to respond. She'd known for weeks now that Matthew had become more and more aware of her dislike for Curtina, but she hadn't thought he would go as far as confronting her about it.

"It's complicated, Matt."

"But why is it complicated? And why can't you just love Curtina? Because I'm really scared about you and Dad."

"Why do you say that?"

"Because you argue all the time, and you're always mad at each other."

"I'm really sorry that you've had to witness some of

our disagreements, but please try not to worry. Everything will be fine, and more than anything, what I want you to remember is that we both love you and will always be here for you."

"I love you, too, Mom. But Curtina is only a little girl, and it's not her fault that she was born with a different mother. Just like it wasn't Marissa's fault that she was born with a different father."

Charlotte wanted to break and run. If she could, she would leave the room by any means necessary, as long as it meant she no longer had to face her son and hear him speaking the truth. The kind of truth she didn't want to acknowledge and refused to admit to anyone.

"I know that, Matthew, but like I said, it's complicated, and I don't want you worrying about any of this."

Matthew stared at her for a few seconds, clearly wanting a better answer, but gave up on trying to talk to her about it. "I need to work some more on my English project before going to bed, so I'd better get back upstairs."

Charlotte kissed him good night, but she felt horrible. If nothing else, Matthew's grave concern was yet another reason she couldn't leave Curtis. She had to stay there for him, at least until he graduated high school next year. The road ahead would be tough and at times, she was sure, unbearable, but she would do what she had to for her son. She would forget about her own wants and needs and make Matthew's well-being and peace of mind her priority. She would continue being a good mother to him and also play her part as Curtis's wife whenever they were in public. She would do this and more, but she wouldn't stop seeing Michael Porter. She wouldn't give up the one thing she now had to look forward to.

Chapter 19

*I*t had been a long, tiring, and very emotional day, and Curtis was glad it was over. When he'd left the church, he'd picked up Curtina from Aunt Emma's, driven straight home, put Curtina to bed, looked in on Matthew, and then showered. Charlotte hadn't said a word to him, of course, but it wasn't like he had anything to say to her either, so their feelings were mutual.

Now, Curtis lay wide awake in the guest room, thinking about everything imaginable. He thought about his past, his children—specifically Curtina—and also about his deteriorating marriage. He was so unsure about his future, and he didn't like that. He hated not knowing what was to come and not having any control over it. He didn't like waiting for one bad thing to happen after another, and he certainly didn't want to deal with any unwanted surprises. He also didn't want to go through yet a third divorce with a third wife and then have to start all over again. It was bad enough he'd married three different women and had been unfaithful to each of them. But marrying a fourth was simply ridiculous, and it wasn't a road he wanted to travel down.

Still, Curtis didn't have a clue as to where things were headed with him and Charlotte, and had no choice but to sit back and wait to see what she would do. There was no telling with her, so he knew her next move was anybody's guess and definitely not predictable. What he did know, though, was that Curtina would be there with him until she left for college. That was a long time off, but he was very happy and very honored to be able to raise her up and offer her the most blessed life possible. Yes, she'd been born into the wrong circumstances, and yes, he never should have taken a chance on getting another woman pregnant. But it had happened, and now he had to make the best of it. He'd hoped Charlotte would do the same, however . . .

Another hour passed, but Curtis still lay awake, thinking. Except at the moment he wasn't thinking about Charlotte at all and thought more about his attraction to Anise, Raven, and Sharon, and how all he had to do was make a quick call to either of the latter two and they'd come to him. Or he'd easily be able to go to them. With Anise, he wasn't sure how she felt about him, but he'd already made the decision not to approach her because, after all, she was his wife's first cousin. He felt comfortable around her and knew from years ago that there had been a connection between them, but he wasn't the kind of man who consorted with multiple family members. He had kissed Anise that one time, but only because he'd been hurt about Matthew. He'd been very vulnerable, but today was a different day and he knew better. He also would never do anything to hurt Aunt Emma, not with how good she'd always been to him. Since Anise was her daughter, he knew anything that might occur between him and Anise only meant disaster. A lot of people would be hurt, and there would be no taking it back.

The night continued, and after three hours of tossing and turning, Curtis knew why he couldn't get to sleep.

It was because of all these urges and sexual desires that were successfully consuming him. Curtis had tried to focus on something else, but he now yearned for pleasure and the kind of satisfaction that only a beautiful and very skilled woman could give him. Beautiful because he could never be attracted to a dreadful-looking woman, and skilled because his kind of woman had to know what she was doing and how to make him content.

These compulsive aches and cravings were getting worse by the second, so Curtis started praying. He prayed because he didn't know what else to do, and he didn't want to break his promise to God. He'd told God that if He brought him through that last scandal, he would do right from then on. He would be a good and dedicated servant, and he would make everyone around him proud. He would be an example to all young ministers and be the kind of leader his congregation was proud to have.

So, there was no doubt Curtis wanted to remain faithful, but he loved sex. He loved it and needed it. And it had been four full days now since he and Charlotte had been together in that way. It had been Saturday night, to be exact, and now here it was the wee hours on Thursday morning, which meant he was actually working on day five of going without. But then he realized something: Charlotte loved and needed sex as much as he did, and it had never mattered if they were angry with each other and not speaking—and sometimes they would still not be speaking even after the fact. No matter how serious their issues were, they still shared a frequent and deep level of intimacy. They rarely missed a day and never more than two days, so he knew she had to want him just as badly.

He got up from the bed and went down the hall to his

own bedroom, walked in, and eased into bed with her. He never said a word, but instead, he moved closer to her in a spoon position and wrapped his arm around her. He could tell she was fast asleep, so he kissed her neck in multiple spots from behind. Soon, Charlotte moved her body slightly, but when she realized what was happening, she reached her hand behind her and pushed him away. Then, she turned on her nightstand light and sat up.

"What in the world?"

"Look, baby. I know things are bad, but I still need you. And I know you need me, the same as always."

Charlotte frowned with fury. "You must be crazy if you think I'm having sex with you."

"And why not?"

"You know why."

"Because we're having problems? Because you're mad at me?"

"What other reason would it be?"

"You tell me. Because being mad has never stopped you before."

"Well, this is a new day, and you might as well get used to it."

Curtis got out of the bed. "So it's like that?"

"It is. And it's going to stay that way until you do right by me."

Curtis walked over to the door but then looked back at her. "Fine. But when it's all said and done, I want you to remember something. I really tried. I did everything I could."

"And what is that supposed to mean exactly?"

"Just what I said," he told her and left her sitting there.

Chapter 20

*M*ichael was a drug. The kind Charlotte simply couldn't get enough of. It was Super Bowl Sunday, four days since she'd given Curtis that ultimatum about his daughter, and Charlotte was having the time of her life. She and Michael were locked away in a fabulous five-star hotel suite at a well-known resort down in West Palm Beach, Florida, one that offered mouthwatering meals and the best spa services.

As it had turned out, a few months ago Michael had booked a Super Bowl trip with a few of his friends, but a couple of days ago he had come up with the perfect idea: Charlotte would fly to another city in Florida so that he could skip out on the Super Bowl in Miami and come spend all his time with her instead. Needless to say, Charlotte hadn't hesitated and had quickly told Curtis that she needed a vacation. She needed to get as far away from Illinois as possible. Curtis hadn't commented or objected, which was strange, so on Friday morning, she'd caught the first flight available out of O'Hare.

She was thrilled about it, too, because right now she was lying next to Michael, reminiscing about the five times they'd made love over the last two days. Michael made her feel as if she was the most important woman in the world, and she needed that. She needed what Curtis was no longer giving her: his undivided affection and attention. She needed the kind of love and attention that little heifer Curtina had stolen from her.

"Gosh, baby, you have no idea how much I wish we could just stay here from now on," Michael said as he walked away from the balcony doors with a bath towel secured around his waist.

"I know. I've had an amazing time here with you, and I hate for it to end."

"If I didn't have to be back in my office on Tuesday to meet with some very important clients of mine," he said, sitting down on the bed next to where Charlotte was leaning against two pillows, "I would ask you to stay here until next weekend."

"That would have been wonderful."

Michael locked eyes with her. "You might not believe this, but I haven't been this happy with a woman in a very long time. I've dated other women, which I've already told you about, but I never felt anything like I'm feeling with you. You and me, we're so right together. So in sync and we understand each other."

"I know, and it's weird, isn't it?"

"Very. Especially since we hadn't spoken in so long, but now I don't want to be without you. What I want is to see you all the time," he said, leaning forward and kissing her.

Charlotte's body shivered. It did this every time Michael touched her—or when he did anything to her, for that matter. He was driving her wild and completely out of her mind. She could barely think straight, and at this very moment, she felt like calling Curtis and telling him that she wanted a divorce just as soon as he could give her one. But then her phone rang, interrupting her daydream. This was part of the reason she'd wanted to turn her phone off and keep it off the entire time she was gone. But she'd known Matthew would want to call her, and she didn't want to disappoint him. Ironically, it was him now.

"Hey, Mom. Are you having a good time down there in sunny Florida?"

"I am, honey. I really needed this," she said. Michael kissed her on the cheek and went back over near the balcony. "But how are *you*?"

"I'm great. Can't wait to get over to Elder Jamison's in a couple of hours, though. Remember, I told you he's having a big Super Bowl party for some of the men at the church and their sons."

"I know you'll have a wonderful time."

"That's for sure," he said. "And hey, do you wanna speak to Dad?"

"No, not right now, sweetie."

"Why? You haven't spoken to him since you left, have you?"

"Matt, your dad and I are having some problems."

"Because of Curtina still?"

"Honey, let's not talk about this, okay?"

"Mom, I really, really don't get it."

"Don't get what?"

"You. And the way you hate Curtina. I don't get how you could make a mistake with that Aaron dude and have Marissa by him, but now you're mad at Dad for doing the same thing with Miss Tabitha."

Charlotte's heart sank. Just the other night, Matthew

had questioned her about Curtina and compared her to Marissa, but she'd never expected him to ever bring up Aaron to her. She heard about Aaron all the time from Curtis but never thought her own son would even think on that level, and she was mortified. She was ashamed and humiliated.

"Mom, you there?" he asked.

"Yes, I'm here, but Matt, it's like I told you. I really don't want to talk about this. What your father and I are going through is very complicated and not something you're old enough to understand—"

"Mom, I'm seventeen, remember?" he said, interrupting her.

"Still, you're much too young to understand these kinds of adult matters."

Matthew sighed but digressed. "So, are you still coming home tomorrow?"

"Yes, I'll see you tomorrow evening."

"I miss you, Mom. And I love you."

"I love you, too, sweetie. And you enjoy yourself, okay?"

"I will."

Charlotte told him good-bye and set her phone on the nightstand.

Michael strutted back over to the bed and sat close to her again. "That can't be easy on you."

"It's horrible."

"It's never easy when children think their parents are going to separate or that things just aren't quite right between them."

"No. And especially for a kid like Matthew who knows his parents have had trouble in the past. Then, add in the nationwide embarrassment we caused him just a couple of years back, and you end up with a child who is terrified that the same thing will happen all over again. It was so bad last time, he wanted to change schools."

"Wow. Not good at all."

Charlotte rested her head against the shiny, cherry-wood headboard.

"So, this might not be the best time to ask you this, but since we're kind of on the subject of you and your husband, do you still love him?"

"Yes," Charlotte said.

"Man. So, it's not like you even had to think about it. That hurts."

"I'm sorry. I just want to be honest with you about everything. I don't know how long I'll be in love with him because right now, I certainly don't like him very much, but I can't deny that I do still love him. I always have."

"I appreciate that. I guess I was just hoping you didn't because ever since we were together on Wednesday, I haven't been able to take my mind off you. Then, now after being with you these last two days...Charlotte, I think I might actually be falling in love with you."

Charlotte hadn't expected to hear anything like this so soon, but his words gave her a warm feeling. "I didn't know you felt that strongly. But I can't deny that I have very strong feelings for you as well," she said. She didn't know if it was love, but her feelings for him were definitely intense.

"Lie all the way down," he told her. Then he moved on top of her and stared straight into her eyes. "Promise me that you won't stop seeing me."

"I don't know if I can do that."

Michael kissed her rough and then asked her again. "Promise me." Then, he kissed her entire neck like a madman. "Promise me."

Charlotte grew weaker by the second. She was under some forceful spell and was tired of fighting him. She was so tired, she told him what he wanted to hear. "I promise, I promise, I promise."

She lay there, enjoying the magnificent way Michael was pleasuring her, and she blocked out all that normally mattered to her. She let herself go completely just like he wanted her to. She lay there in absolute heaven.

Chapter 21

$\mathcal{M}$atthew was at school, Curtina was in her room, sitting on the floor watching a video, and Agnes was downstairs washing a load of clothes and cleaning up the kitchen. Curtis, against his better judgment, was on the phone with Sharon, the woman who'd claimed she wanted prayer—and him at the same time.

"I knew you couldn't wait to call me, and I'm so glad you did."

"Oh yeah? So, how did you know?"

"Because you need me."

Curtis relaxed his body on the chaise in his bedroom and crossed his legs. This woman didn't beat around the bush, and he sort of liked that about her. "No, I called because I was simply looking for good conversation."

"Okay," she said, laughing, obviously not believing him.

"I'm serious."

"Well, if that's true, then why can't you just get that from your wife? And why did you keep making eye contact with me during service yesterday?"

"It's complicated. But let me be very clear on something. When we talk, my wife and my children are off-limits."

"No problem. I'm fine with that."

"Good."

"So what *do* you want to talk about then?"

"You."

"What do you wanna know?"

"Anything you wanna tell."

"Well, let's see. I'm past thirty but not quite forty. I've never been married, don't have any children, and I plan to do whatever it takes to make you fall in love with me."

"Hmmm. Now, that's funny."

"Maybe to you."

"So what do you do for a living?" he asked, dismissing her last statement.

"I'm an IT manager."

"Is that what you've always done career-wise?"

"Pretty much. But I love it even more now that I can basically work from home if I choose to."

"Is that where you are now?"

"I am. Why?"

"Just asking."

"Maybe you're asking because you want to come over."

"No. That's not it at all."

"You sure?"

"Positive."

"So what else do you wanna know?"

"Are you seeing anyone?"

"No. Just you."

Curtis laughed. "Well, we both know that's not true. But since we're on the subject, why did you take it upon yourself to approach me the way you did?"

"It's like I told you in the letter. From the moment I saw you at that conference last year, I wanted you."

"But why?"

Sharon paused. Then said, "Truthfully?"

"Of course."

"Because you're a powerful, attractive man who is known everywhere."

"Well, at least you're honest."

"Honest is the only way to be. As long as you can handle it."

"It's better than being lied to."

"I agree."

There was a bit of silence, and then Sharon said, "So does that answer all your questions?"

"For the most part. Although, I am wondering why you left the great city of Chicago for a small town like Mitchell."

"I told you that in my letter, too. I did it so I could be closer to you."

"So, you moved all this way just to be near someone you don't even know?"

"I did. I even made sure the home I bought was out in the country and very secluded so you wouldn't have to worry about anyone seeing you. I know it sounds strange and maybe a little naïve, but some things are meant to be."

"You're right. Some things are, but I'm not sure that's true where you and I are concerned."

"Trust me. It is. You just don't know it yet. Either that or you're in denial."

"You're a very aggressive woman."

"You think so?"

"You are."

"I'm not afraid to go after what I want, if that's what you mean."

"I figured that out when you came up to me after Bible study and passed me that envelope."

"Life is too short, and fear gets you nowhere. But enough of all that. When exactly are you coming to see me?" she said matter-of-factly.

"Maybe in the future."

"What's wrong with coming today?"

"Can't."

"Can't or won't?"

"Both."

"If you come see me, I promise to make it worth your while. I promise to do whatever you ask and then some."

Dear God, please give me the strength to say no to this woman.

"Are you there?"

"Yeah, I'm here."

"So do you want my address?"

"No. And actually, I have to go now."

"So you're not coming?"

"No."

"That's too bad."

"Sorry."

"It's okay. I'm a very patient woman, and I know you'll change your mind eventually. You'll be ringing my doorbell sooner than you think."

Curtis told her good-bye and hung up. Last Wednesday night, after reading Sharon's note, he'd told himself that he wouldn't call her. But after Charlotte had denied him sex later that evening and then hopped up at the last minute and left for Florida, he'd had the entire weekend to think. Charlotte had claimed she needed a break, but Curtis wondered who she might be taking a "break" with. He didn't want to think the worst, but he also knew who his wife was and what she was capable of. He was going to give her the benefit of the doubt, though, something he rarely did with anyone who had betrayed him previously, and it was the reason he'd made the decision to only *talk* to Sharon for the time being. Now, he wished he hadn't contacted her at all because he found himself still thinking about her.

Thankfully, though, his daughter Alicia called, and that allowed him to focus on something else.

"Hey, sweetheart," he said. "How are you?"

"I'm good, Daddy. What about you?"

"Can't complain."

"So did you guys make it over to Elder Jamison's for the Super Bowl? Matt told me on Saturday night that he was having a party."

"Yep. We did, and it was a great time."

"I'm sure it was. And what did Charlotte and Curtina do?"

"Curtina stayed with Aunt Emma, and Charlotte flew down to Florida for a spa weekend."

"Really? Without me? I can't believe she didn't call and ask me to go with her because she normally hates going to those places alone. Did Janine go?"

"No, as far as I know, she went by herself. Said she just needed a break," he said, not wanting Alicia to think anything was wrong. "I'm sure she'll ask you next time."

"I hope so. But I'm still giving her the business when I talk to her," Alicia said, laughing.

Curtis forced himself to laugh with her but then changed the subject. "So, how are things going with Phillip?"

"Oh my God, Daddy, they couldn't be better."

"Yeah, I know," he said, chuckling.

"You're a trip."

"Phillip talks about you every time we speak, but I just wanted to hear your take on your relationship with him."

"I'm so happy, Daddy, and so glad to be back seeing Phillip. I know I messed things up pretty badly the first time, but I really hope to marry him again."

"I'm hoping the same thing, baby girl. Phillip is one of the best men I've ever known, and you're blessed to have another chance with him."

"I know. And I'm very grateful."

"But tell me. What have you heard about that fool JT?"

"Well, actually, one of his former members called me a few days ago, saying she heard that a lot of the members who left are slowly but surely rejoining. I mean, can you believe that, Daddy? Even when they know JT used to be a pimp and then got a woman pregnant while he was married to his first wife and then did the same thing when he was married to me?"

"Yeah, I believe it. It happens all the time," Curtis said, thinking how his own congregation had stood by him, too, even after they learned about his affair with Tabitha and about the birth of Curtina.

"I just don't get it. They couldn't possibly think he's sorry or that he's really changed. Not to mention, he's still out on bail and is sure to get at least some prison time after trying to forge your name on those recommendation letters."

"The trial is coming up in three months, so it'll be interesting to see what happens."

"I know I've said this before, Daddy, but I'm so sorry I didn't listen to you. You tried your best to warn me about JT, but I completely ignored you. I married one of the worst men alive, and I'll always regret that."

"But the good news is that it's all in the past now. You got your divorce, you moved on, and that's all that matters."

"Still. I just wish I hadn't gotten involved with him."

"Like I said, it's all in the past."

"I guess," she said. "So what else is new?"

"Well, I'm almost finished up with the revisions for my second novel, and my publicist has just about finished confirming all my tour events. I can't believe my first book is actually being released in four months."

"I believe it."

"It's so exciting, and I hope it'll be a good time out on the road."

"You'll have the best time ever, and you know I'll try to make it to as many of your events as I can."

"I really appreciate that, Daddy."

"I'm glad it's in the summer so Matt won't have to miss any school. You know he would die if he couldn't come see you."

"Isn't that the truth. But you know I want him there, too. I want everyone there."

Curtis walked down the hallway to Curtina's room to check on her. "Oh, and hey. How's your mom?"

"She's fine. Actually, she asked about you, too, just this morning. She wanted to know if you were also working on another book and how you were doing."

"You'll have to tell her I said hello when you speak to her again."

"I will."

"Hey, you wanna speak to your big sister?" Curtis said to Curtina and then gave her the phone. He smiled as she spoke nonstop gibberish. When he figured Alicia had heard enough of it, he took the phone back and Curtina continued watching her video.

"Okay, it's me again."

"Curtina is so funny," Alicia said. "But I love hearing her voice."

"You'll have to come visit us when you get some time."

"Actually, Phillip and I were planning on coming down on Sunday for service, but since it'll be Valentine's Day, we decided to celebrate here. We'll be down the next Sunday, though, for sure."

"Sounds good. Can't wait to see you."

"I can't wait either. Anyway, Daddy, I'd better get back to my revisions and then get something to eat. But I'll call you in a couple of days."

"You take care, sweetheart."

"You, too, Daddy. Love you."

"I love you back."

Curtis ended the call and thought about calling Charlotte. They hadn't spoken since before she'd left, and he wondered how she was doing. But then he thought about the fact that she hadn't bothered to contact him either, and how even when Matthew had asked her if she'd wanted to speak to him yesterday, she'd said no. Matthew hadn't told Curtis what she'd said exactly, but Curtis had been standing around the corner and had heard Matthew's part of the conversation. He'd even heard him questioning her about her dislike for Curtina and had wondered what Charlotte's response had been.

Curtis continued debating whether he should call Charlotte, but then something came over him: resentment, disappointment, and anger. So much so that at that very second he decided he was through begging and pleading with her to work things out with him. From this point on, he would leave their reconciliation up to her. He would wait until she came to him, saying how sorry she was and how she was finally ready to call a cease-fire. He would wait for a little while, but if she didn't come to her senses soon, well…

Chapter 22

The long, sleek, black stretch limo wound around the curve of the subdivision and turned into the driveway. Next, the driver stepped out of the vehicle and opened the door for Charlotte, and she got out and typed in the code to open the security gate. As it slid open, Charlotte got back into the vehicle, and the driver continued up to the house. This morning, Charlotte had really started to miss Matthew and couldn't wait to see him, but she already dreaded seeing Curtis and his baby sidekick. She'd had a wonderful time in West Palm Beach, and thanks to Michael she hadn't had to think about her husband or his daughter for three full days. As a matter of fact, this was part of the reason she couldn't wait to see Michael again. He'd been the perfect gentleman, and even now she couldn't stop thinking about the effect he had on her sexually. She couldn't get over how good he still was in bed. Even during her three-hour flight home, she'd spent most of it fantasizing about him and daydreaming about the next time they would have a chance to be together.

When they arrived in the circle portion of the driveway and directly in front of the house, the driver got out and opened the door for Charlotte again. Then he pulled her luggage from the trunk. Charlotte walked up the steps and opened the front door with her key, and the driver walked in and set down both her garment and overnight bags.

"Thanks so much for everything, Carlisle," she said, passing him a fifty-dollar bill. "I know the standard gratuity is always added on to the bill when the reservation is made, but I just want you to have a little extra."

"That's very kind of you, Mrs. Black, and I really do appreciate it."

"No problem, and you take care."

"You, too. I'll see you next time." Charlotte closed the door behind him, but as soon as she did, Matthew came down the stairway.

"Hey, Mom," he said, hugging her. "I'm so glad you're back."

"Hi, honey. It's good to be back, too."

"You want me to take your stuff up to your room?" Charlotte smiled at how thoughtful her son was. "That would be nice, so thank you for that."

Matthew picked up her bags and started back up to the second level. "So, you know the Saints won, right?"

"Yeah, I saw that. And I'm sure you're thrilled to death about that," she said as she followed him.

"I am. I told Dad they were going to win, but he decided to keep rooting for those losers. And I've been razzing him about it ever since."

Charlotte laughed. "I'm sure you have. But hey, how was school today?"

"Well, while we were in the cafeteria having lunch, the police showed up and finally arrested Mr. Rush."

"Good."

"They didn't handcuff him at first. But then, a few of us got up and looked out of the window and saw his hands bent behind his back and the police helping him into one of their cars. It wasn't a regular police car, though; it was the kind detectives drive. We also heard that a second girl has come forward, but we don't know who it is yet."

"That really saddens me to hear that, Matt, but I'm glad you realize that not everyone can be trusted. Not even people you should be able to trust no matter what."

"I realize that now, Mom, because I never would have thought anything bad about Mr. Rush. None of the kids would have." Matthew walked into the master bedroom and set her luggage down. Then he pulled his iPod Touch from the lower front pocket of his Mitchell Prep Football hoodie and read a text someone had just sent him. He scrolled through it and then cracked up laughing. "Elijah is too loony," he said and quickly texted a response to his friend.

Charlotte pulled off her jacket and kicked off her shoes.

Matthew read another text and laughed out loud again. "I'll be back, Mom," he said.

Charlotte shook her head and smiled. She wondered what these kids would do if they couldn't text each other a zillion times per day. It was all they seemed to do anymore, and they couldn't seem to live without it.

But Charlotte's smile vanished when she saw Curtina walking into the room.

"Mommy!" she said, all bright-eyed and happy.

Charlotte stared at her in a not-so-pleasant way and hoped it was enough to make her leave. There was no such luck, though.

"Mommy!" Curtina repeated. This time she walked right in front of Charlotte and reached her hands up.

Charlotte gazed down at her with folded arms and spoke in a harsh but low volume. "If you think I'm picking you up, you've got another think coming. Now, get out of here and go back to your room where you belong."

Curtina's smile disappeared, but she didn't move.

So, Charlotte took her little hand, forcefully escorted her across the room and then right out of it. Curtina burst into tears, but Charlotte quickly closed the door in her face. Curtina stood outside, weeping, but it wasn't long before Charlotte heard Matthew.

"What's wrong, Curtina? It's okay. Stop crying. You can come in my room," he said. Charlotte knew he must have picked her up because all of a sudden she didn't hear anything.

Good. She was finally gone. Although, Charlotte was glad Curtis hadn't caught that little brat bawling because she could only imagine the crazy fit he would have thrown. Actually, she wondered where he was since she still hadn't seen him yet. Ironically enough, she heard his voice barely ten minutes later, and it sounded as if he was talking on the phone. She couldn't tell who he was chatting with but knew it had to be someone from the church because he was raving over how spectacular the lighting system was going to be in the new building. At first, she'd wondered if maybe he'd been gone, but now she knew he'd obviously been downstairs in his study all along but just hadn't bothered coming out to say anything to her.

Curtis walked into the room as he ended his call. Then he looked at her. "So did you have a good time?"

"Yes. Actually, a great time."

"Good for you. Lots of sun and spa treatments every day?"

"Lots."

"Good." He picked up one of his many Bibles from the dresser and headed back out of the bedroom.

Charlotte watched him and knew she didn't have the right to expect any excitement from him, not with what she'd been doing with Michael all weekend down in Florida, but it felt strange seeing how nonchalant he was about her arrival back home. He acted as though it was no major deal at all, and she'd be lying if she said her feelings weren't hurt at least a little. He seemed to have a whole new attitude, much different than the one he'd possessed only a few days ago, and she wondered why. She didn't want to think the worst, that he'd washed his hands of the situation and no longer cared about their marriage, but she couldn't help feeling a bit concerned. She couldn't help wondering if maybe Curtis had found someone else to be with, the same as she had. He wouldn't do that, though. Maybe years ago he might have, but the new Curtis had promised her he would be faithful to her until the end. And she believed him. It was true that *she* was committing adultery again, but not Curtis. No, Curtis truly did want to live a respectable and decent life, and he was serious about being a good father and husband. He was committed to both God and his ministry, and regardless of how bad things had gotten between them, he wouldn't take up with another woman. He'd said he wouldn't, and Charlotte knew she was silly for thinking otherwise. She knew she'd gotten herself all worked up over nothing.

Chapter 23

Curtis sat reading the book of Romans, chapter seven to be exact, and hated that he was starting to identify with Paul all over again. He'd known talking to Sharon was wrong, but for some reason he'd called her a second time this afternoon and had chatted with her for another two hours. When he'd hung up from her this morning, he'd told himself that he wouldn't make communicating with her a habit, but the more he'd played with Curtina and tried to busy himself with reading and watching CNN, it hadn't been long before Curtina had gotten sleepy and Curtis had put her down for a nap. He'd taken her into her bedroom and dialed Sharon's number immediately following.

Now he wanted to call her a third time but hesitated for two reasons. First, Charlotte was back in town, and he didn't want to take the chance on her hearing his conversation. Sure, he was downstairs and on a totally different level of the house; however, he still didn't want to be careless. But it was his second reason that was most important and the one that affected him greatly: the Scripture he'd just finished reading. He sometimes studied the King James version of the Bible, but tonight he focused on the

New Living Translation. Romans, chapter seven, verses fourteen through seventeen: "The law is good, then. The trouble is not with the law but with me, because I am sold into slavery, with sin as my master. I don't understand myself at all, for I really want to do what is right, but I don't do it. Instead, I do the very thing I hate. I know perfectly well that what I am doing is wrong, and my bad conscience shows that I agree that the law is good. But I can't help myself, because it is sin inside me that makes me do these evil things."

Curtis took a deep breath. *Why is this happening? After all this time of doing what's right and being content with it. Why, God? Why am I so tempted to sleep with another woman?*

It just didn't make any sense, regardless of how bad his marriage was because, like Paul, he knew right from wrong. He'd known the difference between the two since he was a child, so there was no excuse for the way he was feeling. His thoughts and actions were uncalled for, but, also like Paul, he simply couldn't help himself. He knew the best thing for him was praying and asking God for help, but shamefully, he hadn't. He hadn't gotten on his knees the way he normally did whenever he wanted to converse with God about a serious matter, and he knew it was because he'd enjoyed his time on the phone with Sharon. He'd tried to tell himself that she was nothing special, but in truth, he was fascinated with the sound of her voice and flattered by her great desire to be with him. She was so easy to talk to and seemed willing to do whatever he wanted on a moment's notice.

Another half hour passed, and Curtis struggled with the idea of calling her again. He knew he shouldn't, but it wasn't long before the good in him lost the battle and he dialed her number.

"Hello?" she answered.

"Hey. How's it goin'?"

"Wow, three times in one day. I'm impressed."

"Is that right?"

"Yes. I'm glad you called back. Although I knew you would."

"How?"

"Just had a feeling is all."

"Not sure I like that."

"What?"

"Being predictable."

"Well, I don't see anything wrong with it."

"So what are you doing?" Curtis leaned back in his chair and flipped on the flat-screen television mounted on the corner wall. He did this for added sound, just in case Charlotte did decide to come downstairs.

"Lying here thinking about you," she said.

"Yeah, right."

"I'm serious. I told you I want you. And I meant that. I wanna do the kinds of things to you that some folks might consider illegal."

Curtis's body heated up. "I don't know if I like the sound of that."

"Trust me. You'll love it, and you won't be able to get enough of it. You'll crave everything about me from then on."

"Sounds to me like some sort of voodoo," Curtis said, slightly laughing.

But Sharon stayed serious. "No, nothing like that. But once you've been with me, you definitely won't be able to think about much else. You'll be back again and again and again."

Now Curtis got serious. Years ago, he would have taken words like that to heart. He would have seen them as a challenge and would have been out the door, in his car, and on his way to prove that *he* was the one women couldn't stop thinking about. Not after having sex with him. It had been that way for years, and while he hadn't slept around as of late, his skills hadn't changed. He still had the ability to drive any woman mad if he wanted to.

"So you think so?" he finally said.

"I'm positive."

"Well, maybe we'll have to see."

"I agree. And since you've decided to put it out there, I say there's no time like the present."

Curtis hated the way she kept tempting him. She was doing all that she could, trying to get him over to her place and into bed with her, and he could barely contain himself. She was driving his curiosity wild, and he wasn't sure about anything anymore. But maybe if he went to visit her that would be enough. Maybe once he saw her again, he'd realize she wasn't all that and he'd be over her just as quickly as he'd become attracted to her.

But Curtis knew that wouldn't happen because he *was* attracted to her. He didn't know her from a bag of jelly beans, but he already liked multiple things about her. Her boldness, her beauty, and her irrefutable willingness to please him. So what was a man to do? How was any man expected to ignore a woman like Sharon and just forget about her?

"All you have to do is get in your car and drive over here. It's as simple as that."

"No, I don't think so," he struggled to say.

"Curtis, please. Please just give me a chance. Let me satisfy you."

Curtis sighed and rolled up his shirtsleeves. It was the second week in February and exceptionally cold outside, but he felt like turning on the central air. Sharon was starting to get the best of him, and he wasn't sure how much longer he'd be able to deny her. He knew he shouldn't go to her, *but* at the same time, he didn't know why he shouldn't. Especially since Charlotte had decided to drop off the face of the earth for an entire weekend like a single woman. He'd tried to convince himself that maybe she truly had taken a trip all by herself and, as she'd said, "just needed to get away," but his gut told him otherwise.

But was it really that? Did he really believe Charlotte was having an affair? Or was he merely looking for a way to justify his own thoughts and desires? Was he mainly just trying to find a way to rid himself of guilt?

Curtis glanced over at Romans chapter seven again and came to his senses. "I can't."

"But why? Why won't you come to me when you know you want to so badly? I can hear it in your voice."

"Because I'm married."

"I realize that, but you're not happily married. You won't admit it, but if you were happy you wouldn't have called me in the first place. Not just once or twice, but three times today."

Curtis knew she had a point, but he wasn't going to give in. He wouldn't let her control his emotions and make him do things he would regret in the end.

"I'm going to hang up now," he told her.

"I wish you wouldn't."

"Well, I am. But you take care, okay?"

Sharon chuckled. "You're afraid of me, aren't you?"

Curtis raised his eyebrows, wondering how she knew. He tried leading her to believe otherwise, though. "Afraid? Are you kidding?"

"You are. You're afraid because you know what I'm capable of. You can feel it all through your bones, and that's why you won't come to me."

She was right again, but there was no reason to confirm her thinking. "You're wrong."

"Say what you want, but I know what I know."

"Like I said, I'm hanging up now, and you take care."

"You take care as well, Curtis, and I'll speak to you tomorrow."

"No, I don't think so."

"Of course, I will. Either that, or I'll just plan on seeing you when you get here. Late afternoon or anytime in the evening would work best for me. But I also have no problem switching one of my appointments around if you wanna come by earlier."

"Good-bye, Sharon," he said.

"See you soon."

Chapter 24

*B*eads of sweat lined Charlotte's forehead and trick-
led down the sides of her face. Her chest, stomach, and back were soaking wet, too. She'd been
on the treadmill for nearly fifty minutes, power walking
at a speed of 4.7 miles per hour, and she'd never felt better. Her brain had released a huge amount of endorphins,
and she absolutely loved this feeling. There was only one
other form of activity that could compare to this kind of
natural high—that being sex—and it was the reason she
worked out so religiously. As a matter of fact, she hadn't
felt this good since yesterday morning, the last time she
and Michael had made love. They'd awakened bright and
early, pleasured each other one last time, and then gotten
dressed and headed to the airport in separate cars. They'd
even taken different flights as a precaution, even though
they'd both flown back to O'Hare.

Charlotte glanced at the number of calories and car-
bohydrates she'd burned, watched the last five minutes of
The Young and the Restless, and then thought about Curtis. He'd slept in the guest bedroom again, of course, but
when he'd come into their room this morning, he'd taken
a shower, shaved, and gotten dressed, and he'd seemed

very pleasant. He hadn't said anything at all to her except, "Good morning," but what puzzled her was how normal he acted. He hadn't seemed annoyed by her presence, frustrated by what they were going through as a couple, or bothered by much of anything, for that matter, and she couldn't help speculating why that was. She wondered why his demeanor was noticeably calm when their marriage was in an uproar—admittedly a silent uproar, but an uproar nonetheless. They were no longer screaming and yelling at each other, but they still had serious issues to contend with. Yet now they connected more like roommates than they did as husband and wife.

But Charlotte decided this wasn't the time to focus on Curtis. Not when she was overcome with such mesmeric euphoria. So, she upped the treadmill to 5.0 for the final two minutes of her sixty-minute session and then dropped it back to 4.0 for the start of her cooldown period. She breathed heavily, wiping her face with a plush white towel, and when her cooldown ended, she read the final reading on the digital display, stepped off of the belt, stretched, and picked up two eight-pound hand weights. She watched the news while toning her biceps and triceps, then sat on the Bowflex seat and worked her legs. After that, she positioned herself on the floor and did two hundred crunches. Now she lay there with her eyes closed, resting.

Finally, she got herself up, went up to the main floor, and grabbed a bottle of water from the fridge. She had already downed one about thirty minutes into her workout, but she was still pretty thirsty.

"That whole Emily and Patty story line is really starting to get to me," Agnes said, complaining about one of the current *Y & R* story lines.

Charlotte took a swig of her drink. "I know. I was watching it downstairs. What I wanna see play out, though, is this whole thing with Adam. He's gotten away with all his dirt for much too long, and it's time he got what's coming to him."

"You got that right. I can't wait," Agnes said, laughing.

Charlotte smiled. She and Agnes rarely missed a day of their favorite soap opera, and they talked about the characters as if they were real. Even when she couldn't be home at eleven, she never worried because the family room DVR was set to record it like clockwork. She'd been watching Victor, Nikki, Jack, and the rest of them for years, and it was by far one of her guiltiest pleasures. Well, it used to be her guiltiest pleasure—that is, before Michael had come back into her life. Gosh. She just couldn't stop thinking about Florida, and she needed to talk to him. Needed to hear his voice. Wanted to know what he was doing at this very moment. So she quickly went up the stairs and called him.

"Michael Porter," he said.

"Hey."

"Hey, yourself. I was just thinking about you."

"Oh yeah? What were you thinking?"

"How I haven't felt this good about anything in a long while."

"We did have a good time this weekend, didn't we?"

"The best," he said and then asked her to hold on for a second. She heard him talking to someone in the background, but then he was back with her.

"So have you had a busy morning?" Charlotte asked.

"Very. But it's been good, though. One of my top clients who's worth millions just decided to move his entire portfolio over to me. I've handled a good portion of his money for a few years, but a couple of hours ago he came in and said he couldn't be more happy with my services and saw no reason to deal with anyone else from this point on."

"That's wonderful, Michael."

"It is. I'm pretty excited, to say the least."

"Good for you. I can only imagine how great it feels to have a career you love, and I really miss that."

"Then, why don't you go back to work?"

"I don't know. I worked as a paralegal at a top law firm, but when we founded Deliverance Outreach, Curtis wanted me to quit so that I could focus on the church operations with him."

"That's all fine and well, but that's his dream. Not yours. Am I right?"

"To a certain extent. When we first moved out here, I fully supported his desire to start his own church, and I had no problem helping him do it. But I also wanted to keep working as a paralegal."

"Then, you should do what makes you happy. And if your husband truly loves and respects you, he'll encourage exactly that."

"Maybe I'll think more about it."

"I hope you do. Because no one should put their dreams on hold. No one should deny themselves of being happy."

"I wish life was really that easy."

"It can be."

"Maybe in a perfect world, but not in real life."

There was silence, and then Michael said, "So when can I see you again?"

"I don't know."

"What about this Sunday? Valentine's Day."

Not once had Charlotte ever considered the idea of spending the most romantic holiday of the year with anyone else, not since marrying Curtis, and a certain sense of sadness besieged her. Although, if she were honest with herself, she knew Curtis probably didn't even care.

"I'll have to see," she finally said.

"Why? Do you think it would be hard getting away for a few hours?"

"No. Not really. Especially since Curtis is acting so laid-back."

"So he wasn't upset when you got home?"

"No. He seemed more at ease than before I left."

"Does that bother you?"

"Well, I'd be lying if I said it didn't, at least a little."

"Well, just so you know, Sybil didn't have much to say either. She was very calm, and for the first time, she didn't complain about the fact that I didn't call her once while I was gone. Normally, she rants and raves for hours, so what I'm hoping is that she's finally realizing it's all a lost cause."

"Being in a bad marriage is tough."

"Tell me about it. Actually, I'm tired of the whole situation, and I'm this close to asking her for a divorce. I want to end things with her so badly, and if you ever made up your mind to leave Curtis, I would tell her in a heartbeat."

Charlotte had threatened Curtis with a separation and possible divorce, but deep down, she wasn't ready for any of that. "I can't think about that right now, and I honestly don't know what the future holds for Curtis and me."

"But you know you're not happy with him."

"Yes, but divorce is a major and very permanent step. And while I really care about you and enjoy my time with you, I haven't stopped loving Curtis either. I have to be honest with you about that," she said, trying to determine if what she mainly loved about Michael was the passionate way he made love to her and how attentive he was to her needs.

"I do believe that you still love him, but I'm not so sure you're *in* love with him. Not anymore, anyway. And there is a difference."

"Yes. I know that. But I guess I just need some time to sort things out."

"No problem. I told you before that I'm willing to wait, and I really meant that."

"I appreciate that."

"But in the meantime, let's just enjoy each other as much as we can. Okay?"

"Okay," she said.

"And I'm serious about Valentine's Day. I really want to see you."

"I want to see you, too, and I'll let you know in a couple of days."

"Sounds good. All right, well, I have another meeting, so I'd better get going."

"It was good talking to you."

"Same here. And call me later if you get a chance."

"I will."

Charlotte laid the phone down, but as soon as she did, her phone rang again. She frowned when she saw the word Private displayed, and wondered who it was.

"Hello?" she answered.

"Well, well, well," the man said. "I can't believe I actually caught you on my first try."

"Excuse me?"

"Oh, come on now. Don't tell me you've forgotten my

voice already. Not when we were just together barely a week ago."

Charlotte widened her eyes. *It couldn't be.*

"It's me. Tom. You know, the guy who rocked your world when we left the jazz club last Tuesday."

Charlotte's heart raced. "How did you get my number?"

"Well, remember after we made love? And you fell asleep? Well, I got kind of bored sitting there all alone, and the next thing I knew, I was rummaging through your purse and found your phone. So I figured what the heck. Might as well dial my number with it. That way I'd have your number and could store it into my own phone."

"But why?"

"So we could keep in touch, of course."

"I guess I don't understand."

"You will. All in good time."

"What is that supposed to mean?"

"Let's not worry about that now. I do, however, wanna see you again. And that same little sleazy motel we went to last Tuesday is more than fine."

"Well, I'm sorry to tell you this, but that's not going to happen."

"Sure it will. You'll see me or else."

"Or else what?"

"I'll be calling your husband, your parents, your son, and a whole slew of other folks I got from your contact list. I copied down one name and number after another, and I know they'll love hearing about our little sexcapade."

Charlotte swallowed hard and tried steadying her shaky hand. "Why are you doing this?"

"I told you. Because I wanna see you. I wanna see the freak come out in you again like it did the first time."

"Look," she said, trying to scare him. "I don't know who you think you are, but if you call this number again I'm—"

"Are you threatening me?" he interrupted her. "Because I don't take very kindly to threats."

Charlotte was devastated. She couldn't fathom why he was doing this. He had no reason. "What is it you want from me?"

"I already told you. So, either you plan on meeting me at our same little love nest or I'm calling Pastor Black. Understood?"

Charlotte knew he wasn't playing. The tone in his voice confirmed it, and she could only think of one way out of this. "I'll do anything but that. I'll even pay you. All you have to do is name your price."

"I don't want money."

"Why?"

"Because."

"Because what?"

"What I want is to have my way with you whenever I want."

Charlotte was speechless.

"I know this must be a lot to take in so suddenly, so I'll tell you what. I'll give you two or three days to get used to the idea, and then we'll schedule a time to meet."

"But—"

"But nothing," he said. "I'll call you soon."

Charlotte waited for him to say more, but he hung up. She couldn't believe this was happening. Worse, she couldn't believe she'd been stupid enough to get drunk and sleep with this lunatic. He'd been a complete stranger, but to her, it really hadn't been all that big of a deal. Simply about two people having a good time and then moving on with their lives. But apparently Tom had decided otherwise.

What really worried her, though, was that he didn't want money. He was blackmailing her but didn't want to be paid in dollars and cents, and that made her nervous. What he wanted was for her to have sex with him again, and she couldn't do that. Sleeping with Michael was one thing, but sleeping with Tom or any other stranger on a regular basis wasn't an option. Or did she even have a choice? Especially since Tom had made it clear that he would tell Curtis about them if she didn't do what he asked. So what was she going to do? How was she going to fix this latest debacle she'd created?

Truth was, she had no idea. She hadn't a single clue, and all she could hope was that this new dilemma would go away quietly. Maybe Tom would forget about her and that would be the end of it. Somehow, though, she knew this was wishful thinking and that she would have no choice but to deal with him head-on. She could just kick herself for being so foolish.

Chapter 25

"This is a quick summary of what we'd be looking at interest-wise and how much we'd be paying back over a period of thirty years," Raven said, passing around copies of a document that outlined information for the additional loan they were considering taking out. Curtis, all the elders, and a few other finance committee members were in the conference room discussing the possibility of purchasing a pretty nice-sized piece of land situated next to the new building. Raven passed Curtis his copy but could barely look at him, and Curtis knew it was because of the way she'd tried to come on to him last week. She was having a tough time being in his presence, and he couldn't deny that being around her felt a bit awkward as well, especially since he couldn't ignore how radiant she looked today.

Curtis scanned the sheet of paper. "This all looks good, and of course, the plan will be for us to pay the entire loan off much sooner than thirty years."

"Exactly," Elder Jamison added. "So, if you ask me, we can go ahead and take a vote right now, because the last thing we want is to take a chance on someone else coming along and buying it before us."

"I agree," Curtis said. "There's so much public enthusiasm

about the new church that we'll need to build on an addition in no time. And when that time comes, I want us to be ready."

Elder Dixon set the document down in front of him. "You know the old saying, 'When you snooze you lose,' so we need to jump on this immediately. Need to snatch that property up before it's too late."

Everyone else in the room agreed, but they took an official vote anyway. The outcome was unanimous, and after discussing a few other minor items, Elder Jamison adjourned the meeting. As everyone got up, preparing to leave the room, Curtis asked Raven to stay.

Elder Jamison was the last person to exit, and when he closed the door behind him, Curtis looked at her.

"I thought it might be best if we had a conversation about the other day."

Raven made direct eye contact with him, but only for a second, and then glanced away.

"Look, the bottom line is this. I don't want you feeling bad about any of what you said, and I don't want things feeling strange between us. We've always had a great working relationship, and there's no need for that to change now."

Raven looked at him again. "I never should have said those things to you, regardless of how I was feeling. I had no right approaching you that way."

Curtis smiled. "But everything you said was the truth, though, right?"

"Yes."

"Then, there's nothing for you to worry about. I wasn't offended. Shocked, maybe. But not offended or upset with you."

"Thank you for saying that."

"I mean it. There was no offense taken, and I don't want you walking around feeling embarrassed or out of place."

"That really helps, and I have to admit, I'm very relieved. I was so worried that you were angry with me and that my job might be in jeopardy."

"No, not at all."

"If I could take everything back, Pastor Black, I would. And again, I'm really sorry."

"Apology accepted. Now get back to work," he said, smiling.

Now, Raven smiled as well. "Oh, and were you able to contact Richard Cacciatore okay?" She was referring to the attorney she'd recommended to Curtis.

"Yes, I did, and we had a good conversation. I like him already and can tell he's as knowledgeable as you said he was. I'll definitely be hiring him on at some point to handle a few items for me."

"Great. I'm glad you felt comfortable with him."

"I did, and thanks again for the recommendation."

"No problem." Raven slid her seat in close to the table and left.

Curtis leaned back in his chair, thinking about a number of things, mostly stuff he wasn't proud of. For one, he replayed the way he'd just scanned Raven's body from head to toe as she'd turned and walked out of the conference room and how he'd then imagined what it might feel like to be in bed with her. The temptation was killing him, and between her and this Sharon woman, he could barely think straight. He knew he was wrong, but he was also human, and humans just weren't perfect. They had flaws. They were blemished, and even Romans 3:23 talked about all human beings committing sins and falling short of the glory of God. It was just the way things were, and there was no getting around it. Curtis didn't want to fall short, but suddenly, he was having a hard time trying to do the right thing. He was starting to feel that he was fighting a losing battle and that it wouldn't be long before he lost control. He'd been trying to talk to himself daily, but for some reason he wasn't getting through to himself, and sadly, all the praying he'd been doing didn't seem to be helping. But then he thought back to Romans 7 again. He'd focused on verses fourteen through seventeen the other night, but this morning he'd read verses eighteen through twenty, which repeated much of the earlier passage but still made a lot of sense. "I know I am rotten through and through so far as my old sinful nature is concerned. No matter which way I turn, I can't make myself do right. I want to, but I can't. When I want to do good, I don't. And when I try not to do wrong, I do it anyway. But if I am doing what I don't want to do, I am not really the one doing it; the sin within me is doing it."

So maybe his lustful desires couldn't be helped after all. Maybe committing certain sins was his destiny, and there wasn't a thing that could be done to change it. He didn't want to believe that, but he also didn't see any other reasonable explanations. Maybe some people just weren't meant to walk the straight and narrow. No matter how hard they tried. Maybe some people were simply meant to wreak havoc and cause heartache—for themselves as well as those around them.

Curtis closed his eyes and sighed deeply. He was so tired of feeling this way. Tired of teetering back and forth and trying to do God's will when there was this nagging, immoral part of him wanting to do otherwise. He was exhausted from all the fighting inside of him and ready to succumb—to whatever his fate might be. And he would, unless something or someone stopped him.

Chapter 26

*I*t was shortly after eleven o'clock. Now that Curtis was back in his office, he flipped through the file of the couple he'd be meeting with in a few minutes. Bruce Betts and Stephanie Moss had been members of Deliverance Outreach for a little over a year and had set their wedding date for October. That was eight months away, but they'd decided to schedule their first pre-marital counseling session for today. Actually, Curtis preferred that couples come in as soon as possible, so this was a good thing.

In the meantime, though, he thought about Curtina and decided to call Aunt Emma to check on her.

"So, how's my little princess doing?" he asked.

"Just fine. She played all morning, and now she's taking a nap. She'll be up in a while, though, and I'll give her some lunch. She's such a good little girl, and just a joy to have around."

"I'm glad you feel that way, Aunt Emma. Glad you don't mind keeping her for me."

"Not at all. I told you that from the beginning, and actually, I look forward to when you drop her off every morning. Then I miss her on the weekends."

"She is a good kid, and I just wish Charlotte could see

what you and I do. I wish she would rethink how she feels about Curtina."

"Maybe in due time," she said.

"I hope so. Because things aren't good between us. They're worse than ever."

"I'm sorry to hear that, Curtis. I thought maybe once Charlotte got away for the weekend, she would feel a lot better about things when she was back home."

"I was hoping that, too, but nothing has changed."

"Has she said anything to you at all about Curtina?"

"No. I've been cordial to her, and she's been pretty cordial to me, but that's pretty much it."

"Cordial isn't good for either one of you because my experience is that when husbands and wives become cordial, they're leaning toward the idea of giving up. They're deciding that the whole marriage is a lost cause and that they might as well just accept it."

Curtis didn't comment because he knew she was right. Before Charlotte had left he'd been furious with her, but now he didn't feel as angry, and he was relieved not to be arguing with her anymore. He was happy to have at least some peace in his household, and, yes, was on his way to accepting things as they were.

Curtis finally spoke. "Even three months ago, I wouldn't have expected our lives to be like this. I knew we had problems, and I knew Charlotte wasn't thrilled about Curtina being around, but not ever did I think we'd be at some sort of standstill with neither of us willing to budge."

"Well, it's not like you really have that much room to budge, because there's no way you can kick your own child out of your house. And Charlotte shouldn't even expect that."

"But she does. She expects me to send Curtina to live with one of Tabitha's family members and just forget she ever existed."

"And she really doesn't see that you could have said the exact same thing about Marissa? I know you've told me that before, but I just have to ask again, because it doesn't make any sense."

"No. She doesn't see that as being the same. She says it's different and doesn't have anything to do with this since Marissa is no longer with us. She's constantly reminding me that her daughter is dead."

"Mm, mm, mm. That poor niece of mine. Just pitiful, I say."

"I hadn't told you this, but last week, she brought up the idea of us having another baby."

"Why?"

"For some reason she thinks that will make things better for us."

"I don't see how. Not when you and her are so at odds about Curtina."

"That's what I told her. She doesn't get that either, though."

"Lord have mercy on Charlotte's soul. She's got a lot to learn and a lot of growing up to do."

"I agree, but she doesn't see that."

"Then, I just don't know what to tell you, Curtis. My prayer is that the two of you will soon work this out, but I don't see how you can do that if Charlotte doesn't realize how wrong she is."

"I didn't want to say that to you, but unfortunately, you're right."

"I'm really sorry."

"I am, too, but in all fairness to Charlotte, this isn't all her fault. Because had I not gotten caught up with Tabitha, there would be no Curtina."

"But what's done is done, and sadly you can't change what happened. All you can do now is go forward."

"I know," Curtis said, looking at his watch. His office phone rang, and he knew it was Lana, letting him know that Bruce and Stephanie had arrived. "Well, hey, Aunt Emma. It was good talking to you but I need to get going here."

"Anytime."

"Thanks for everything, and I'll see you this evening."

"You take care, now, Curtis."

He set his cell phone down, called Lana back, and told her to send Bruce and Stephanie in.

When they entered, Stephanie, a short, petite young woman, smiled and shook Curtis's hand. Bruce, a tall, bodybuilder type, did the same, and they both sat down. Curtis smiled to himself when he realized how much Bruce towered over Stephanie; he could probably pick her up with one hand.

"Thank you so much for seeing us," Stephanie said.

"I'm glad to do it and glad both of you think enough of your relationship to go through this process," Curtis said.

"Yes, thank you very much, Pastor," Bruce added.

"You're quite welcome. So, first of all," Curtis continued, "how did the two of you meet?"

They both looked at each other and laughed.

"Wow, so is the humor a good thing or a bad thing?" Curtis said, chuckling.

"Should we tell him, baby?" Bruce asked her.

"I don't see why not. We're totally different people now, anyway."

"We met at a strip club," Bruce said with no hesitation. "I used to work there, and Steph used to come in sometimes with some of her girlfriends to watch my show."

"We used to be ashamed to tell people, but not anymore."

"And you shouldn't be because everyone has a past. All of us have done things we wouldn't do today, and the important thing is that we've changed for the better." Curtis thought about his own yearnings toward repeating history. He even wondered if he was qualified to give this couple any advice at all, what with how rocky his own relationship was. Not to mention how pessimistic he was these days about the institution of marriage.

"Yes," Stephanie said. "Bruce and I finally realized that, and we've even started sharing it with others as a testimony. We've been sharing our story with friends and letting them know just what can happen once you allow God to take charge of your life."

"Good for you. That's what I like to hear," Curtis said. Then he changed the subject a bit. "So, how long have you been engaged?"

"We dated for about six months, but we've been engaged for a year now," Bruce said.

Stephanie nodded in agreement. "So all told, we've been together for eighteen months."

"Good. Then, you've had a nice amount of time to get to know each other."

"Yes, we have," Stephanie said.

"We've learned a lot about each other, too," Bruce said.

"And are you pretty much in agreement on most things?"

Bruce twisted his mouth to the side. "For the most part."

"Is there something in particular that you're not quite on the same page about?"

"Money," Stephanie blurted out immediately.

"Uh-oh," Curtis said.

"But we'll work all that out as time goes on," she said.

"You might," Curtis told her. "But chances are you won't. Finances can cause more problems in a marriage than infidelity as well as lots of other issues. Money can make people do some strange things and make you despise each other. My daughter and her ex-husband are a prime example, and they don't mind me telling their story to any of the couples I meet with."

Curtis could see how disappointed Stephanie was to hear this, but he had to be honest with them.

"So, what is it the two of you disagree on?" Curtis asked.

Bruce answered first. "I think our money should all be deposited into one account, and that's what our bills should be paid from. To me, there shouldn't be any of that fifty-fifty stuff. You know, that craziness where we both pay one half of every bill we have. To me, we should both pay a hundred percent of everything together."

"Not me," Stephanie added. "Our marriage is going to be a partnership and normally partners split everything fifty-fifty. Especially since I'm coming into the marriage with basically no debt, and Bruce owes just about everybody."

Bruce shifted his body toward her, and Curtis knew this was a constant debate between them. "But if we're going to become one the way the Bible says we are, then we should become one with everything we have."

"I disagree," Stephanie said, then looked at Curtis. "But what do you think, Pastor Black?"

"Well, I have to admit that every situation is different, but I am a believer in joint bank accounts for all married couples. I do think you should each have your own checking or savings accounts on the side so that you can save your own emergency funds, but the majority of your salaries should go toward paying your bills and toward your retirement accounts."

"See," Bruce said, laughing.

Stephanie smiled but said, "I don't see what's so funny."

Bruce rubbed her hand affectionately. "It's not like I'm trying to get over on you, baby, but if we start out with all this separate-what's-mine-is-mine-and-what's-yours-is-yours jazz, our marriage will be over before it gets started. I admit that I do have a lot of debt, but I'm willing to do everything I can to get it paid down as quickly as possible."

Stephanie didn't comment one way or the other, so Curtis said, "Maybe you could at least think about it. And Bruce, since it sounds like Stephanie manages her own money pretty well, maybe you could let her help you manage yours starting now and not just when you get married."

"I'm all for that," he said.

"Stephanie?" Curtis said.

"That's fine. I can do that."

"Good. Because in order for your marriage to start out on the right foot, you're going to have to settle on this."

"There is one other thing," Bruce said.

"What's that?"

"My mom was a stay-at-home mom, and that's what I want Steph to be when she has our first child. I want her to be the one to take care of our children and not some babysitter or day-care provider. At least until our last one turns five."

"But Bruce, it's like I keep telling you," she said, sounding aggravated. "I'm not the stay-at-home type. I love being an attorney, and I don't think it's fair for me to have to give up my career. Plus, sweetheart, you know you don't make enough money for us to live on one salary."

"But, baby, it wouldn't be forever."

"It would be long enough, and the last thing I want is for us to struggle financially. I won't do that."

Curtis relaxed further into his chair and locked his hands together. He listened as they debated one subject after another and wished he had better news for them. Their marriage was already ruined. It was over and they hadn't even taken vows yet. He hated seeing them this way and wondered which was worse: realizing you're probably not meant to be together beforehand, even though you really do love each other, or realizing this unfortunate fact ten years later, the way he was starting to realize about himself and Charlotte. To him, it was better to figure things out before the wedding, and he hoped Bruce and Stephanie would consider cutting their losses now. It was best for them to leave well enough alone and look for people they were more compatible with. What he hoped was that they wouldn't get married in spite of their problems and then end up like him and so many others. Miserable and rethinking everything.

Chapter 27

*C*harlotte finished applying her champagne-colored lipstick, powdered her nose again, and picked up her Marc Jacobs hobo. She had a number of errands to run but mainly wanted to stop at the beauty supply store to grab a few hair products and then stop at the bookstore. Two of her favorite authors had just released their latest novels, and she couldn't wait to read both of them. She loved reading because it allowed her to leave her own world for a while and enter someone else's. Something she especially needed now, after hearing from that Tom character. She was still stunned by his call and hoped he'd never contact her again. Although, to be honest, she already had a bad feeling about this and just wished she knew why he was trying to force her to be with him. There had to be some sort of personal reason. That was always the case whenever a person blackmailed you but didn't want large sums of money.

As Charlotte grabbed her keys, she heard her Black-Berry chiming. This meant she'd just received a text, so she pulled it out to see who it was from. When she clicked on the text icon, she saw the name Portia Melvin, which was the name she'd given Michael Porter in her phone.

She also now kept the sound alerts on silent whenever Curtis was home so that she wouldn't have to worry about him checking to see who was trying to contact her. He rarely picked up her phone under any circumstances, but she never knew what he might do now that they had issues. It was the reason she'd told Michael to never send her any incriminating texts, and she was glad this text only said, Long time no hear from.

She dialed his number. "Hey," she said.

"Hey, yourself."

"So what's with the 'long time no hear from' thing?" she said, teasing him. "Because I just talked to you a couple of hours ago."

"You said to be discreet. So that's what I'm doing."

"I know. I'm just messing with you."

"So what were you doing?"

"Getting ready to head out to a couple of stores."

"Why don't you come see me instead?"

"I don't know, Michael."

"I realize we just saw each other yesterday in Florida, but I really need to see you again. So how about it? Why don't you meet me at Gerald's place this evening?"

"I really wanna see you, too, but I also don't want to make Curtis suspicious."

"I understand that, but baby, I can't stop thinking about you. I'm so caught up, I can barely focus on my work."

Charlotte's phone beeped, but she ignored it. "I've been thinking about you as well. All last night and then again this morning. But I don't know. Maybe we can see each other tomorrow."

"Tomorrow is a very long time."

Charlotte's phone beeped a second time, so this time

she looked at the screen and saw that it was Matthew. "I'm sorry, Michael. This is my son calling. Can you hold on?"

"Sure. Go ahead."

Charlotte pressed the button with the green phone symbol. "Hey, Matt."

But there was no one there, so she switched back to Michael.

"I guess I didn't answer in time. I know what he wants, though. To hang out after school at one of his friends' houses. I'll just call him back later."

"Pretty please," Michael continued, as if she'd never stopped talking to him.

"You're making this very hard, you know that?"

"That's why I'm doing it."

They both laughed.

"Okay, then, what about this?" he said. "I'll see if I can get off early and then you and I can meet in a couple of hours. That way you'll be home pretty early."

Charlotte debated what she should do and finally said, "Okay, I'll see you then."

"Miss Charlotte!" Agnes screamed up the staircase. "Miss Charlotte, come quick."

"Michael, something's wrong. Our housekeeper sounds upset, so I'll call you later."

"Talk to you then."

Charlotte dropped her phone and purse onto the bed and ran down to the kitchen. Agnes was hysterical. "Miss Charlotte, look. It's Matthew's school!" She pointed at the television.

Charlotte's mouth dropped open and she wanted to die. There was a breaking news report plastered across the screen: Gunman holding students hostage at Mitchell

Prep Academy. Then the announcer said, "The gunman is believed to be Harold Rush, the well-liked history teacher who was recently arrested because of child molestation allegations."

"Oh my God, Matthew!" Charlotte exclaimed. "Oh my God. He just tried calling me."

She rushed back up the stairs and checked to see if he'd left her a voice message. But he hadn't. So she tried calling him back. His phone rang and rang and rang until his outgoing message began, so Charlotte picked up her handbag and flew back down to the kitchen.

"Agnes, I'm going to the school, and please call me if you hear from Matthew or anyone."

"I will. And what about Mr. Curtis?"

"I'll call him while I'm driving."

"Try to stay calm, Miss Charlotte, and please be careful."

"I will," she said and was out the door and inside her car in seconds. When she left the driveway, she dialed Curtis's cell phone immediately, but he didn't answer. So she called Lana's number directly.

"Pastor Black's office. Lana speaking."

"Lana, it's Charlotte. Hey, do you know where Curtis is by chance?"

"He had a counseling session and then a phone conference, so now he's out taking a late lunch. He should be back in an hour or so, though, because he has another meeting."

"We have to get in touch with him. There's trouble at Matthew's school, and some students are being held hostage."

"Oh dear Lord," Lana said. "And where are you?"

"I'm on my way there, so if you hear from Curtis before I do, please tell him to meet me."

"I will, and you know I'm going to start praying as soon as we hang up."

"Thanks, Lana."

Charlotte pressed the End button and dialed Curtis's cell phone again, but when he still didn't answer, she yelled out loud, "Curtis, where are you?"

She was so frustrated and wondered where he was. She waited a few seconds and then pressed Redial. As the phone rang, she stepped on the accelerator and said, "Come on, Curtis, you have to answer this time. I really need you."

&a &a &a

When Curtis glanced at his phone and saw that Charlotte was calling him, he clicked Ignore and slipped his phone back inside the inner pocket of his blazer.

"So who was that?" Sharon asked.

But Curtis didn't respond. He had tried his best not to call this woman again or come see her, but once Bruce and Stephanie had left his office and he'd found himself thinking way too much about Raven, he'd decided to contact Sharon. His hope had been that if all he did was talk to her, it would take his mind off physically being with Raven. But one word had led to another and the next thing he'd known, Sharon had talked him into coming to visit her. They'd spoken by phone for maybe a half hour, and she'd promised him that if he wanted, they could take things very slow, chat like old buddies even, and simply enjoy each other's company. This, of course, had sounded fine to Curtis, and so far, talking was in fact all they'd been doing. He was also glad she was sitting on the love seat adjacent to the sofa he was relaxing on.

"So I guess you don't want to tell me who's blowing up your phone, as my girlfriend's son would say," Sharon said.

"It's not important," Curtis said, noticing how captivating her light brown eyes were and then admiring how thick her hair was. It was almost the same color Charlotte had been dyeing her hair for the past couple of years, except Charlotte had beautiful highlights mixed through hers and Sharon's was all one shade.

"You sure I can't get you anything?" she said.

"Positive. I stopped and grabbed something to eat on my way over here." Curtis looked around the place. It was small and quaint, but immaculate. "So, did you decorate this yourself?"

"Every bit of it."

"You have excellent taste."

"Thank you."

There was silence, but when Curtis's phone vibrated again, he scooted to the edge of the sofa. "Well, I really need to get back to the church."

"But you've only been here for maybe thirty minutes at the most."

"True. But just the same, I need to get going," he said and his phone vibrated again. When he pulled it out, he saw that it was Charlotte and that she also must have left him a voice message the last time she'd called, because his message alert symbol was displayed. He wondered why she was all of a sudden calling him, because right now, he really didn't want to be bothered. Especially since she hadn't tried calling him once when she'd been vacationing like a queen miles and miles away. Actually, the only reason he kept checking his phone was because he'd missed a call from Matthew during his drive over to Sharon's. It had happened when Curtis had called Sharon to double-check the directions she'd given him. Curtis had typed her address into his navigational system but since she lived in the country, one of the roads she'd mentioned hadn't shown up. After he'd hung up with her, though, he'd tried calling Matthew back, but he hadn't answered.

"Wow, looks to me like somebody needs to speak to you pretty badly," Sharon said.

Curtis stood up. "It's nothing, but I really do need to go."

Sharon got up as well. "I really wish you would stay."

"I wish I could, but I can't. I do appreciate you inviting me over, and I enjoyed our conversation."

Still, Sharon moved closer to him. "Look, Curtis. Why are you trying to fight these feelings you know you have for me?"

Curtis gazed into those pretty brown eyes of hers, felt his legs weakening, and wished she would step away from him. But Sharon moved even closer, caressed his chest with both hands, and pushed his blazer back and partway down his shoulders. Thankfully, though, his phone vibrated again, and Curtis was glad for the interruption. He quickly pulled his jacket back over his shoulders and looked at his BlackBerry. This time it was a text from Matthew, saying, 911 cant call u.

Now Curtis panicked. He wondered what was wrong with Matt and if maybe this was the reason Charlotte kept trying to contact him. So he dialed into his message system. His heart skipped a beat when he heard how frantic

Charlotte's voice was: Mr. Rush was holding a group of students hostage in a classroom. There was also a message from Lana saying basically the same thing and that he needed to call Charlotte as soon as possible. Curtis wasn't even sure how he'd missed Lana's call, although maybe she'd tried calling him right when Charlotte had.

"I have to go," he told Sharon and rushed out of her house and into his SUV. He drove out of her driveway, sped down the road like a madman, and called Charlotte.

"Oh my God, Curtis, I think Matthew is one of the kids still inside," she cried.

"Are you at the school?"

"Yes. And where are you?"

"I'm on my way. I'll be there in twenty minutes. But in the meantime, you try to stay calm, baby, okay?" he said but deep down, he had never been more frightened or worried about anything. He was terrified, to say the least, and he wondered if this was all his fault. He couldn't help wondering if God was already punishing him for consorting with another woman—for almost giving in to her sexual demands—for wanting her to do all the things she'd been promising she could and would do to him if he let her.

Curtis would never forgive himself if something happened to Matthew, and he prayed his son was going to be okay. Then he thanked God for allowing Matthew to send him that text when he had. If he hadn't, Curtis knew things would have gone too far with Sharon, and there would have been no turning back for him. The day would have ended on a very shameful note, and Curtis was grateful he'd been stopped. He was glad God had stopped him cold.

Chapter 28

*W*hen Curtis arrived near the school, squad cars, detective cars, personnel from all the local media outlets, and many others were scattered throughout the street. As he drove closer, he even saw a large number of students standing around as well, some who were in tears and already embracing various adults, probably their parents, and some holding on to each other. Sadly, though, Curtis did not see Matthew, and his stomach knotted.

After driving as close as possible to the scene, Curtis finally found a parking spot on a residential street, grabbed his full-length, black cashmere coat from the passenger seat, and went looking for Charlotte. He pushed through groups of people, many of them speaking to him along the way, but turned around only when he heard Charlotte calling his name. She was only a few feet away. To his surprise, she hurried toward him and fell into his arms, crying.

"Hey," Curtis said, smoothing his hands across her back. "Matt is going to be fine. God is going to fix this, and we can't think anything different."

"But what if he's not all right? What if . . . oh God, no. Not my baby," she said, weeping loudly.

Curtis's eyes watered, and as he looked around and

saw tears rolling down the faces of other parents, those who obviously hadn't seen their children come out of the school yet either, his faith was shaken. He wouldn't let on to Charlotte or to anyone else how he really felt, but he struggled with utter fear for the first time in a while.

He struggled for a few minutes. However, it wasn't long before he remembered his strong belief in God and how God could do all things, no matter how impossible they might seem. Needless to say, his faith was quickly renewed, and he had no doubt that Matthew would soon come walking out safe and sound, and this would all be over.

When Charlotte had settled down a little, she said, "He tried calling me, Curtis, but I didn't answer the phone in time."

Curtis frowned. "He tried calling me, too, but when I dialed him back I couldn't reach him."

"Why do you think he didn't leave a message?"

"I don't know. He did finally send a text, though, saying he couldn't call but that was it."

Curtis looked up when he saw a band of teenagers, heading toward them, one of whom was Elijah, Matthew's best friend.

"Elijah," Curtis said. "What happened?"

"I don't know. Matt just flipped out, I guess. He had a chance to flee just like the rest of us, but when he saw who Mr. Rush wanted to keep in there, he wouldn't leave."

"Mr. Rush said he only wanted those two girls to stay," one of the girls in Elijah's crowd said. "Those girls who made those accusations against him."

"I just don't get it," Elijah continued. "Because the next thing we knew, Matt was telling Mr. Rush he wasn't going anywhere and that if he was going to shoot those girls, he would have to shoot him, too. So, Mr. Rush told him fine and that he could die right along with those—excuse my language, Mom Black and Pastor Black—but he said Matthew could die right along with those sluts because it made no difference to him."

"Why did Matt do that?" Charlotte blurted out. "Why didn't he run out with the rest of you?"

"We don't know," another student said. The rest hunched their shoulders.

Charlotte burst into tears again and laid her head on Curtis's chest.

"So it's not a whole class of students in there?" Curtis asked. "Just Mr. Rush, Matthew, and the two young ladies?"

"Yep," Elijah said.

"Did Mr. Rush say why he was doing this?" Curtis asked.

"He told Jennifer and Tasha that they never should have snitched on him, so now he had no choice but to kill them. Said they should have kept their mouths shut like he told them."

Curtis shook his head and prayed like never before. He prayed that God would soften Mr. Rush's heart and bring this sick man to his senses so he would release Matthew and the two girls he was holding without harming them. He just couldn't lose Matthew, and while he didn't know Jennifer and Tasha well, he didn't want to see anything happen to them either.

Another couple of hours passed. Charlotte was on the phone with her mom, who was en route to Mitchell with Charlotte's dad, and Curtis could tell the police were at a standstill. They'd tried calling Mr. Rush on the phone inside the classroom, but he wouldn't answer it. They'd also tried calling Matthew's, Jennifer's, and Tasha's cell phones, but none of them had answered either. Presently, the officers wanted nothing more than to storm inside the building, rescue the three children, and take Mr. Rush down. But they knew it wasn't that simple, and that Mr. Rush might pull his own trigger before they finished their operation. They worried that Matthew, Jennifer, and Tasha would end up casualties, and Curtis agonized over the same thing. He was still trying to keep his faith strong, the same as he had right after arriving on the scene, but now too much time was passing.

When Charlotte hung up with her mom, she clasped her gloved hands together and huddled close to Curtis again. "It's cold out here."

"You wanna get in the car for a while?"

"No. I wanna be right here when Matthew comes out of there."

Curtis felt the same way and wondered how much longer Mr. Rush was going to keep at this.

Over the next thirty minutes, Curtis and Charlotte spent time with Jennifer's and Tasha's parents, who were beyond distraught. Then Alicia arrived, hysterical about her brother, and they tried settling her down. But suddenly, Curtis's phone rang, and when he saw that it was Matthew, he discreetly ushered Charlotte and Alicia away from the swarm of innocent bystanders and over near a tree.

"Matt?" he said, when he was sure no one other than Charlotte and Alicia could hear him.

But there was no response.

"Matt?" he repeated. "Matt? Matt?"

Still nothing. As Curtis held the phone for a few more seconds, though, he heard Matthew say, "Mr. Rush, you're a good person and you don't have to do this. All the kids here love you. Don't you know that?"

Curtis thought he heard Mr. Rush crying. He also heard him mumbling something back to Matthew, but Curtis couldn't understand what he was saying.

Charlotte and Alicia wanted to know what was going on, but Curtis raised his forefinger, politely asking them to keep silent, so he could listen in a little more. He also pressed the Mute button just in case Matthew had his volume up pretty high. That way Mr. Rush wouldn't be able to hear any of the background noise from Curtis's phone.

"They're going to lock me up and throw away the key," he heard Mr. Rush say.

"No, they won't. You're not well, Mr. Rush. You're a little confused, and you just need a little help is all."

"No one understands me. They don't understand what I went through as a child. They don't know about all the horrible things those men did to me. All those men my mother dated."

"That's why you have to stop pointing that gun at us, so I can help you," Matthew said. "You have to let Jen and Tasha go, and then you and I can walk out of here together. Nobody is going to hurt you, Mr. Rush. Not as long as I'm with you."

Curtis heard one of the girls whimpering and pleading with the teacher. "Please, Mr. Rush. I'm so sorry I told on you, but when my parents found out I was pregnant, they made me tell who the father was. I didn't want to, but they forced me."

"Pregnant?" Mr. Rush said. "No one told me you were pregnant!"

"My parents didn't want anyone to know," the girl said. "They're so ashamed and so upset, and I don't know what

I'm gonna do. My life is ruined, Mr. Rush. But if you kill me, you'll also be killing your own child."

"Oh God," Mr. Rush bellowed out, then bawled like a baby. "I'm so sorry, Jen. I'm so, so sorry. And I'm sorry for what I did to you, too, Tasha. I couldn't help myself. I'm sick. I'm really sick, and I don't deserve to live anymore."

"You do deserve to live," Matthew told him. "Everyone deserves to live."

"No. People like me can't be helped, so what I want is for you kids to leave. Go on now. Get out of here."

Curtis saw three detectives and Mitchell's chief of police heading their way.

"Pastor Black," the chief said. "We've been notified by Verizon that your son's phone is currently in use and that it's connected to one of the other phones on your account. So are you on with him?"

Curtis kept the phone up to his ear but told him, "Yes." He knew they would want to know about the call, but as he'd listened to Matthew trying to reason with Mr. Rush, he'd decided it was better to just hope and pray Matthew was successful. He hadn't wanted the police to know what Matthew was doing because he couldn't take the chance on them ending the call and then attempting to call Matthew back. Not when it was clear that Matthew had secretly dialed his number and then probably kept it inside the front pocket of his sweatshirt. He'd done this so Curtis would know he was okay and that he was trying his best to talk Mr. Rush down from whatever trip he was on.

"Is your son okay?" the chief asked.

"So far so good. The girls are fine as well, and it sounds like Mr. Rush is going to let them leave."

"Cecil," the chief said to the older of the detectives.

"Let your men know that the three hostages may be coming out soon and to make sure everyone is in place."

"No," Curtis said, putting the phone down to his side. "They have to stay clear of the doorway and the sidewalk because my son is planning to walk out with Mr. Rush. He's talked him into letting the girls go first, and then he and Mr. Rush will exit together."

"Can you at least put the phone on speaker?" the chief asked.

Curtis hadn't thought of that before now, but it was actually a good idea. He still had the call muted, but he was sure his BlackBerry would allow the call to be on speaker at the same time. So he pressed the button for it, and it worked fine.

"Matthew, you're a good kid, you know that?" Mr. Rush said. "Your parents have raised you very well."

"They have, Mr. Rush, and I know they can help you, too. Especially my dad. You know he's a pastor, right?"

"Yes, but it's too late for all that, son. What I've done is completely unforgivable, and there's no hope for me."

"God forgives everyone. And He'll forgive you, too. He forgives all His children because He loves them," Matthew told him. Tears streamed down Charlotte's face, and Curtis couldn't have been more proud of his son than he was right now. He was so brave, and the idea that he was telling Mr. Rush what he knew about God brought tears to Curtis's eyes as well.

Curtis looked over toward the front door of the school and saw it opening. The crowd cheered and applauded when Jennifer and Tasha walked out of the building. Two officers quickly pulled them to the side and away from the entrance, and their parents made their way over to them.

"Thank God," Curtis said.

"Thank God indeed," Charlotte added, and she and Alicia hugged each other.

"Matthew, I want to thank you for everything, but son, I really need you to leave now," they heard the history teacher say.

"No, Mr. Rush. If I leave, you might try to hurt yourself."

"Matthew, please. I'm begging you to go."

"Why won't he just come out?" the police chief said. "Why won't he escape while he has the chance to?"

Curtis could tell by the look on Charlotte's face that she was thinking the same thing, but not him. Not anymore, anyway, because he now knew Mr. Rush wasn't planning to hurt Matthew, and that the reason Matthew didn't want to leave him was because he knew what the result would be. He knew Mr. Rush was planning to kill himself.

"I won't leave without you, Mr. Rush," Matthew told him.

"But you have to. You have to go before those officers come in here and start shooting."

"They won't do that as long as I stay here with you."

"Well, we can't stay in this classroom forever. You do know that, don't you?"

"I don't want to stay in here forever, but I'm willing to stay as long as I have to. I'll do whatever I have to if it means saving your life."

"But I already told you. I don't deserve to live anymore. I'm all washed up now. I'm a filthy disgrace to this school and my family, and I've hurt two innocent girls. I violated them, and there's no making up for that. So, I'm asking you to please get on out of here. Your parents must be worried to death about you."

"Of course they are, but they wouldn't want you to kill yourself either. No one wants that."

"I'm not leaving," Mr. Rush said matter-of-factly.

"Okay, then, at least give me the gun."

Charlotte sucked in her breath, and tears gushed down Alicia's face. "Matthew, no," Alicia said, as if he could hear her. "Please just come out of there."

"If I give you the gun, will you leave?"

"Yes. But I still want you to come out with me."

"Fine," he said. "Here."

"I'm really proud of you for doing that, Mr. Rush. Now, let's go so we can get you to a hospital."

The chief and the three detectives who'd been standing near Curtis, Charlotte, and Alicia for the last few minutes rushed back closer to the building.

Charlotte grabbed Curtis tighter. "Matthew *is* right, isn't he? The police won't shoot at Mr. Rush as long as Matt is with him. Right?"

"No, they would never put Matthew's life in danger like that."

Curtis held the phone but didn't hear much of anything. Finally, however, the front door of the school eased open. Curtis wanted to shout with joy when he saw his son's face, but suddenly, Mr. Rush grabbed the gun from Matthew, shoved him forward and slammed the door back shut. Matthew turned, beating on the door with both his hands. "Mr. Rush, please don't do this! Please! Mr. Rush, please!"

But the gun went off.

Mr. Rush had shot himself as planned, and there wasn't a thing Matthew or anyone else could have done to stop him. Mr. Rush's mind had been made up, and this was the outcome.

Chapter 29

hank God you're all right," Charlotte said, practically squeezing the life out of Matthew. The two of them were standing next to Curtis's SUV, waiting for him to unlock the door so they could get inside of it. They'd all driven their own cars to the school, but since Matthew and Charlotte had still been so upset, Charlotte's dad had agreed to drive Matthew's vehicle home, and Janine's husband, Carl, had agreed to drive Charlotte's. Janine had finally gotten there, too, but she'd left about twenty minutes before to go pick up Bethany from the babysitter.

"But what difference does any of that make, Mom? Who cares if I'm okay, if Mr. Rush still dies?"

Charlotte felt bad about Mr. Rush, but the good news was that he was still alive. He'd shot himself in the stomach, and the paramedics had quickly rushed him off to the emergency room. Charlotte hoped he was going to be okay, but she couldn't help wondering if Mr. Rush had truly wanted to die. If he had, she wondered why he hadn't shot himself in the head the way most suicide victims did. In most cases, people who wanted to die knew a gunshot wound to either their head or their heart was much more of a sure thing.

But that was neither here nor there because Matthew was completely distraught over the entire situation, and Charlotte knew she had to treat this whole hostage-shooting incident with kid gloves. She was angry with Mr. Rush for placing her child's life in danger, not to mention the despicable things he'd done to those young girls, and she wanted to see him rot in prison. But she also knew Matthew wasn't focusing on the crimes Mr. Rush had committed, and instead was mainly concerned about Mr. Rush's well-being.

Curtis turned the ignition, pulled the vehicle in gear, and drove away. Charlotte relaxed her head against the leather headrest, relieved the day hadn't turned out worse. The three of them were headed home together as a family, and most important, Matthew was safe. He'd walked away from this tragedy fully unharmed, at least physically, anyway, and Charlotte was very grateful. God had watched over Matthew, protected every inch of his being, and then kindly returned him to her—even though she'd betrayed Curtis to the *n*th degree. She'd slept with not one but two men behind his back and had been planning to meet Michael again this evening. She'd even been on the phone with him when Matthew had tried calling, and all she could think was, *What if the situation had been different?* It was true that Matthew had found another opportunity to call Curtis again so that they'd be able to listen in on his conversation with Mr. Rush, but what if Matthew had been calling for a different reason? What if he'd needed her to do something, and it had been his only chance to contact someone? What if he'd been calling her right before Mr. Rush had stormed into the school and that had been her last chance to speak to him? *Oh*

God, what's wrong with me? Why can't I just be happy with Curtis and be a good wife to him? Why can't I just do the right thing?

Charlotte thought about one thing after another and burst into tears.

Curtis reached across the console and grabbed her hand, but this made Charlotte feel even worse. Why? Because she knew Curtis was under the impression that her tears were related to what had occurred at the school. He had no idea she was crying over the one-night stand she'd had with that Tom guy as well as the ongoing affair she was having with Michael. Curtis was being kind and loving and acting as though they were happy with no problems. He held her hand in a way that told her he was still in love with her. Deeply in love with her and ready to reconcile.

"Mom, don't cry," Matthew said. "I'm okay. So, there's nothing for you to worry about now."

"I know," she said, sniffling. "But I'm not sure what I would have done if something had happened to you."

Curtis stopped at the red light. "I know the feeling. I worked hard to keep my faith strong, but just the thought of you not being here with us, son, was almost too much to bear."

"I don't think we could go on without you, Matt," Charlotte said. "I really don't."

"I get that, Mom. And while I don't mean any disrespect to you, how do you think I feel when you and Dad don't speak to each other? Or when you do speak, it's mostly because you're arguing about something. I mean, how do you think it feels to wonder how long it's going to be before your parents break up?"

Charlotte hadn't expected to be chastised this way and was at a loss for words. She couldn't even turn and look Matthew in his face or even at Curtis for that matter. She was ashamed of herself and all that she was doing and sorry that they were letting Matthew down—again. She was sorrier about what she was doing individually, though, because she knew Matthew mostly blamed her for the breakdown in her and Curtis's marriage. He blamed her more than he did his father because he knew she didn't like Curtina. It was the reason Matthew was posing these questions to her directly.

She still didn't say anything, not even when she saw Curtis looking at her, and continued focusing straight ahead.

"Dad, aren't you going to pick up Curtina?"

"No, with all that's happened, I think I'll just ask Aunt Emma if she'll keep her overnight."

"She's not gonna be okay with that," Matthew said. "Not when she's so used to seeing us every night before she goes to bed."

"She'll be fine," Curtis told him. "Curtina loves Aunt Emma, and Aunt Emma loves having her there. I'll pick her up tomorrow after I leave the church."

Good. Charlotte would never say it out loud, of course, but she was glad to finally have an evening at home without her. It would feel like old times—pre-Curtina, that is—and for the first day in weeks, Charlotte looked forward to being alone with Curtis. She needed to be with him and hoped he felt the same way. She wasn't sure what had come over her, but she knew it had a lot to do with what they'd just experienced and how this whole disaster had got her thinking. Made her realize what was important: family, loyalty, and everything else she'd been blessed with. Made her consider how it wasn't good to take the people who cared about you for granted. Made her rethink her relationship with Michael and wonder if it was time to end things with him.

Chapter 30

After they arrived home, and Alicia and Charlotte's parents had left on their way back to Chicago, Matthew had finally eaten one slice of the deep-dish pizza they'd ordered from his favorite pizza place, Maciano's, and had gone up to bed. It was still pretty early in the evening, but he'd said he was exhausted and wanted to lie down. Charlotte knew he was more emotionally drained than anything else, and that he was sad about Mr. Rush. He'd even tried calling the hospital as soon as they'd walked in, but they'd told him they couldn't release any updates to non-relatives. He'd seemed very disappointed, so for his sake she hoped Mr. Rush wouldn't end up dying, because she had a feeling Matthew would somehow blame himself. He would be convinced that he hadn't said the right things to Mr. Rush, and that he should have handled things a whole lot differently. This would, of course, be very untrue, but Charlotte knew her son and how he always wanted to save people. He wanted to protect them, make them happy—she saw that more than ever before whenever he was with Curtina—he wanted to show as much love as possible to everyone. He had a huge heart, and while it was much softer than her own, Charlotte admired him because of it.

Charlotte made sure Curtis was still in his study and then went upstairs to check her BlackBerry. Sure enough, Michael had sent her ten text messages, the last just five minutes ago, and she knew he was wondering why she hadn't called him back yet. Especially after so many hours had passed. So, she closed the bedroom door and then went down the hallway toward the bathroom and called him.

"Hey," she said.

"Hey, yourself. What happened to you? I was worried sick."

"It's a long story," she said, keeping her voice down. "But long story short, one of the teachers held some students hostage and my son was one of them."

"What? Is he okay?"

"He's fine. We're home now, and in time he'll get beyond this."

"I'm glad to hear it. I knew something was wrong when I didn't hear back from you."

"I'm sorry I couldn't call."

"No. I completely understand."

"Anyway, I just wanted to let you know, but I'll have to talk to you later."

"Can I see you tomorrow?"

"I don't think so. Matthew is really hurt over what happened, and I really need to be here for him."

"What about Thursday or Friday then?"

Charlotte didn't know how to tell him she wouldn't be able to see him for a while. Not until she knew Matthew was back to normal. Or maybe never again. She just didn't know anything anymore, now that Matthew had openly expressed how troubled he was over her and Curtis's constant bickering, silent treatments, and marital breakdown.

She loved being with Michael and didn't want to give him up, but Matthew was more important. Her son was her life, and she would make whatever sacrifices she had to if it meant keeping him happy. She wanted him to be content and to not have to worry about anything until he finished both high school and college. Matthew, like most children in a two-parent household, couldn't imagine his parents not being together, so she knew she had to make some changes. She had no choice but to bypass some of her own wants and desires and make him her priority again.

"I don't think that will work either," she finally said.

"Well then, when?"

"I don't know, but it won't be soon."

"Why?"

"Because of Matthew and everything that happened today."

"I understand how you must be feeling, but baby, please don't shut me out."

"I'm sorry."

"Charlotte, I love you. I knew it when we were down in Florida, but now I'm positive."

"Maybe you just think you are because of all the problems you're having with your wife."

"No, that's not it. I stopped loving her years ago, but I've never fallen in love with anyone else until now. I'm so sure about my feelings for you that I asked Sybil for a divorce two hours ago and told her I was moving out by the end of next week."

"Michael, you shouldn't have done that."

"Why?"

"Because I'm not leaving Curtis. I'm not leaving my son."

"Maybe you can't right now, but you will in due time.

You don't love Curtis. I know you keep saying you do, but that's only because you've been with him for such a long time and you have a child together."

Charlotte was a little shocked by the things Michael was saying, and she hoped he wasn't planning to cause the kind of trouble Aaron had caused a few years back. Now that she thought about it, ten text messages was a lot for anyone to send, even if the person hadn't been able to get in touch with you. But, no, Michael was far too sophisticated and too levelheaded to fall into the "fatal attraction" category, so she refused to even think on that level. He was nothing like Aaron, and she knew Michael's tiny obsession with her was clearly being fueled by his miserable marriage to Sybil. He wanted out and had been hoping Charlotte was the answer to his problem.

"Charlotte," he said. "Baby. Please don't stop seeing me. I mean, go ahead and spend some time with your son, and then I'll just see you for Valentine's Day. We'll talk tomorrow about the details."

"I can't see you on Sunday either."

"You don't mean that."

"I do."

"I don't understand. You contacted me on Facebook, slept with me one day later, and then flew to a whole other state to spend an entire weekend with me. And now you're ready to just cut me off?"

"No, I didn't say that."

"Then, what are you saying?"

Charlotte walked back toward the bedroom, making sure the door was still shut. "That I can't see you for a while."

"How long is a while?"

"I don't know. I can't put a time frame on my son and how soon he'll be feeling better."

"Baby, your son is seventeen. He's had a tough time today, but he'll forget about this whole hostage business in no time."

"I hope he does, but until I'm sure of that, I'm going to be here for him."

"And who else are you going to be there for? Curtis?"

"Michael, let's not do this, okay?"

"Do what? Tell the truth?"

"Look, I really have to go now."

"So basically what you're saying is that you pretty much used me," he said, ignoring her last comment.

"No. I would never do that."

"Of course you did. You hated the fact that your husband moved in his daughter, that innocent child you hate so much, and then you came looking for me. You were looking for a way to pay Curtis back because you couldn't get your way with him, but now you've decided you do want to stay with him after all."

"I never lied about my feelings for Curtis. I always told you that I loved him. I was always honest with you about that."

"Well, if you love him so much, then why were you so quick to lay up with me? You opened your legs faster than a track star last Wednesday afternoon and then acted like some porn queen when we were in Florida. You gave me sex so many times, my heads were spinning—both of them. You couldn't get enough of me. But now you're so in love with your husband. Yeah, right."

Charlotte was flabbergasted. She listened but didn't want to believe the man she was talking to was really

Michael Porter. He sounded like Michael Porter, but his words were those of a stranger. He was talking crazy, and his attitude was very bizarre. It was almost as if he had two personalities, and today was the day he'd decided to expose his evil side. It was as if she'd never even met him before.

"I'm sorry if I led you to believe I was going to leave my husband."

"I'm sorry, too. Especially since you made me ask my wife for a divorce."

Charlotte frowned. "I didn't make you do anything. You did that on your own."

"When you slept with me multiple times a day this past weekend and told me this morning how you couldn't stop thinking about me, I knew that you wanted me to leave my wife. So that's what I'm doing."

"That's fine, Michael, but just know that you're not doing it for me. Also, I may as well just tell you, I can't ever see you again. What we had is over, and I wish you all the best."

Michael laughed out loud. "You're a real slick piece of work, you know that? A common whore. The slut of sluts. No better than an average prostitute."

"Why are you talking to me this way?" Charlotte said loudly. "What's wrong with you?"

"*You're* what's wrong with me. But I've got something for ya. I took all kinds of naked photos of you when you were asleep, and I'm going to hand-deliver them to your husband at his church tomorrow. Then, I'm going to burn down that mansion you're so proud of."

"What's wrong with you?" Charlotte screamed. "What's wrong with you? Why are you doing this?"

"Baby, wake up," Curtis said. "Wake up."

Charlotte struggled back to consciousness and sat straight up. She looked around and realized she was in bed.

"Baby, are you okay?" Curtis asked, stroking her back. Charlotte breathed heavily, perspiration covered her face and chest, and the temperature of the room felt like a hundred degrees.

"You were having a bad dream," Curtis told her.

Charlotte's heart beat the same as if she'd been running a marathon, and she wanted to jump out of her skin. There were times when she didn't remember her dreams when she woke up or, in this case, remember her nightmares, but she remembered every aspect of this one. Michael had turned on her and threatened to tell Curtis about their affair, the same as Aaron had. He'd even threatened to burn their house down. Talk about déjà vu.

"What were you dreaming about?" Curtis asked.

"I don't know," she said, flicking on the lamp on her nightstand.

"Well, whatever it was, it really had you worked up."

Charlotte looked at him and then thought about something. They'd come home from the school, Matthew had called to check on Mr. Rush and then gone to bed just like in her dream—but the only difference was that instead of her coming upstairs to call Michael, she and Curtis had taken a shower together and then made love. They hadn't said more than a few words to each other, but Curtis had made her feel like a brand-new woman. He'd made her feel better than Michael had, and now she knew she must have been out of her mind to have ever considered leaving him. Yes, they had their problems, and yes, she had this deep-rooted dislike for Curtina, but after today—after

Matthew's near-death experience and her realization that her love for Curtis was so eternal she couldn't even explain it—she was going to be a better person. She would call Michael first thing tomorrow morning, letting him know she couldn't see him anymore, and she would work harder at trying to accept Curtina. It wouldn't be easy, but she loved Curtis with all her heart and was willing to do what she had to.

Charlotte eased her body down flat onto the bed and looked at Curtis. "I'm so sorry."

"For what?"

"The way I've been acting this last month. But I promise you, things are going to be different."

"This whole hostage thing really puts things into perspective, doesn't it?"

"Like you wouldn't believe. But even outside of all that, Curtis, what I realized is that I really do love you. I never stopped."

Curtis leaned over and kissed her. "I never stopped loving you either," he said. Then he devoured her lips and kissed what seemed like every area of her body. He took total control, just like he used to, and she begged him to continue. She pleaded with him to do whatever he wanted, and he did. He had his way with her, and she was thrilled about it. Her husband—*the* Reverend Curtis Black, the incredibly gorgeous pastor whom every woman in America loved—gave her exactly what she wanted. He proved once and for all that he was a master at his craft. The reigning champ. The one no other man could beat out. He was everything to her and then some, and she was glad she'd finally wised up. Glad she'd had sense enough to keep him.

Chapter 31

*C*harlotte passed the glass pitcher of orange juice across the table to Matthew and couldn't have been happier. It had been two days since the hostage situation, but ever since then, she and Curtis hadn't been able to keep their hands off each other. They'd made love twice that evening, and then yesterday, he'd decided to stay home, and they'd done the same thing before getting up and then again in the afternoon, once Matthew had left the house. Matthew had decided not to go to school and had lain around most of the day, but when he started to feel better emotionally, he'd gotten dressed and told Charlotte and Curtis he was going out for a while. Curtina had still been at Aunt Emma's, and Agnes had left early for her granddaughter's dance recital, so Charlotte and Curtis had found themselves alone. It was almost as if they'd fallen in love all over again and were enjoying a mini honeymoon.

Charlotte bit into a piece of buttered toast. "So, sweetie, do you think you're really up for going back to school today?"

"Yep," Matthew said. "I'm good, Mom."

"Because if you don't feel like going, you don't have to."

"No. I'm really okay."

Curtis set down the sports section of the newspaper and drank some of the espresso Agnes had made for him. With the exception of an occasional vanilla latte, Charlotte wasn't a huge coffee or caffeine fan, but Curtis loved just about any kind. "I know I've said this more than once already, son, but your mom and I are very proud of you. You put your life on the line for those two girls, and then you did everything you could to try to help Mr. Rush."

"I tried to do the right thing, Dad. Just like you've always encouraged me to do."

"Well, you did an awesome job."

"But it still wasn't good enough, because look what happened. Mr. Rush shot himself, and Elijah and Jonathan were telling me last night that he's in critical condition."

"Nonetheless," Curtis said, "you did your best and that's all God ever expects from us. It's all we expect from you, too."

"Exactly," Charlotte added.

Curtina clapped her hands and picked up her sippy cup. Agnes had filled it with apple juice, and Curtina seemed to love it. Actually, she'd probably loved it for some time now, but until today, Charlotte had never paid much attention to her likes, dislikes, or to her, period. She was really trying, though. It wasn't easy, but she was trying not to feel any animosity or hatred toward her, not when things were going so wonderfully with her and Curtis. Things were fabulous, and Charlotte could even see how elated Matthew was about the two of them being on happy terms again. He'd let her know how he felt during the drive home from the school, so Charlotte was glad she and Curtis were now in a different place.

"You love that stuff, don't you, little girl?" Matthew said. Curtina grinned, nodded, and took another sip.

Curtis smiled at his daughter, and Charlotte thought about Marissa. Oh, how she missed her child and would do anything to have her back. It was clear that Marissa had been born with a few "issues," so to speak, and she hadn't been the nicest child in the world, but Charlotte had still loved her. Plus, it wasn't like she could help who she was. Yes, she had a demented personality, did devious things to people, but it was only because she'd inherited serious mental problems from her psycho father. Charlotte still remembered the day she'd caught Marissa waving her hand through a flaming burner on top of the stove and looking as though this was something normal.

If only Charlotte hadn't been in denial for so long and had tried to get her some help a lot sooner, things might have turned out differently. There was a chance she would have gotten better and would have been much more equipped to deal with the news she'd overheard Charlotte and Curtis arguing about—that Curtis wasn't her biological father. She'd heard the truth, taken it badly, and had plummeted down the stairway accidentally.

"Hey, baby," Curtis said. "When you finish up at the hair salon, why don't you meet me for lunch?"

"I can do that. I won't be finished until around two, though."

"That's fine. I won't be finished with my one o'clock meeting until around then, anyway. So, let's just meet at two-thirty. Actually, I'll probably just take the rest of the afternoon off."

"Sounds good."

"Can I get you more espresso, Mr. Curtis?" Agnes asked, clearing away Matthew's plate.

"No, I think I'll pass."

"You sure?"

"Yeah. I'm good. Well, I'd better get going." Curtis scooted his chair back from the island. "I have a couple of meetings this morning, and since I was gone yesterday, I have a few things to catch up on."

Matthew stood as well. "I need to get out of here, too. See you later, little girl," he said, kissing Curtina on her forehead.

"Bye-bye," she said, waving at him.

Curtis slipped on his navy blue pinstriped jacket, and Charlotte admired how classy he always looked. Always picture-perfect by anyone's definition. The perfect tie, the perfect tailor-made French cuff white shirt, the perfect suit.

"I guess I should get dressed myself," Charlotte said. "My appointment isn't until eleven-thirty, but I need to run a couple of those errands I never got around to the other day."

Curtis walked over and kissed her. "I'll see you in a few hours."

"Okay."

Matthew hugged her good-bye, and Curtis pulled Curtina from her high chair, removed her jumbo-sized bib, and put her coat on. Within minutes, they were all on their way to their respective destinations.

About an hour later, Charlotte was finally in her car, heading to the beauty supply store. She had driven for all of two blocks when she heard her phone chiming. There was no doubt that it was Michael again, because she still hadn't called him back. He'd sent her a couple of text messages the evening of the Mr. Rush incident and then again yesterday morning, but all she'd done was delete them. She'd been solely focused on Curtis over the last forty-eight hours, and she didn't know what to say to Michael. She knew she wanted to tell him the truth, but after that dream she'd had, she was a little nervous. She knew she owed him an explanation, though, so when she slowed at the stop sign, she pulled out her phone, adjusted her earpiece, and dialed his number.

He picked up on the second ring. "Wow, I can't believe it. You finally called me."

"I know. I'm really sorry that I haven't before now but a lot has happened."

"Yeah, I assumed as much when I saw on WGN that a teacher in Mitchell had shot himself after holding three students hostage. They didn't mention your son's name but they did say one of the kids was the son of the popular pastor Curtis Black."

"I wanted to call you, but it was never really the right time."

"No problem. You had to take care of your son, and I understand that."

When the light changed, Charlotte proceeded through the intersection but dreaded breaking the news to him.

"Why are you so quiet?" he asked. "Is something wrong?"

"Sort of."

"Should I be concerned?"

"You probably won't be happy about it."

"Hmmm. I don't think I like the sound of this."

"I can't see you anymore," she said, as quickly as she could.

"Whoa. You're right. I'm not happy to hear that at all."

"I know. And I'm sorry. But Curtis and I have reconciled."

"Really? In a matter of two days?"

"I know that sounds fast, but I did a lot of soul-searching and regardless of what has happened between Curtis and I in the past, I love him."

"Gosh. So, *you* love him, and *I* love you."

Charlotte hated this and couldn't have felt worse. "I never should have started seeing you, Michael, and I apologize for that. I'm sorry for getting involved with you when I knew I was married."

"But that's just it, baby. We're both married and very unhappy."

"I *was* unhappy. But not anymore."

"And you're even okay with having your step-daughter live with you? You're fine with being a mother to her?"

"Not exactly. But I think I can be in the future. Especially if it means keeping our family together."

"Well, if you don't mind my saying so, I think you're making a pretty big mistake."

"I disagree. Curtis and I have history and the kind of love that will never die. We've been through lots of storms together, but one fact always remains: we don't want to live without each other."

"So, there's nothing I can say to change your mind, I guess."

"No."

"Well, this is definitely a huge blow for me. Not what I expected to hear first thing this morning at all."

"I know. And I really do feel bad about this, Michael. You and I had a good time together over this last week, but it was wrong."

"No. Actually, I hadn't felt so good about anything in

years—and if you want to know the truth, I really did have high hopes about you leaving Curtis and marrying me."

Charlotte turned into the parking lot of the strip mall and felt horrible. "Maybe you can work things out with Sybil," she said, for lack of anything better to say.

Michael laughed.

"What's so funny?"

"The irony in what you just said."

"I don't understand."

"I was so sure about you and me that I contacted an attorney yesterday afternoon. To get my divorce proceedings started."

"Does Sybil know about that?"

"Yes. I told her last night."

"Please don't tell me I was the only reason you did that," she said, thinking how dead-on her dream had been.

"I was planning to end things with her, anyway, but after spending time with you, I decided to do it immediately. I wanted to be free and ready for a new life. Which I thought included you."

"I know I sound like a broken record, but Michael, I'm so, so sorry about this."

"Hey, it is what it is. I knew you were married, so it's not like I should have expected anything one way or the other."

"I never should have contacted you on Facebook."

"Maybe. But I was the one who responded and then asked you to get together with me. So, I'm just as much at fault."

"Well, for whatever it's worth, I did enjoy my time with you. You're a wonderful guy, Michael, and any woman would be lucky to have you."

"Yeah, but it's you I really wanted."

Charlotte sat with the car running and wished she'd thought long and hard before being with him. She'd made a careless and very selfish mistake, and now Michael had been hurt in the process. Not to mention, she'd hurt Curtis, too, except he just didn't know about it.

"Well, hey," he said. "I have to head out for a meeting, but you take care of yourself, okay?"

"I will. And you do the same, Michael."

Michael told her good-bye, and Charlotte wanted to cry. What was wrong with her and all these terrible decisions she kept making? She had a whole list of things she'd done since marrying Curtis and even before she'd married him, she'd started sleeping with him while he was still married to his first wife, Tanya. Charlotte hadn't thought twice about it at the time. Although, back then she'd been very young and hadn't known any better, but today was different. Right now, she was in her thirties, and there was simply no excuse. It was almost like she felt entitled when it came to doing whatever she wanted as long as it made her happy, regardless of whom she ended up harming in the process.

Charlotte reached to turn her ignition off but stopped when her phone rang. Her stomach stirred when she saw the word Private.

"Hello?"

"So how are you on this beautiful but very cold morning?"

"Why are you calling me again?"

"I told you I'd give you some time to get used to all of this. Remember?"

"Well, I don't have anything to say to you."

"Oh, I think you do. You'd better have a lot to say or

else I'll be calling the good Reverend Black with the quickness."

"So is this a regular thing for you? Meeting women, sleeping with them, and then threatening to tell their husbands?"

"No. Not a regular thing at all. Actually, this is only my first time."

"But why me?"

"Like I told you the other day," he sang. "All in good time. When I'm ready, you'll know everything."

"You know what?" Charlotte said, tiring of him. "You go ahead and call my husband or anyone else you want to, because he'll never believe you. He'll just think you're some crazy person who doesn't have anything else better to do."

"I don't think you want that."

"My husband knows I love him, and by the time I tell him *my* truth, he'll laugh in your face."

"I'll tell you what. I'm going to end this call with you and send you something. Then, I'll call you back," he said and hung up.

Charlotte waited for a couple of minutes and then heard a text message coming through. "Oh, God, no," she said after opening it. The text contained a photo of her, lying naked across the bed at that motel she'd gone to with Tom. Her eyes were closed, so he must have taken it when she'd been asleep.

This couldn't be. Not now. Not when all she'd done was sleep with this man one time.

Her phone rang again. This time when she pushed the button to answer it, she didn't say anything.

"So as you can see," Tom said, "I'm not playing with you."

"What do you want from me?" she yelled.

"You. Nothing more, nothing less."

"But I already told you the other day that I can't do that."

"You can, and you will."

"Please. I'm begging you."

"Was I that bad in bed?"

Charlotte pretended she didn't hear him.

"Of course, I wasn't," he said. "Remember, you told me how great I was."

Charlotte cringed, and a sharp pain shot through her heart. "I was drunk."

"Drunk. Sober. Makes no difference. Not to me, anyway."

"I can pay you," she pleaded.

"And I already told you I don't want that. This thing here is about so much more than a few dollars and cents."

"But I'm not talking about that kind of money. I'm talking about a lot of it."

"No. What I want is for you to meet me at our friendly little motel on Saturday."

"That's only two days away. And what am I supposed to tell my husband?"

"Tell him whatever you want. Just make sure you're there at six o'clock."

"That's too late."

"Well, we could meet earlier in broad daylight, if you prefer that."

Charlotte felt like she was suffocating.

"Look, I'm not going to argue with you about this.

Either meet me on Saturday or tell your husband to expect a copy of that photo I just sent you. I do have his cell phone number. Or have you forgotten that?"

Charlotte knew there was no way out of this and hung up the phone. She tried figuring other options, but in the end she knew she had to do what this man demanded. She had no choice but to drive over to Chicago on Saturday to have sex with him, just one day before Valentine's Day, and she could barely fathom the thought of it. She could hardly stand the idea of being forced to sleep with a total stranger and then betraying Curtis all over again. She hated herself more than ever.

Chapter 32

Curtis strapped the seat belt across his body and backed out of Aunt Emma's driveway. He'd just dropped the little one off for the day and was still in awe of how well things were going between him and Charlotte. She even seemed a bit more tolerant of Curtina, strangely enough, and all he could hope was that it would continue. He prayed her tolerance would soon become total acceptance and ultimately a normal mother-daughter relationship. He knew this would probably be a long time off, but Charlotte's new attitude was very encouraging. He also knew this total change was a result of Matthew's hostage situation. Curtis would never have wished such a dangerous experience on his son, but he was glad it had made Charlotte think. The whole scenario had truly opened her eyes, and life was better for all of them.

Curtis was glad about something else, too: that he hadn't slept with Sharon. He had certainly come close, that much he couldn't deny, but what mattered was that he'd walked away with no regret. Sure, he'd been attracted to her and had gotten himself caught up in the idea of sleeping with her, but that was already in the past. It had been over before it ever got started, and he was at peace about it. So at peace he picked up his phone to call her. He could easily never speak to her again, but he wanted to tell her where things stood with them. He wanted her to know that his coming to visit her never should have happened, and that this would be his last time speaking to her by phone.

But before he could dial her number, Raven called him.

"Hey, Raven," he said.

"Hey, Pastor. I tried you at home, but your housekeeper said you were already headed to the church."

"I am. Wanted to get in early this morning."

"Oh. Well, anyway, the reason I'm calling you is because I won't be in today. My car won't start, and I'm having it towed to the dealership."

"I was really hoping you'd be at our monthly budget meeting."

"I know. But when I called the service department a few minutes ago, they said all their loaners were either gone already or had been promised to other people who have repair appointments."

"Well, if you want, I can swing by and pick you up."

"You don't mind?"

"Of course not. I should be there in about twenty minutes."

"I really appreciate this."

"See you soon," Curtis said and then dialed Sharon.

"Hello?" she said.

"Hey, how are you?"

"Now that I'm talking to you, I couldn't be better."

"Well, that's sort of why I'm calling. Look, I never should have started calling you, and I definitely shouldn't have come to your home. It was wrong, and I apologize. But this will be my last time phoning you."

"I'm really sorry to hear that. I'm not upset about it, though, because whether you think so or not, you *will* call me again. It might not be tomorrow or even next week, but you'll contact me sooner or later."

"No. I won't."

"But you wanted me too badly the other day not to. I saw the look in your eyes, and had your phone not vibrated with that text message from your son, you would have stayed. You would have made love to me, Curtis, and you know it."

"But things are different now."

"Is that right?"

"It is."

She chuckled like she didn't believe him. "Whatever you say. Nonetheless, I'll be waiting on you for however long it takes. You and I have this thing between us. This burning desire that will never go away. But like I told you before, I'm very patient."

"I won't call, and from now on, the only time I'll see you is at church."

"You do know what this is about, don't you?"

"Yes. Me doing right by my wife and my children."

"No. This is about your son and that incident at his school. I saw the whole story on the news. Things like this tend to bring families very close together and can even help sustain a bad marriage. But only for a little while."

"That's where you're wrong."

"No, I don't think so. But you'll see."

"Well, that's all I called to tell you."

"Talk to you soon," she said.

Curtis hung up and turned into Raven's driveway. She wasn't standing in the doorway and he didn't see her looking out, so he called her cell.

"Hey," he said when she answered. "I'm here."

"Oh, okay. Um, Pastor, there's something I really need to talk to you about. So, would you mind coming in for just a few minutes?"

Curtis glanced at the clock on his dashboard. "No, actually, I need to get to the church. But we can talk on the way if you want."

"That's fine. I'll be down shortly," she said.

Curtis wondered what that was all about. Especially since she sounded disappointed about his not agreeing to come in. Now he wondered if there was something wrong with her car after all.

He sat for a few minutes, and Raven finally came out and got into the truck. She didn't say anything, though, and looked out of sorts.

"So, what's up?" Curtis finally said, heading down the street. "What is it that you wanted to speak to me about?"

"Us."

"I'm not sure I know what you mean by that."

She turned her body toward him. "Us. You and me."

"But I thought we already cleared that up."

"I thought so, too, until you asked me to stay after when our meeting was over on Tuesday."

Curtis squinted his eyes. "And?"

"You told me I shouldn't feel bad about these feelings I have for you."

"No. What I said was that you shouldn't feel bad about the things you told me."

"That's the same thing."

"No. Not to me it isn't."

"You also said you weren't offended."

"Okay, but what does that have to do with anything?"

"It means you understand and that you don't have a problem with it."

"I think you misunderstood our whole conversation. The reason I had that little talk with you was so you wouldn't feel uncomfortable about anything. I was trying to clear the air so that it wouldn't be hard for us to work together."

"What about the way you look at me whenever I'm leaving your office? You did the same thing when I left the conference room. Even without looking back, I could feel your eyes all over me."

Curtis wasn't sure how she'd sensed it, but she was right. He had scanned her entire body. But that was two days ago and this was now. Two days ago, he'd been a confused man who was being ignored by his wife. Today, he was happily married and had no desire to look at another woman in that way, let alone be with her.

"Look," she said. "I won't tell anyone. This can be our little secret. No one else will ever have to know. We can enjoy each other, and then you can go home to Charlotte. I won't cause any trouble. I just want to be with you. That's all."

"Raven, I don't wanna talk about this anymore. I'm married, I'm not getting involved with you, and that's that."

"But why?"

"I just told you."

"So are you saying that if you weren't married to Charlotte, you and I could be together?"

"I couldn't guarantee it, but the bottom line is that I *am* married. So none of what we're talking about really matters."

"It matters to me, Pastor."

Curtis decided to leave well enough alone and not say anything else. But he wondered what was going on with Raven. She'd been so apologetic the other day, but now here she was coming on to him again. He also had a feeling she'd staged her so-called car problem, and that her plan had been mainly about getting him inside her house. Women.

They rode the rest of the way to the church in silence but when they parked, Raven switched gears on him again.

"Pastor, please forgive me. I don't know what came over me. I'm very sorry. My actions were completely uncalled for and if you want to fire me, I will totally understand. You certainly have every right to."

"No, that won't be necessary. We all make mistakes."

"I promise I won't approach you like this again. I'll get over these feelings I have, and things will go back to the way they used to be with us. Everything will be strictly business."

"I'm glad to hear it," Curtis said, and they both got out and went inside the church.

Chapter 33

Curtis hadn't been sitting at his desk for more than an hour when he asked Lana to summon Raven into his office.

"You wanted to see me, Pastor?" Raven said, walking in.

"Yes, and please close the door behind you."

Raven did as she was told and took a seat.

"I know we basically finished this conversation during our ride here, but I just want to make sure we're on the same page about everything."

"Okay."

"You keep saying you have all these feelings for me, and I keep telling you that I'm married. But what if these feelings of yours don't go away?"

"They will. It might take a while, but they will go away eventually."

"I can live with that. But what I can't live with is the way you've been approaching me. When you first did that in my office, I sort of blew it off, but now today, this was something different."

"What was different about it?"

"Well, first of all, you lied about your car needing to be repaired. Am I right?"

Raven stared at him, clearly caught and definitely embarrassed. "I just didn't know any other way to get you to my house."

Curtis sighed. "Well, you know how I feel about people I can't trust."

"I know. And I'm sorry. It's like I told you earlier. I don't know what came over me. I won't ever lie to you again, though, Pastor. That I can promise you."

"Can you imagine how upset my wife would be if she ever found out about all of this? And what if I had come into your house like you wanted me to and someone saw me?"

"But you didn't come in. And it's not like your wife will hear about any of this, anyway."

"Well, actually, she will, because I'm planning to tell her everything," Curtis said, lifting his phone. "Lana, please tell Barry and Joel they can come in now."

Barry and Joel were two of the security guards who worked for Deliverance Outreach on an as-needed basis, whenever Curtis had "issues" that needed to be dealt with. Curtis had asked Lana to call them right after he'd arrived this morning.

They both strolled in and Barry, the more muscular of the two, walked right up to Curtis's desk and stood next to Raven.

"What is this?" she asked.

"Ms. Jones, we need you to come with us," Barry said.

"For what?"

"You're being let go, and we've been asked to escort you from the building."

"Pastor, what are they talking about?"

"Your services are no longer needed here."

"You're firing me? After you told me you wouldn't do that?"

Curtis glared at her.

"Ms. Jones," Barry said. "Please come with us."

Raven stood up. "I don't believe you. But that's okay because when your wife hears that you were at my house this morning and that you've been coming on to me for weeks now, we'll see who gets fired."

"Now, Raven, you know that's not true."

"Sure it is. And it's not like you can deny it because all of your staff members just saw us walk into the church together."

Curtis pulled the miniature tape recorder from his lap and placed it onto his desk. "Like I said. You know that's not true."

"You were taping me? You actually set me up?"

Joel took her by her arm. "Let's go, Ms. Jones."

"Let me go! And I hope all of you know I'm not leaving here until I box up my things."

"That won't be necessary," Barry told her. "We've already collected your purse for you, and we'll have the rest of your items delivered this afternoon."

"No! I'll do it myself."

"Let's go," Joel said, and the three of them left Curtis's office.

Lana rushed in right after. "Pastor, what's going on?"

"I didn't have time to tell you this when I first got here, but Raven came to me last week, saying she had feelings for me."

"What?"

"Yeah. And then this morning, she called to say her car wouldn't start, but when I arrived to pick her up she tried to get me to come inside."

"Please tell me you didn't."

"No. But then on the way here she kept trying to come on to me and then, all of a sudden, she started apologizing again. And that's when I knew she was going to be a problem."

"Oh my. I'm stunned. Raven? Of all people."

"Yeah, I was shocked, too."

"Well, you sure didn't waste any time getting rid of her," Lana said, laughing. "I mean, I know this isn't funny but you got her out of here lickety-split."

"I had to. Raven knows everything there is to know about our financials, and I couldn't take any chance on her doing something dirty. That's why I wanted to record our conversation and then get her out of the building. If I hadn't, she would have tried going back to her office and doing only God knows what."

"I guess you're right."

"I know I am. Especially since right after I told her she was fired, she tried to threaten me."

"Goodness. What is the world coming to? You just can't trust anybody these days."

"No, you can't. Not even the most innocent person."

Chapter 34

Charlotte walked inside Robin's Hair Creations and laughed to herself. Some things never changed, and one would think that after coming there for as many years as Charlotte had, it wouldn't bother her. But it did. She knew it wasn't her business, but she just couldn't understand why every stylist in the place continued stacking clients on top of clients when they knew they were only able to work on one head at a time. It was ludicrous to think they could do more, although Charlotte knew that, actually, they didn't think anything of the sort. What they wanted was to make as much money as possible, even if it meant making customers wait more than an hour before they were even shampooed. Robin, Charlotte's stylist and owner of the salon, sometimes did this, too, but not with her. No, with Charlotte, it was a much different story because Charlotte still paid her double the price so that Robin wouldn't book anyone else during Charlotte's two-and-a-half-hour time slot.

It was amazing how Charlotte played this entire scenario through her head every time she came there, but again, it really bothered her. It was one of her pet peeves, she guessed, and she couldn't help herself.

Charlotte hung up her coat and then spoke to the three women who rented booth space from Robin.

"Hey, Charlotte," Robin said, already waiting for her.

Charlotte went over and sat down in the styling chair. "So how are you?"

"I'm good, and I'm loving those jeans you have on, girl. Who are they?"

"Donna Karan."

"Nice. I'm also lovin' that sweater and those boots, too."

"Thanks."

Robin wrapped a cape around her. "So what are we doing today?"

"Just a wash and condition."

"Let's go then," she said, starting toward the shampoo bowl.

Charlotte took a seat and leaned her head back, and Robin turned on the water.

"So how's Matthew doing?" Robin asked.

"He's fine, and thanks so much for calling to check on him yesterday."

"I still can't believe that happened. But I'm glad he made it out of there okay."

"We all are. Such a blessing."

"Definitely. And how's Pastor Black doing?"

"He's fine as well."

"And Curtina?"

"She's good."

"Glad to hear it."

"And what about you?" Charlotte asked. "How's everything on your end?"

"Girl, don't even ask."

"Why? What's wrong?" Charlotte was glad no one else was back in the shampoo area, so they could talk a little more freely.

"Shoot, where do I begin?"

"This sounds bad."

"It is. Reggie just told me last weekend that his former girlfriend is eight months pregnant."

"What?"

"Yeah. That was my response exactly."

"How long have you guys been together?"

"Only for six months, but still."

"Did he just find out?"

"No, and that's part of the reason I'm so pissed off. He knew right away when we started dating, but he didn't tell me. Claims he was afraid I wouldn't keep seeing him if I knew."

"Wow. So what are you going to do?"

Robin reached for the bottle and added more shampoo to her hands. "I don't know. But I really hate this because now I feel like I can't trust him. He shouldn't have kept this from me. Plus, I'm not sure I wanna deal with any baby mama drama. Actually, I'm not sure I wanna deal with another woman's baby, period. But there's one problem with that."

"What?"

"I love Reggie. I mean I really, really love him, Charlotte."

"That's hard. And you know I understand that better than anyone."

"I can't even imagine."

"It's hard, and while I've never shared this with you before, ever since Curtina came into the picture, I've been miserable. At first, it was because of Tabitha and how she kept trying to be with Curtis. Then, when Tabitha starting being sick all the time, Curtina started staying at our house more and more. But the worst has been since Tabitha died."

"Why is that?"

"Because Curtina now has to live with us for good."

"Do you think you'll ever feel better about it?"

"I don't know. But for the sake of my marriage, I'm really trying."

"Just knowing that Reggie is about to have his first child with another woman really hurts," Robin admitted.

"I'm sure it does. I was devastated when Curtis first told me Tabitha was pregnant. But at least with Reggie, he didn't start dating you until after the fact."

"But he still kept it from me."

"He definitely should have been up front with you, but if you love him maybe you should just see how things go."

"I guess. I won't have him hanging out at her house all the time, though. He can either pick his baby up when he wants to see it and bring it to his house or not see it at all."

"I don't blame you. Because some women never move on. They always feel like they have a connection with a man if they have a child with him, and they never get past it. That's how Tabitha was, anyway."

"That's what I'm afraid of. Reggie claims she's not like that, but that remains to be seen."

Robin lathered Charlotte's hair twice, rinsed it one final time, and saturated it with conditioner, and then placed a clear plastic cap on her head. As they walked over near the dryers, Robin said, "Oh no. Look."

They both moved closer to the TV screen.

"We've just learned that Harold Rush, the history teacher who held three students hostage earlier this week, has died," the female anchor stated. "Rush had also been in the news because of child molestation charges and had just been arrested one day before the hostage incident. However, he posted bail the very next day, went to his home and picked up a handgun, and then drove to Mitchell Prep Academy. Rush is survived by his wife and a stepdaughter. This story is continuing to develop, and we will bring you more during our five o'clock broadcast."

"Matt is going to be so hurt over this," Charlotte said and then heard her phone ringing. She grabbed her purse, and ironically, it was Matthew calling. "Hey, sweetie."

"Mom, did you hear?" he said, choking up.

"I did. And I'm so sorry, Matt."

"I knew he was gonna die. I knew it."

"Well, at least you did all you could."

"But it wasn't enough. I just wish I'd known what it was I was supposed to say to him."

"Mr. Rush was a very sick man, sweetie, so please don't beat yourself up over this. It's not your fault."

Matthew sniffled, and it killed Charlotte to hear so much pain in his voice. She hated that he was blaming himself for Mr. Rush's death.

"I'm going home."

"I don't think you should be driving. So, why don't you call your dad to pick you up?"

"I'll be fine."

"You don't sound fine."

"I'm just a little upset is all."

"Are you sure?"

"Yes. I just wanna go home."

"I wish you would call your dad, but okay. Straight home. And I'll be calling you in about twenty minutes."

"Okay, Mom," he said, sounding slightly irritated, and Charlotte knew it was because she was babying him again.

"I love you, and you drive safely."

"I love you, too, and I will."

Charlotte got under the dryer and called Curtis.

"Hey," he said.

"Hey. You busy?"

"A little. But I have a few minutes. What's going on?"

"Mr. Rush died."

"That's too bad. Have you spoken to Matthew?"

"Just hung up with him, and I could tell he was crying. He said he was going home."

"That's probably best," Curtis said.

"I agree, but I wish he didn't have to drive himself. I told him to call you, but of course, he didn't want to."

"He'll be okay. I'll check on him in a little while."

"I told him I'd call him, too."

"I'm sure he's taking this hard."

"He is, and it's all because he was right there when that gun went off. He didn't actually see it, but he was right there."

"We're probably going to have to get Matt counseling."

"I think that's a good idea, and I don't think we should go to lunch now," Charlotte said.

"No, I'll just come straight home when I finish up with this last meeting. Oh, and I have some other news for you, too. It's about Raven."

"What about her?"

"I'll tell you later. You won't believe it."

"Okay, well, I'll see you soon."

"I love you, baby."

"I love you, too."

Chapter 35

*W*ell, I'll say this much," Charlotte said. "You were definitely right when you said I wouldn't believe it. I mean, Raven was always so nice. So pleasant to be around."

Curtis lifted one of the smaller barbells from the floor. "She fooled all of us."

Normally, Curtis did his workouts first thing in the morning before anyone else got up, but with all that had gone on over the last couple of days he hadn't gotten around to it. Now he was warming up his biceps, but it wouldn't be long before he lay on the bench and lifted more pounds than Charlotte cared to think about. In the meantime, she sat around watching him. They hadn't done this in a long time, talking nonstop about everything going on in their daily lives, and Charlotte was glad to be doing that again.

"So, did you get all the locks changed?" she asked.

"Is your name Charlotte Black?"

Charlotte chuckled and so did Curtis.

"Did you call Carl?" she said, asking about Janine's husband since he owned a locksmith business.

"Yep. I asked Lana to call him as soon as Raven was out of there, so it's all taken care of."

"Good."

Curtis raised the weight with his right arm and lowered it. "All I know is that I'll be glad when this week is over."

"Me, too. First this whole Mr. Rush situation and now Raven. Although, I was really happy to see Matt doing a lot better when we got home, because he was so sad when he called me at the hair salon."

"He was definitely in much better spirits, and I think he'll feel better all the time."

"I hope so."

"He will. And hey, this is completely on a different note, but earlier I was thinking about Valentine's Day. It's coming up this weekend, and I thought maybe I would ask one of the associate ministers to deliver the sermon on Sunday, so you and I can spend the night in downtown Chicago on Saturday. We've had such a rough couple of months, so I really want that day to be special for us."

Charlotte would have loved nothing more than to spend a romantic evening with Curtis on Saturday, but she couldn't. She had to meet Tom instead.

"Oh, baby, I'm so sorry," she said, already preparing the lie she was going to tell him. "But when you and I weren't really speaking, I planned a spa afternoon with Mom and then dinner at six. And while I know she would understand if I canceled, I really hate doing that because we haven't done anything together in months."

"Don't even think twice about it. Go have a good time. We all only get one mother, and if mine were still here I'd be doing everything I could with her."

Charlotte hated deceiving Curtis. He was being so sincere and so understanding, but it wasn't like she could tell him the truth. She wouldn't tell her mother the truth either and would simply call her and tell her she needed her help. She would tell her that if she somehow spoke to Curtis after Saturday and the subject came up, that she needed her to lie for her—convince him that they had in fact spent the afternoon at the spa and had then gone to dinner in the evening. Charlotte would also ask her mother not to answer the phone at all on Saturday or any day before that, just in case Curtis tried calling. The only thing that might go wrong with this plan was if Curtis called his in-laws and Charlotte's dad answered, because he would never lie for Charlotte under any circumstances.

"I wish the timing was better," she said. "But I'm glad you don't mind."

"Of course, I don't." He did the last of his repetitions and set the weight back on the floor. "Come here," he said, grabbing her and pulling her closer to him and relaxing his arms around her waist.

Charlotte clasped her hands behind his neck. "You have no idea how happy I am right now."

"I know the feeling, baby."

"I really am sorry about this weekend," she said again, feeling guilty.

"Will you stop talking about that, woman? I'll make reservations at one of our favorite restaurants right here in town and then, if you want, we'll still book a hotel room in Chicago for that evening and just come back on Monday."

"I would really like that."

"I think I'll go ahead and do the message on Sunday morning after all, but I'll keep it short. Then, we can spend the rest of the day with just the two of us."

"I love you so, so much, Curtis," she said, kissing him.

Curtis kissed her back but they stopped abruptly when Matthew said, "Get a room, lovebirds."

He was grinning at them, and even Curtis laughed and bumped fists with him, but Charlotte was a little embarrassed. Clearly this was a guy thing, but Charlotte still wasn't comfortable having her son see her kissing Curtis as passionately as she had been when Matthew had walked into the workout room.

"So how are you feeling?" Charlotte asked him.

"Better than I did when I was at school."

"I can tell that, and I'm glad," she said.

"Seeing you guys happy again has really helped me, too."

"I'm sure it has, Matt," Curtis said. "And we're sorry for making you worry about us the way I know you have been."

"I was worried for all of us. Our whole family."

Charlotte caressed her son's face. "Well, you don't have to do that anymore, because your dad and I are fine now."

"That's right," Curtis said. "We're good."

Matthew raised both his arms, stretching his body like most growing boys do. "I think I'll go get a pizza, so do you want me to pick up Curtina while I'm out?"

"Yeah, actually, I do," Curtis told him. "Make sure you get her car seat out of the truck, though."

"I will. Oh, and can we go to Mr. Rush's funeral?"

Charlotte wanted to tell him no, but didn't want to hurt his feelings. "We can if you want."

"I do."

"Then we'll go," Curtis said.

"Okay then, I'm out of here."

"Drive safely," Charlotte told him. But when he was

gone, she said to Curtis, "If we go to that funeral, what will the other parents think?"

"I don't know. To be honest, I would rather not attend either, but this isn't about us. It's about Matthew and what will make him happy."

"I know a man died, but that same man sexually molested those two girls and got one of them pregnant. Then, on my way home, Elijah's mom called and told me that there's a rumor going around about him having done the same thing to his stepdaughter."

"How sick."

"Very sick, and that's why I have no desire to be there."

"All we can hope is that Matthew somehow changes his mind."

Charlotte leaned against the wall. "I know Matt has a big heart, but it's almost as if he's forgotten the reason Mr. Rush was arrested in the first place."

"No, he hasn't forgotten. Because yesterday, I heard him talking on the phone to Jonathan. He was saying how even though Mr. Rush was wrong for the crimes he committed and deserved to be in prison, he still didn't think he had deserved to die. Plus, you know Matthew has never thought anyone should have to die because of wrongdoing. Remember when he wrote that lengthy paper back in junior high, explaining why the death penalty should be eliminated?"

"How could I forget? He took it so seriously, he drove both his English teacher and debate coach crazy."

They both laughed at how persistent Matthew had been, but Charlotte couldn't deny how many valid points he'd made back then. He'd only been maybe thirteen, but he had easily caused many adults to rethink their positions. Mr. Rush hadn't been executed, but somehow this whole dilemma made her think about Matthew's passion toward anything he fully believed in or his passion toward anyone he thought needed help.

"So," Curtis said, pressing his body against her. "Where were we before our wonderful son came down here and interrupted us?"

Charlotte smiled. "I think you know."

"I do, and since Matt will be gone at least an hour, maybe we should take this party upstairs."

"Maybe. Or we could also keep our little party going right down here."

"Makes no difference to me. Here. There. Because either way you know what's about to happen."

"No. But I can't wait for you to show me."

Chapter 36

Saturday had arrived in record time, and Charlotte had tried her best to reschedule her meeting with Tom. She didn't have his cell number, what with him always blocking his number whenever he called her, but thankfully he had phoned her yesterday morning. She'd begged, groveled, and pleaded with him to change the date or cancel it altogether, but Tom had straight out refused. He'd even become a bit indignant in his tone and had told her he didn't want to hear another word about it, and that she had better be there at six p.m. sharp.

So now, Charlotte had just left the mall and was heading in the direction of the motel. She'd been gone most of the day, hanging out with her mom, shopping and then having lunch, so at least this part of her lie to Curtis had worked out perfectly. She'd called her mom as planned, and while she hadn't told her about her blackmail situation, she had reminded her that if Curtis asked, her mother needed to say they'd had a girls' spa day and had then gone to dinner. Charlotte could tell her mother hadn't felt comfortable with it, but as always, she'd agreed to do what she'd been asked. She did whatever she thought was necessary to keep her daughter's marriage intact. Then, as more luck would have it, her father was away on an NBA trip with some men's organization, so there wouldn't be a problem with him either. She knew anything was possible and that Curtis might just up and call her dad out of the blue on his cell phone, but it wasn't likely.

Charlotte drove onto the interstate and looked at her navigational screen. She was only about thirty minutes from her destination, but it was barely four-thirty. Maybe she could stop at another mall on the way and see what new makeup the M.A.C. store was promoting. Either that, or she could park and call Alicia or Janine to see what they were up to. But as she debated whom to call first, her phone rang. Charlotte cringed when no number showed up.

"What is it?" she said.

"There's been a change of plans," Tom told her.

"What kind of change?"

"The location. I'm up in Madison, Wisconsin, visiting some relatives so I want you to meet me at this motel outside of Fontana instead."

"But I'm already in Chicago. So, if it's okay with you, I'd rather meet at the original spot."

"No. Fontana is a lot more convenient for me, so Fontana it is."

"What's the name and the address?" Charlotte asked, not wanting to argue with him.

Tom rattled the information off. "And please don't keep me waiting."

"Whatever," she said and hung up.

But Tom called her right back.

"One more thing," he said. "I've already checked in, so just come to room number eight."

Charlotte hung up again without saying a word. This was ridiculous, and she was tempted to call her cousin Dooney, who would jump at the chance to help her. But she couldn't take the chance on him finding out she'd been silly enough to sleep with a stranger. She also didn't want him knowing she'd messed around on Curtis, because it just wouldn't sit right with Dooney. He was a thug, but he loathed women who slept around on their boyfriends or husbands.

Charlotte pulled to the side of the road, entered the new address into her nav system, and started back on her way. Rose, the nickname she and Curtis had given both their extremely polite guidance experts, recalculated the distance, and Charlotte saw that Fontana was sixty miles from where she was currently. Meaning there wouldn't be any time to spare after all.

Charlotte turned her radio to XM 33, the Praise channel, and heard one of Shekinah Glory Ministry's latest singles. Sometimes she listened to XM 62, Heart & Soul, but today she needed to be uplifted. She needed to hear a song of hope as well as one about forgiveness, because after all the many sinful things she'd done, she needed God and Curtis to forgive her. She needed them both to understand that she was only human and that humans didn't always make the right decisions. Sometimes they tried, tried, and tried, and still failed at it miserably.

As the music played, Charlotte traveled closer and closer to her dreaded destiny. She just didn't want to do this, and she wondered how long Tom was planning to keep this pathetic game of his going. She also wondered for the hundredth time why he was doing this. She'd come up with all sorts of ideas, but none of them made any sense. The whole thing was a total mystery, and Charlotte wanted to get to the bottom of it.

After taking the last exit, Charlotte drove down a two-lane street, turned onto a second one, and then drove onto the frontage road where the motel was located. It looked just as unglamorous as she'd expected, and she couldn't wait to be out of there.

She drove around until she found the room Tom was holed up in and parked. Suddenly, though, her nerves got the best of her, and she could barely will her legs out of the car. But she knew Tom wouldn't be happy about her not showing, and she just couldn't have Curtis learning about this. She couldn't and wouldn't allow Tom to ruin her life or her happy marriage.

Charlotte left the car and knocked on the door.

Tom opened it, smiling seductively. "Well, don't you look as beautiful as ever?"

Charlotte walked in and felt dirty already. She had never felt filthier and wondered how many prostitutes had turned multiple tricks in there.

Tom reached his arms out to hug her, but she pushed him away.

"Awww. Now, don't be like that, sugar boo," he said, taunting her.

Charlotte's skin crawled.

"Have a seat," he instructed.

"You know what?" she said. "Let's just get this over with."

"What's the big hurry? Especially since we have all night together."

"No, we don't."

"Oh yeah. I forgot. You have to get back to the good reverend, don't you?"

"Exactly. So, like I said, let's get this over with."

Tom ignored her. "Have a drink."

Charlotte watched him pour what looked to be some sort of cheap wine into two glasses. "No, I don't think so."

"You know, I'm really not liking this little uppity attitude of yours. You're really killing the vibe in here."

The television played and the volume was turned down pretty low, but Charlotte kept her eyes glued to it. She pretended to love whatever sitcom she was watching, but if she could somehow get away with murdering Tom, she would.

Tom sat enjoying himself like he was at a ritzy country club. "Sure you won't have some?" he said, lifting his glass toward her.

Charlotte didn't even bother responding.

Finally, after another ten minutes or so, he said, "Take all your clothes off. Every single stitch."

His tone was angry, but Charlotte still hesitated. She didn't move.

"Did you hear me?"

"I heard you fine."

"Then, I suggest you do what I told you. Either that or I'll send that photo of you to your husband right now."

Charlotte closed her eyes, stood up, and undressed herself. Then she slid into bed very quickly. Tom stripped off his shirt, pants, and underwear faster than a few seconds and got in next to her. He kissed her wildly, and she wanted to vomit. Then, he did what he'd come there to do, and now Charlotte knew what it felt like to be raped. It was almost as if she was having an out-of-body experience, so she went to a whole other place, far away from this roach-motel room and was glad when Tom had finished and rolled off of her.

He panted like a thirsty bloodhound, and this time Charlotte really did throw up. She'd never felt more sick, and all she wanted was to be out of there and on her way back home where she belonged.

"You were even better this time than before," he struggled to say between breaths.

But just when Charlotte got out of the bed, someone knocked on the door. They knocked once, twice, and then a third time, and Charlotte was terrified that someone might recognize her. So she hurried to get her clothing on.

"Uh-oh," he sang. "Sounds like we have a visitor."

Charlotte didn't like the sound of that and knew something wasn't right.

Tom slipped on his pants and then went to the door. Charlotte pulled up her jeans without having a chance to zip them and rushed to put on her sweater. Still, Tom opened the door before she'd had a chance to get on her boots or comb her hair, which was scattered wildly on her head.

But none of that mattered anymore when she saw Matthew walking in.

"Mom?! What are you doing? And who is this man you're with?"

"Oh God, Matt. Who told you to come here?"

"I got a text from a Chicago number saying that you wanted me to meet you here, but that you didn't want me to tell Dad."

"What?"

"That's right," Tom said with great pride. "It *was* a Chicago number, and the call came from me. I sent it so your son could see just how slutty his mother is. I wanted him to see with his own eyes."

Matthew tossed Charlotte a dirty look. "Why, Mom?"

"Sweetie, it's not what you think."

Matthew glared at her, and Charlotte had never seen him more disappointed.

"Matt, please," she said, walking toward him. But he turned and left her standing there. He walked out into the night, and Tom shut the door behind him.

"What kind of sick monster are you?" Charlotte yelled.

"Hmmph. Darlin', this is only just the beginning," he said.

Charlotte burst into tears.

Chapter 37

There was a time when Valentine's Day had been one of Charlotte's favorite holidays of the year, but not this one. Not when she'd been forced to have sex with some heartless maniac less than twenty-four hours ago and her son had nearly caught her in the act. She'd tried finding words to describe what it felt like, having your innocent child witness something so crass, but there weren't any. Your child whom you'd carried around for nine whole months and would give your life for. The child you'd been trying to protect since the day he was born—the child who hadn't spoken to you since he'd seen you standing in the middle of some tenth-rate hole in Wisconsin.

Last night, right after walking inside the house, Charlotte had spoken to Curtis, who'd been down in his study working on the last part of his sermon, and then she had gone straight up to Matthew's room to talk to him. But when she'd knocked on his door, he'd asked who it was, she'd told him, and he hadn't responded. So Charlotte had eased his door open and gone in anyhow. As soon as he'd seen her, though, he'd turned his back to her and slipped on his iPod earbuds. He'd wanted nothing to do with her, and she'd had no choice but to leave him alone.

Curtis strutted into the bedroom, dressed in a charcoal suit, pure white shirt, accented with a turquoise tie and matching silk handkerchief. "Don't you look gorgeous on this beautiful and very blessed Sunday morning," he said, complimenting her newest cream-colored, custom-made suit and matching four-inch, pointed-toe pumps.

"Thanks," she said, trying to sound upbeat. "You look pretty handsome yourself. Same as always."

"Here," he said, passing her an exquisitely wrapped silver box.

Charlotte was a little surprised because he'd already had the florist deliver two dozen roses to her this morning and had also given her a five-hundred-dollar gift card to her favorite local spa, along with a Jimmy Choo handbag. So she wondered what this was.

"Wow," she said, untying the wide red ribbon and removing the lid. She felt like melting when she saw a stunning pair of diamond and sapphire earrings. "You didn't have to do this," she said, hugging him. "Baby, thank you."

"I wanted to do it. You deserve that and so much more, and that's why I spent the better part of the afternoon yesterday looking for them. So, as it turned out, I was glad you spent the day with your mom because it gave me an opportunity to go shopping for you."

"Now I feel like I should have gotten you something more, too."

"Please. You got me a Cartier watch, so what more did you need to get?"

"Still," she said, feeling even worse about taking a shower last evening and then telling him she was too exhausted to make love. But she just hadn't been able to fathom doing something like that all the while knowing she'd had sex with that jerk, Tom, only a few hours before.

"You're funny," he said, pecking her on the lips. "But hey, since we still have a little more time before we have to leave, I'm going to head back downstairs so I can trim down my sermon a little more."

"Okay. I'll be down soon," she said, still fighting back tears. She was terribly distraught, but when Curtis was out of sight, she went down to Matthew's room. The door was slightly ajar, so she knocked and walked in. "Matt, I really need to talk to you."

Matthew acted as though he hadn't heard her and never stopped looking at the television. He also still had on pajama bottoms and a T-shirt, so his decision to skip church was pretty evident.

"Matt, please. I never wanted to be there. You have to believe me."

Matthew still ignored her.

"Sweetie, you have to talk to me about this."

Matthew put on his earphones, the same as he'd done last night, and Charlotte knew there was no sense staying. As she walked back to her room, tears flowed down her face, and she couldn't stop them. When she was back sitting on her bed, she cried more. *Oh God, please give me strength. Father, please console my heart, and give me peace of mind.* Charlotte prayed and then, suddenly, Curtina appeared out of nowhere. Charlotte looked at her and wiped her face with both hands.

Curtina walked closer. "Mommy cry."

Charlotte wasn't sure what to say, but Curtina took her little hand and now she wiped one side of her stepmother's face, too.

"Mommy cry," she said again and Charlotte grabbed her into her arms, crying uncontrollably.

Charlotte held her close, and to her surprise, she was comforted. She cuddled this child whom she'd walked around ignoring, resenting, and hating—this child she'd wanted out of her life forever. Charlotte hugged her, and Curtina finally said, "Up Mommy."

Charlotte knew what that meant, so she lifted her onto her lap, and Curtina tried wiping her tears away again. She stroked Charlotte's face with both her tiny hands, and Charlotte had never been more grateful for anything. She also couldn't remember having her prayers answered so quickly. She'd asked God for peace and consolation, and He'd given it to her through Curtina. It was all very strange, but it just went to show that God truly did work in mysterious ways. He was true to His Word, and Charlotte was quickly reminded of one of her favorite Scriptures, Matthew 11:28: "Come to me, all of you who are weary and carry heavy burdens, and I will give you rest."

Charlotte had gone to Him, and He had delivered, like always.

Chapter 38

They'd been sitting and having breakfast for nearly an hour, yet Matthew still hadn't said a single word to Charlotte. He simply had nothing to say, and there was only so much opportunity she had to try to talk to him when Curtis wasn't around. She certainly didn't want to beg and plead for his forgiveness and then have Curtis asking what she needed to be forgiven for. So she'd been very careful about the times of day she'd approached Matthew. Actually, she hadn't thought she would have any chance trying yesterday evening at all, but then she and Curtis had decided not to drive over to Chicago the way they'd planned. They hadn't gone because Curtis had insisted something was wrong with Matthew, and he hadn't thought they should leave him. Charlotte had agreed wholeheartedly because she knew there *was* something wrong with him. Something major and extremely heart-wrenching. Curtis, of course, had thought maybe he was having a minor setback relating to Mr. Rush's passing, but Charlotte knew otherwise. She knew Matthew was mainly distressed about his mother.

She was just sick over Matthew making that trip up to Wisconsin and then finding her with another man, because she knew he would never forget it. Even when years passed and he had found a way to forgive her—she hoped—he would always remember that cold Saturday night in February when he'd driven a half hour from home, only to have his heart ripped out. Charlotte hated herself for this.

"Son, what's wrong?" Curtis asked.

"Nothing."

"Are you depressed about Mr. Rush?"

"No."

"Well, you're not yourself."

"I'm fine, Dad."

"Do you still want to attend his services tomorrow?"

"No. I changed my mind."

"Why?"

"I just did."

Charlotte saw the concerned look on Curtis's face, and she was worried, too. It was bad enough Matthew had already been on an emotional roller coaster over the last week, and now there was this daunting thing with her. He seemed so downtrodden, and what hurt her the most was that he wouldn't even look at her.

"Mommy, look," Curtina said, showing her some little doll she'd been playing with.

Charlotte forced a smile on her face. "I see it, sweetie. She's beautiful just like you are."

Matthew jerked his head up and finally *did* look at his mother. Even Curtis raised his eyebrows in disbelief and then smiled at her. This was the first time the two of them had seen Charlotte acknowledge Curtina genuinely, and she was glad they'd been able to witness it. To be honest, she was still a little shocked herself because not once had she ever believed she would feel good about Curtina, and she certainly had never counted on caring about her. It was as if she'd been changed in the blink of an eye, and some sort of spell had been cast upon her. But she definitely didn't believe in witchcraft and knew, without a doubt, her astonishing change of heart was all God's doing.

Matthew slid his chair back, stood up and grabbed his book bag. "See you, little girl," he said to Curtina, kissing her as usual.

"Bye-bye."

"See you, Dad," he said, bumping knuckles with him and then left for the garage. Charlotte wanted to cry, but knew she couldn't. Matthew was really through with her, and she was glad Curtis had been so busy reading the newspaper, he hadn't noticed anything—he hadn't noticed that for the first time since Matthew had been a small child leaving for school, he'd left without hugging Charlotte.

Curtis got up from the table. "Well, I guess I'd better get going, too. But when I get home, I think we should sit down and have a talk with Matthew. See what's really bothering him. I do think it's about Mr. Rush, but I just want us to be sure. I also think it's time to consider counseling for him like we talked about."

Charlotte wasn't sure she liked the idea of the three of them sitting down to do anything together. What if Matthew snapped and told Curtis everything? What if he'd had enough of his mother's shenanigans, those from long ago and now her most recent act of mischief, and wanted to set the record straight?

"Yes, I think we should," she said, but only because she knew this was what Curtis wanted to hear.

"I think he'll be fine, but I also think we should be on the safe side."

"I do, too."

"And thank you, baby," he said, lifting her chin and kissing her.

"For what?"

"Putting forth so much of an effort toward accepting Curtina. You have no idea how amazing that makes me feel."

"It's no problem," she said, wishing she could tell him why she now saw Curtina in a different light: her little stepdaughter had consoled her when she'd been feeling her lowest yesterday morning.

"I really wish you and I could have had an overnight trip, but I still enjoyed our dinner and, well, just being together."

"I enjoyed our time, too."

"We'll still get downtown, though, and soon."

"I wish you didn't have to work on your day off."

"I know," he said and went over and slipped Curtina's coat on. "Me, too. But I still have a lot to catch up on from last week."

"Well, have a good day," she said. "You, too, Curtina."

"Bye-bye," she said.

When they were gone, Charlotte finished reading the latest issue of *Essence* and then called to check on Agnes. She'd arrived right on schedule this morning and fixed their breakfast, but then she'd left because she wasn't feeling well. Charlotte hoped she was going to be okay, because February was definitely flu season.

About an hour later, after getting her walk in, she went up to her office and signed on to Facebook. She hadn't been on in the last couple of days and couldn't wait to see what was new. The first thing she did, though, was check her inbox, and she saw that she had a message from Michael. She wondered why he was still trying to contact her after she'd explained that she couldn't see him anymore. However, maybe he had good reason, so she opened it.

Hey, when you get a chance, please call me. It's urgent.

Charlotte wondered what was so important, and it made her nervous. She called him immediately.

"Hey you," he said.

"Hey. So, what's up?"

"I called to let you know that Sybil knows about us."

"What? How?"

"She says she knew about you when I started seeing you years ago, and she knows you met me at Gerald's a couple of weeks ago. But it gets worse."

"What?"

"She knows I rerouted my Miami flight to West Palm Beach, and that you were there with me. She's been paying someone to follow me, and to be honest, I didn't think she had it in her. I mean, women do that all the time, but not women like Sybil."

"What do you mean by that?"

"She's so laid-back and nonchalant. She's angry as I don't know what, but I just wouldn't have pictured her calling any private detective. If you want to know the truth, I didn't even think she was smart enough."

"So what is she planning to do with all this information?" Charlotte asked, fearing the unthinkable.

"She's threatening to tell your husband."

"You . . . have . . . got . . . to . . . be . . . kidding . . . me."

"No, I'm not. She's blaming you for our breakup."

"Why? Because it's not like the two of you have been happy for years now."

"I know. I told her the same thing but she said that regardless of how many affairs I've had, this was the first time I saw a reason to file for a divorce."

"That's crazy."

"Well, maybe. But, actually, she is right because it was only after I fell in love with you that I knew I couldn't be with her anymore. I knew it was finally over between us."

"Unbelievable. Do you think you can stop her from calling Curtis?"

"I doubt it. She's a woman scorned, and I don't think there's much anyone can say to her at this point."

Charlotte wanted to laugh out loud just to keep from crying. This just couldn't be. Not now, when she was still trying to figure out how to end this Tom foolishness and make things right with her son.

"This isn't good," she said.

"I know, and I'm really sorry to have to tell you all this."

"I'm sorry, too. Very sorry that I slept with you. I never should have done that and now my marriage could be ruined because of it."

Michael didn't say anything.

"Why are you so quiet?"

"You don't wanna know."

"I do. So tell me."

"Look. For your sake, I don't wanna see your marriage broken up. But I'd be lying if I said it would make me sad. Not when that would mean I'd finally have a real chance at being with you."

"I can't believe you're saying that."

"I'm just being honest."

"I have to go," she said.

"Baby, please don't be angry with me."

"Good-bye, Michael."

Charlotte tossed her phone onto the desk. How dare he wish that something bad would happen between her and Curtis? Yes, she knew he'd said he was in love with her, but he also knew she was in love with her husband. Michael knew because she'd told him so. He knew this was the reason she'd made it clear that she couldn't see him again.

But what was she going to do now? What if Sybil was on the phone with Curtis at this very moment, disclosing everything? What if Curtis then called her to confront her about it?

Charlotte paced back and forth, wishing she had a drink to calm her nerves. But she knew alcohol wasn't the answer, because alcohol had been part of the reason she'd been so quick to sleep with that Tom.

Charlotte's phone rang, and all she could think was, *Speak of the devil.*

"What do you want?" she screamed.

"You, of course," Tom said, snickering. "And how's that kid of yours?"

"He's horrible, thanks to you. And why on earth did you involve him in this?"

"All in good time. You'll know soon enough. But in the meantime, I want to see you again."

"No. I'm not doing that anymore."

"You'll do what I tell you, or I'll send that little porn picture of yours to more than just Reverend Black."

Charlotte felt faint and quickly sat down in her chair.

"For example," he went on, "I wonder what your parents would think about it? Wonder how they'd feel about all the whoring around their little girl is doing."

Charlotte couldn't speak.

"What's the matter? Cat got your tongue?"

Charlotte still said nothing.

"Ignore me if you want. But you *will* do what I say or face consequences."

Charlotte just sat there.

"Oh," he said. "And I'll call you with the location and time in a few days. You take care now."

Charlotte set her BlackBerry down and wept. Lately she cried all the time, but she knew she had reason. Plenty of reason and far too much of it.

She wondered if maybe she should simply go ahead and tell Curtis the truth, so this part of her nightmare would be over with. But she knew he would never forgive her for this, just like he would never forgive her for Michael—once he learned about her affair with him.

He would probably never speak to her again, and neither would Matthew. They would shut her completely out of their lives, and she wouldn't be able to bear that. There wouldn't even be a reason to live.

Chapter 39

*C*urtis read through one of the résumés the head-hunter had e-mailed him an hour ago. It was a pretty quiet morning, but he knew that was because not every staff member at Deliverance Outreach worked on Mondays. Many of them had various duties on Sundays just like he did, so it was only right that they only had to work four days during the week.

Curtis set aside the résumés of two potential candidates and skimmed through another. Some lived right there locally and others lived in the Chicago area, but they all seemed very well equipped to handle a CFO position. He was also looking forward to speaking with a guy Anise was highly recommending, since he currently worked as a VP of Finance for a large nonprofit organization. The other plus was that he was a man. Curtis wasn't a male chauvinist and had no problem hiring any woman as long as she was the most qualified and a good fit for the position, but after that whole Raven fiasco, hiring a man would be a welcome change.

Even though four days had passed since Barry and Joel had escorted her out of there, Curtis was still pretty dismayed by her actions. She'd done a great job for the church and had seemed very well put together as a person, but then she'd switched her persona. She'd turned into someone he didn't know, and he was glad he'd never gotten involved with her. Even the thought of what she might have done had he given in to temptation and had actually slept with her was disturbing, because there was no telling what the outcome would have been.

Then there was Sharon, who hadn't been able to take her eyes off of him during service yesterday. He knew this not because he'd been staring at her nonstop but because every time he occasionally looked her way, her eyes were fixed on him. He wouldn't deny that she made him feel a bit uneasy because of the chemistry they definitely had between them, but he was serious about not calling or seeing her again. He'd made up his mind about that and was very proud of his decision.

Curtis's phone rang. "Hello?"

There was no response.

"Hello?" he said but then saw the call ending.

He wondered if someone's mobile device had dropped the call or if someone had simply dialed the wrong number. He looked up when Lana knocked on his door, which was already open.

"I've got a few other items for you to look at and about five letters for you to sign, but it's no rush."

"Sounds good. I'll try to get to them today, but if not, tomorrow."

"So, how are things at home?" she asked.

"Actually, they're a hundred percent better. Charlotte has done a total turnaround, and she's even warming up to Curtina in a way like I've never seen her do before."

"Praise God. What a blessing."

"I know. And I have to tell you, being happy with her again has dropped my stress tremendously."

"I'm sure it has, and I'm so happy for you, Pastor."

"I appreciate that, Lana."

"Also, I let my niece read the early review copy of your book, and she said she's never been more inspired."

"Well, good. And thank you for giving it to her."

"Now, she's waiting on the next one just like the rest of us."

"I've been gradually mapping out the outline, but with all that I've been dealing with personally, I haven't done nearly as much as I would like."

"Well, at least you got this one finished pretty early."

"Yeah, and I'm glad because once we move closer to the dedication ceremony and begin all the other activities for the new building, there won't be much time for anything else. I'm also glad it won't be out until early next year, so that I'll be here regularly for at least the first six months after we move in."

"Oh that's right. You're doing a pretty extensive tour this time around."

"Yeah, it's time. I did maybe five cities for each of the last two books, but I haven't done a standard tour since Curtina was born."

"You haven't traveled much at all. Not even for general speaking engagements, because I'm still getting no less than two calls per week from churches, seminaries, and a lot of other organizations. They're still trying to book you."

"I know. My publicist has been telling me the same thing, but I just don't want to start back being on the road all the time again. Not when Curtina and Matthew really need me here right now, and Charlotte and I are finally content again."

"I completely understand. And by the way, how is Matthew?"

"Still not himself. And over the last two days, he's been more quiet than he was when the hostage incident first happened."

"Poor thing. I will certainly continue to keep him in my prayers."

"Yes, please do," Curtis said right when his office phone rang. "Yes?"

It was one of the assistants who reported to Lana. "Good morning, Pastor Black."

"Good morning to you, Kristen."

"I have a Bruce Betts on the line for you. He says he and his former fiancée came in to see you last week."

"Yes. Please put him through."

"I'll talk to you later," Lana said, and Curtis nodded.

"Good morning, Bruce."

"Good morning, Pastor. How are you?"

"I'm well, but what's this 'former fiancée' news I just heard about?"

"Well, Pastor, I just want to thank you for meeting with us when you did, because that counseling session really opened my eyes."

"It sure sounds like it."

"It did. Stephanie is definitely not the right woman for me, and I've never been more positive about anything. I mean, don't get me wrong. I love her, and it will be a while before I stop loving her, but she's just not the one. Stephanie is a woman with her own agenda and couldn't care less about our plans and our life as a couple."

"Well, I'm really sorry things didn't work out for you, Bruce, but it is better to have realized this now rather than later."

"I agree. Anyway, I just wanted to let you know and to thank you again."

"You take care of yourself, and please call me anytime."

"I will. You have a good day now."

"You, too."

Curtis thought back to his meeting with Bruce and Stephanie and had to admit he wasn't shocked over the breakup. They had two major incompatibilities, and he was sure that if he'd had the chance to counsel them again, he would have learned there were even more of them. He did feel bad for Bruce, but just as he'd told him, it was better to find out beforehand and not years and years down the road.

Curtis picked up another résumé but frowned when he heard his phone ringing again. No number displayed, just like it hadn't the last time, but he still answered it. "Hello?"

Nothing.

"Hello?"

This time Curtis hung up first. He wasn't sure if it was Raven or Sharon, but regardless of which one of them it was, he wouldn't tolerate these kinds of games. He'd ended what brief relationship he'd had with Sharon and fired Raven, and he wouldn't deal with any aftereffects. Not now or in the future.

Chapter 40

At least three hours had passed since Charlotte had spoken to Michael, but she was still nervous and very upset. Worried to death was more like it—over the possibility that Sybil would be calling Curtis anytime now. *How could I have been so stupid? Why?*

Charlotte looked out of the window, then went back to her desk and sat down. She sat there for a couple of minutes but then stood up again. The curiosity was killing her but not more than her fear of Curtis finding out the truth.

Charlotte's cell phone rang, and she jumped. The words Deliverance Outreach displayed across the screen, and she was terrified to answer the phone. She knew it was Curtis, and that he now knew everything about Michael. So, she hesitated. Her phone rang and rang, but she finally answered it before it went to voice mail. She didn't say anything, though.

"Hello?" Curtis said.

"Hey," she responded.

"Why didn't you say anything when you first answered the phone?"

"I did. There must be some sort of glitch with the volume."

"Oh. So what were you doing?"

"Not much. Why?"

"No reason. I just wanted to hear your voice and to tell you I love you."

Charlotte breathed normally again. What a relief.

"I love you, too, baby," she said.

"And hey, did you check on Agnes?"

"I did. She sounds terrible, so I told her to take the rest of the week off if she needs to."

"I'm sure she wasn't happy to hear that."

"No, she wasn't. You know how she hates missing work."

"That I do. I hope she feels better soon, though."

"I'm sure she will. So, have you thought about what you want for dinner tonight?"

"Not really, but I'm fine with just about anything. Actually, I can pick something up on my way home, if you want."

"That would be great, because I really don't feel up to going out today."

"Are you okay?"

"I'm fine," she said, lying. "Just lazy is all."

"Nothing wrong with that. If I were home, I'd be lounging around myself. But duty calls."

"I wish you were here, too."

"Well, baby, I'd better run, but I'll see you this evening."

"I love you."

"I love you, too."

Charlotte set the phone down and thanked God she was still safe. So far, Sybil hadn't called Curtis yet, and the longer she took to do that, the better Charlotte would feel. Maybe—just maybe—Sybil would realize calling Curtis really wasn't going to benefit her in any real way, and she would change her mind about contacting him. Maybe she'd realize it wasn't worth causing problems for someone else just because her marriage was over with. If only Charlotte could be so fortunate.

Charlotte browsed a few department store websites and then read some of the day's headline stories on AOL. She clicked on one after another, but then her phone interrupted her concentration. She looked over at it and saw that infamous word again: Private. It was Tom, of course, but she decided to ignore it. It rang and finally stopped, but then he called a second time. Then he dialed her back again, and also a fourth time. She wasn't sure why he was calling, since she'd just spoken to him this morning, but she couldn't talk to him right now. She couldn't deal with hearing whatever he so desperately wanted to say to her. Not when she had to focus on this Sybil and Michael problem.

Charlotte went back to reading an article on health care and the ridiculous congressional fight that was still lingering because of it, but her phone rang yet again. If this was Tom, she was going to read him his rights and tell him where to go. Thankfully, though, it was Janine instead.

"Hey, J," she said.

"Hey, how are you?"

"Girl, where do I begin?" Charlotte said, ready to pour her heart out. She didn't want to tell anyone, but if she didn't confide her feelings soon she was going to burst.

"Oh, no. This doesn't sound good."

"Do you have a little time?"

"I do. I just finished my last class for the day."

"Well, the thing is, I had an affair on Curtis."

"Charlotte, no," Janine said.

"Yes. I did."

"When?"

"Over the last two weeks. It wasn't long at all, and I've already ended it."

"Does Curtis know about this?"

"No, but Michael, the guy I was seeing, says his wife does and that she's threatening to tell him."

"How did she find out?"

"She had Michael followed. Even when we were in Florida together."

"So that's who you went away with during Super Bowl weekend?"

"Yes, and I'll regret it from now on. I regret the whole thing."

"How did you meet this guy?"

"I dated him right before Curtis and I started seeing each other again. But a couple of weeks ago, I was searching for people on Facebook and decided to look him up." She then told Janine the rest of the story.

"What are you going to do?" Janine asked, sounding very hurt by what she was hearing.

"I don't know. What can I do, except wait?"

"You have to tell him, Charlotte. You have to tell Curtis the truth as soon as possible."

"I can't."

"You have to before he finds out from this guy's wife or maybe even someone else."

"Curtis will never forgive me for this one."

"But if you tell him yourself, he'll receive the news a lot better than if some stranger does it."

"Maybe, but I just can't face him. I can't look Curtis in his eyes and tell him that I've cheated on him and that the reason I did it was because he wouldn't get rid of his little girl."

"So that's why you did this? Because of Curtina?"

Tears filled Charlotte's eyes. "Yes. And I'm so sorry for that, J. I'm so sorry for the way I treated that child and for being so selfish. None of this was her fault, and I finally realize that now."

"Wow, girl, this is bad."

"I know."

"I still say, though, that you have to tell him. Not days from now either. You have to tell him today."

"Janine, please don't hate me."

"Of course I don't. What you did is wrong, but you know you're my girl and nothing will ever change that."

"I really needed to hear that because, suddenly, I'm feeling so, so alone," Charlotte said, thinking about Matthew. She just couldn't bring herself to tell Janine about what was going on with him and why he was so angry with her. She couldn't tell her about any of this Tom madness and how he was blackmailing her.

"Don't think that for a minute," Janine said. "I'm always here for you."

"I hope you mean that because I have a feeling I'm going to need you more than I ever have."

"So are you going to talk to Curtis when he gets home?"

Charlotte sighed. "Yes. I don't know how I'll find the courage, but I will."

"I know it's going to be hard, but it really is the best thing for you to do."

"I just hate this. I hate what I did, but there's nothing I can do to take it back now."

"No; but at least you can tell Curtis the truth and then hope he'll agree to work things out with you."

"I wish I could believe that was possible. Maybe if I hadn't already cheated on him in the past. But you and I both know I did. And then I had a baby."

"You've both done things to hurt each other, and I'm sure Curtis will consider that."

"Maybe. But who knows. I guess time will tell soon enough, though."

"I'll be home all evening, so I want you to call me if you need me."

"I will. And thanks, J. Thanks for listening and for all your advice."

"You're welcome, and I'll be praying."

"Thank you for doing that."

"Talk to you later, and I love you, girl."

"I love you back."

Charlotte hung up and debated calling Curtis right now, so she could tell him she needed to talk to him about something. But maybe she would just wait until he got home. She wasn't sure how she should handle this, however, and before she could think more about it, she saw the word Private on her phone screen again. "Why do you keep calling me?" she yelled. "Why won't you just leave me alone?"

When the ringing stopped, thankfully, Tom didn't call back. But it looked like he'd left a message at some point. The Alert symbol was displaying too soon for him to have left one right now, so he must have done so when he'd called one of the other times.

She signed into the system, keyed in her password, and waited for the message to play.

"Hey, I'm not sure why you're ignoring me, but I wanna see you tonight. I know I told you we'd get together again on Saturday, but I've changed my mind. So you'd better answer your phone the next time I call you."

"Please press seven to delete or nine to save," the lady from the automated menu stated.

This was going too far, Charlotte thought, and now she knew she would eventually have to tell Curtis about Tom, too. But not today. No, today she had to focus on Michael, so she could come up with the best story she could. She would tell Curtis the truth—somewhat—but what she had to work on now was coming up with the right kind of words to say. She had to make him sympathize with her and even feel guilty about the part he'd played in causing this to happen. After all, he'd slept with Tabitha for years and had brought home an illegitimate baby just like she had, so maybe this wouldn't be as bad as she'd been thinking. Curtis wouldn't be happy, but he was a very resilient man, the kind who loved his wife, and that meant there really was hope for them. She'd plead her case and then promise to be the best wife on the planet from this day forth. She would do whatever he asked or wanted until he forgot about this. Either forgot or no longer held it against her.

Chapter 41

*C*urtis glanced over at the clock on the wall and decided he'd work maybe another couple of hours and then head home. He'd gotten a lot of work done today and was thinking he might even take the morning off tomorrow and not arrive until the afternoon. Although, if he did that, he'd slowly start slipping behind again, and he didn't want that. But then again, if he did take off, he'd be able to spend some time with Charlotte, which he was so excited about these days. He would never say it out loud, but he almost felt like some schoolboy who had fallen in love for the first time and literally couldn't think straight. It was strange, but Charlotte definitely had that effect on him. Now more than she had in the past, and he was thankful for it. Thankful for her, their marriage, and the beautiful family they shared.

After reviewing the church calendar for the next three weeks, Curtis went down the list of sick and shut-in members. He normally tried to visit some of his long-time members, but lately he hadn't been able to do that. Partly because his schedule had been very full and partly because of the problems he and Charlotte had been experiencing. His associate ministers had continued making their rounds, so it wasn't like no one was stopping by to check on them, but he still liked going himself sometimes. He would get back to it as early as next month.

Curtis leaned back in his chair and rested his eyes. He'd been looking at multiple documents and gazing into the computer for hours, and he needed a quick break. He relaxed until his phone rang.

He picked it up and slightly frowned when he saw Raven's name. "Hello?"

"Pastor Black, can I talk to you?" she said, sounding pretty cordial, so maybe she'd gotten over being fired.

"What about?"

"My job, and if you could maybe find it in your heart to hire me back."

"No, that's not going to be possible."

"But why? I did an excellent job for you and the church. I worked my behind off."

"I don't deny that. But given the circumstances and the way things turned out, I think it's best you move on to greener pastures."

"But you know how unpredictable the economy is right now, so where am I going to find another CFO job so quickly?"

"I'm sorry, but there's nothing I can do for you, Raven."

"I have bills, Pastor Black, and no savings."

Curtis was a little surprised about that. Mitchell's cost of living wasn't very high, and the church had been paying her a little more than eighty thousand a year. She earned a great salary, so Curtis wondered what she'd been doing with her money.

"I don't know what to tell you," he said.

"I know I was wrong, but Pastor Black, you didn't have

to terminate me. You didn't have to take my job away from me the way you did."

"Raven, look. I'm very sorry things didn't work out for you here, but as I said, there's nothing I can do."

"But Pastor, if I don't get another job very soon, my life might be in danger."

"Why?"

"Because I owe this loan shark thirty thousand dollars."

"For what?"

Raven sniffled. "Gambling."

"Wait a minute," Curtis said, quickly leaning forward onto his desk. "Have you stolen money from the church?"

"No, no, no. But I'll be honest, I was very tempted and it wasn't going to be long before I figured out a way to do it. I didn't have a choice because just a week ago, these guys came to my house, threatening me. They said if I don't have the money by the end of this month, they're going to hurt me."

Curtis was amazed that she would even admit something like this, and regardless of how he felt about her, he respected that. She'd lied about her car being on the fritz, but he sensed she was telling the truth about this gambling addiction of hers.

"Why did they let you keep borrowing if you weren't paying it back?"

"Because the loan shark knew I had a good job, and he was fine as long as I paid back at least two thousand dollars a month. But then I missed six payments, and now he's calling in the whole thing."

"Why did you stop paying?"

"Because I wasn't winning anymore."

"People never win at gambling, Raven."

Raven didn't say anything, and Curtis knew this meant she didn't agree with him. She was an addict who believed she was simply experiencing a dry period but would be back on top any day now.

"What I suggest you do is find another job, so you can pay off your debts. Take two jobs if you have to."

"But if I don't earn enough, it won't matter."

"Maybe you should explain your situation and ask for more time."

"I already did, and D.C. doesn't want to hear that. He wants his money."

Curtis knew the D.C. she was referring to had to be the same D.C. who was close friends with Levi, the drug dealer Alicia had messed around with some time ago. Although, it wasn't like D.C. to threaten women with bodily harm, so there must have been more to the story. Nonetheless, Curtis didn't want to get involved. It was true that D.C. was one of the most well-known loan sharks in the area and didn't tend to play when it came to his business, but like Levi, he had given very generously to Deliverance Outreach. Of course, Curtis had stopped accepting money from both Levi and D.C. right after turning his life around, but he still had no issues with them. They'd understood his reasoning and respected it.

"I can't help you," Curtis told her.

"Can you at least loan me enough to make a couple of payments?"

Curtis was tiring of this. "Raven, your last check went out this morning, but that's it as far as the church is concerned."

Curtis waited for her response but there was empty silence.

"Did you hear me, Raven?"

She boo-hooed again, but then said, "I'll be dead in no time," and hung up.

Curtis now rethought his decision of not contacting D.C. Maybe there was something he could say, because as a man of God, he had an obligation to help people. He wasn't happy with Raven at all, but he also didn't want to see anyone die over money.

He thought about it a little more, and then pulled a leather booklet from his drawer. This was where he'd kept his contact listing before new technology had taken over. He searched through it until he saw "D. C. Robinson" and then dialed the number next to it.

"D.C.," the baritone voice said.

"D.C., Pastor Black here. So, how's it going?"

"Pastor, man, what's up? I'm good. And you?"

"Can't complain."

"No, I guess not because I saw the new church goin' up. Good for you."

"God is good."

"That He is and all the time," he said, and Curtis smiled because D.C. and Levi were two of the nicest criminals a person ever wanted to meet. "So, don't tell me that trick Raven had you call me. With her little sneaky, connivin' behind. Because I know she used to work for you."

"Well, actually, she is the reason I'm calling, but she doesn't know about it. I never even told her I knew you, and I'd like to keep it that way."

"No problem."

"She mentioned your name and said you were threatening to hurt her if she didn't pay back the thirty thousand dollars she owes you."

"That would be correct."

"Now, D.C., you know I've never tried to get in your business, but maybe you could go a little easy on her. Especially since she's now unemployed."

"Doesn't matter. She was behind before she lost her job, so I'm not hearin' that noise from her."

"I just don't understand why she borrowed so much money from you."

"Borrowed?"

"Yeah. She told me she borrowed the money for gambling."

D.C. bellowed with laughter. "That trick never quits. She's such a liar. The reason she owes me thirty Gs is because she stole it from me. I hired her to handle my finances, and that whore started funnelin' money to herself. I had a feeling somethin' wat'n right, and when I called in this other accountant, he confirmed it."

"Oh, I didn't know all of that," Curtis said, now wondering if maybe Raven *had* stolen money from Deliverance Outreach.

"That's because she never tells the truth, and she's always playin' the victim. I mean, she probably does have a gambling problem, but I didn't *loan* her anything."

"Well, I'm out of it," Curtis said, and then he and D.C. laughed and chatted like old friends. They talked about the past and the future, and Curtis even encouraged him to give up the kind of life he was living.

That's when D.C. said, "Okay, now you're startin' to make me feel guilty, so we should probably end this conversation."

They both laughed.

"Maybe one day, though," D.C. said. "Maybe one day I'll give up the life just like Levi claims he has."

"So how is he?"

"He's good. Hanging in there, and he should be out fairly soon. He swears, though, he's done dealin' drugs and has completely turned his life over to Christ."

"Glad to hear it. And when you talk to him again, tell him I'm very proud of him."

"I will."

"Well, it was good talking to you, D.C."

"Same here. I mean, I haven't laughed like this in months, and I enjoyed it. As a matter of fact, you've brightened my day so much, I'm gonna give that trick, Raven, three or four months to find a job. I don't normally soften up like this, you know, but you got me feelin' all sympathetic and compassionate. So, she better thank her lucky stars you called me."

"She was wrong for stealing from you, but I'm glad you're willing to give her a pass this time. A temporary one anyway."

"It's all good. Also, if you don't mind my asking, why'd you let her go?"

"She kept trying to come on to me."

"Really? That's interesting."

"Why do you say that?"

"Because when she suddenly got the hots for me and started claimin' she had all these that's when I got suspicious. That's when my money came up missin'."

"Is that right?"

"Yeah, man, so if I were you I'd call in a few CPAs."

"D.C., I'm already ahead of you."

*ə *ə *ə

When Charlotte's phone rang, she jumped. It was Curtis calling, and since she'd already spoken to him twice today, she knew he could only be dialing her back for one reason. Sybil had blabbed to him. She heard two more rings and finally pressed the Send button.

"Hey," she said, waiting with bated breath.

"Okay, you'll never believe this, but the Raven saga continues."

Charlotte's body cooled down almost instantly, and her muscles seemed less tense. "Now what?"

"She stole money from D.C., but she called me this afternoon, saying she'd borrowed it from him."

"D.C., Levi's friend?"

"That's the one."

"Wow, how did she get caught up with him?"

"She claims it's because of gambling, but who knows? Anyway, I'm not taking any chances, so I've asked Elder Jamison to hire a couple of auditors to go over our books."

"That's a good idea, but I sure hope she didn't take anything."

"Well, if she did, you know I don't take kindly to thieves or to people who betray me."

Charlotte's muscles tensed up again. *How am I ever going to tell him what I did?*

"This is too much," she said.

"Yeah, but we'll see how it turns out and go from there. Oh, and before I forget, Matthew called me earlier to say he was going over to Elijah's after school."

"Did he say how long he'd be there?"

"No, but you know it will be a while. So, maybe I'll

start heading home in about an hour and will pick up Curtina a little later. I think Aunt Emma was taking her over to Anise's for dinner, anyway."

"Sounds good. I'll see you soon."

Gosh, things had really changed. Normally, Matthew always called her when he was planning to visit his friends or go elsewhere after school—but not anymore, she guessed. She couldn't think about that now, though, because she had to calm her nerves, practice her words, and create the saddest possible facial expression. She needed to make Curtis feel sorry for her and like he could never live without her. She had to become a wounded duck, so to speak, so he would pardon her without punishment. She had to hone her acting skills before he got there.

Chapter 42

It had been two hours since Curtis had called Charlotte about that lunatic Raven, and she couldn't wait for him to get there. She'd been a nervous wreck all day but was finally ready to confess about Michael Porter. She was still slightly apprehensive, but in the end she knew Janine had been right and that Curtis had to be told about this. Charlotte had to tell him first, before that miserable Sybil did it for her. It was always better to own up to terrible deeds, anyway, rather than to be caught undercover, so she was glad this was almost over.

Finally, she heard the garage door opening and waited by the island. Thankfully, Matthew still wasn't home yet, because this way she could talk to Curtis calmly and privately. Things would be pretty tough right after she disclosed her secret, but she was confident they could and would get past it. She had to believe Curtis's love for her outweighed the colossal mistake she'd made.

Curtis walked in, looking as though he was ready to kill someone and slammed his keys onto the counter. Charlotte stepped backward.

"So, when were you going to tell me?" he shouted.

Charlotte swallowed hard and knew Sybil had already gotten to him.

"I'm going to ask you again. When were you going to tell me?"

Charlotte covered her mouth. "Baby, I'm so sorry. I didn't mean it," she said, moving toward him.

"No! Don't touch me."

"Please, baby. Let me explain."

"Explain what? That you're the biggest whore of the century?"

Charlotte locked her fingers in a praying position. "Curtis, please, please, please. Please listen to me. This whole ordeal with Tabitha and Curtina had me all messed up, and I just wasn't thinking clearly. I was completely out of my head."

Curtis jerked his tie loose and undid the top button of his shirt. "I just don't understand you. I mean, is it that hard for you to keep your legs closed? Is it that hard to sleep with just one man?"

"No, and I didn't plan any of this. I was hurt, then one day I was on Facebook, and the next thing I knew I was contacting Michael. After that, one thing led to another and before I realized it, I'd let him talk me into flying down to Florida for the weekend. But I never meant for things to go that far, and I ended it right away. I told him last week I couldn't see him anymore, and I haven't."

Curtis looked puzzled. "Michael? Who's Michael?"

Oh God, please don't let this be happening.

"Who's Michael, Charlotte?"

She tried answering him, but she couldn't speak.

"So, what are you saying? You've been sleeping with *two* different men at the same time? Because I'm talking about this guy named Tom." Curtis pulled out his cell phone, pressed a few buttons, and shoved it into her hand. "I'm talking about the man who sent me five different naked photos of you and then called me to gloat about it."

Charlotte slowly dropped down into the chair, and tears slid down her face. She was speechless and knew there was no sense trying to defend herself.

"Why don't you take a look," he yelled. "Take a look at all of them. The three with just you lying across the bed asleep and looking like some filthy prostitute and then the other two with both of you."

"He's been blackmailing me," she said.

"Yeah, I'm sure he has, but did he make you go to that club, get drunk, and then drive to some cheap motel with him?"

"I told you, I was confused. I was still hurt over all those years you slept with Tabitha. I was hurt over the way you snuck her in and out of your hotel rooms whenever you traveled. Then you brought home a baby, Curtis."

Curtis held up both his hands. "Just stop it, Charlotte. Stop all that fake drama, because it's not going to work this time."

"But we've both made mistakes. We've both done things, and now all we have to do is start over."

Curtis laughed. "Start over, huh? You think it's that simple?"

"I do. It's simple because we love each other and we can fix this."

"But what about Matthew? What about the fact that he drove to some grungy motel and found you with another man? Is that simple, too? Can you fix that?"

Charlotte's heart dropped. Tom hadn't left out much

of anything, and she wondered why he'd done this to her. Why he'd chosen her as a target and acted as though he was trying to fulfill some sort of vendetta.

"Yeah, I know all about that," Curtis said, snatching up his keys. "And you make me sick."

Charlotte got up. "Curtis, please don't leave," she said, grabbing his arm. "Please let me talk to you."

Curtis yanked his arm away from her. "Talk to me about what? What is it you have to say that you haven't said already?"

"A lot. So, please, just give me a chance."

"I gave you a chance when you slept with Aaron, remember?"

"And I gave you one when you slept with Tabitha," she shot back.

"And I forgave you for lying and trying to pass Marissa off as my daughter when you knew she wasn't mine. And what about this Michael person and that trip you took to Florida? Am I supposed to forgive you for all that, too?"

There was just no winning with Curtis, and Charlotte no longer had any fight in her.

Curtis opened the door leading to the garage and looked back at her. "You know it's over between us, right?"

Charlotte burst into tears all over again, her chest heaving. "Baby, please."

"It's over for good," he said and walked out.

Chapter 43

Curtis drove to the stop sign located at the entrance of the subdivision, put his truck into Park, and cried his eyes out. His heart ached violently, he was totally humiliated, and the only time he could ever remember feeling such dire pain was first when his mother had passed and then when he'd thought Matthew wasn't his biological son. How could Charlotte do this? How could she look him in his face, day after day, pretending to be so in love with him? How could she stomach the idea of sleeping with two men almost simultaneously? Was she really that much of a whore? Was sex with multiple men just that important to her?

Curtis was so angry with Charlotte he didn't know what to do, and he could literally kill her for hurting his son the way she had. First, she'd treated Curtina like dirt, and Curtis had basically allowed her to get away with it, but now she'd crossed a very treacherous line with Matthew. Curtis could only imagine how that poor child must be feeling after seeing his mother in a motel room with some stranger. He must have been mortified, and now Curtis knew why he'd been so quiet over the last couple of days. He'd been carrying around his mother's dirty little secret and probably dying inside all the time. He'd been carrying the kind of burden no child should ever have to bear, and Curtis despised Charlotte for it. He hated what she'd done to all of them, and he wanted her to pay. He wanted her to feel the kind of lingering pain that wouldn't be forgotten too easily.

Curtis watched as the car behind waited for a few seconds and then drove around him. He didn't even know what to do at this point. Or where to go, for that matter. He was so beside himself, so furious, and he wanted revenge. He needed retribution, and with the way he was feeling he didn't see what would be so wrong with that. What harm would there be in sleeping with Sharon when Charlotte had bedded two men? To him, all this meant was that it was time he leveled their playing ground. Time he showed her how the game was truly supposed to be executed—time he showed her that, compared to him, she was a mere amateur.

But then there was this ugly feeling of guilt that he couldn't seem to shake. Not about anything that had happened between him and Charlotte, but about the awful thing he'd done to Tom. Curtis dropped his head back onto the headrest and replayed their phone conversation from earlier this evening.

"Long time no hear from," Tom had said, but Curtis hadn't recognized his voice.

"Who is this?" Curtis had asked.

"Tom Johnson. Remember my wife, Patricia? The woman you had an affair with a number of years ago? You know, when you were pastor of Truth Missionary Baptist Church? And while you were engaged to your second wife?"

Back in the day, Curtis had slept with so many women, there was no telling who this man was talking about. So, he still hadn't been able to place her.

"Remember how you came to visit her one afternoon and ended up sleeping with her in my bed, and my twelve-year-old son came home early? Remember how he walked in on the two of you?"

It was then that Curtis had recalled everything and couldn't have been sorrier for it. "Tom, I don't know what to say except I'm sorry, and I'm a totally different person now."

"Sorry? What is sorry going to do? My son was so upset, he ran back out of the house, got on his bike, and was hit by a car. It took him over a year to fully recover, and even today, he still has a few aches and pains in his legs. Then, on top of that, once my wife had that affair with you, she kept on having affairs with other men and then one of them finally killed her. She tried to end things with him, but their relationship turned into a fatal attraction."

Curtis hadn't heard about that, but he'd still felt sorry about it, and yes, he felt partly responsible for Patricia's actions.

"So, you see," Tom had continued, "you ruined my life, and it took me years to get it back on track. First, I lost my wife to you, no matter how brief your affair was, then, I lost her to other men, and finally to death. And I almost lost my son to that biking accident he was in. All because you were lowdown enough to sleep with *my* wife, in *my* house, in *my* bed."

"Like I said, Tom, I'm sorry and if there is something I can do. Anything. I will."

"No, there's nothing you can do for me. But over the

last two weeks, I've done a whole lot for you. I've slept with that tramp wife of yours twice and then invited your son to come see his no-good mother at the motel she met me at on Saturday."

"What?" Curtis had said, not wanting to believe any of this.

"That's right, and he was hurt beyond imagination. I saw the kind of hurt in your son's eyes that I saw in my son's eyes years ago. But that still wasn't enough to make me feel better about any of this. You know, they always say revenge is best served cold, so when we hang up, I think you'll see what I mean. Oh, and tell your wife she should have answered my calls this afternoon. I've never liked being ignored, and this is the result."

"So, you actually sought out my wife just to pay me back?"

"No, see, that's the real beauty in all of this. Maybe even divine intervention, because I didn't go looking for her. She just so happened to show up at the club on a night I was there, and I recognized her. Knew her right away, and that's when the wheels started spinning in my head. I saw the perfect opportunity to trash your seamless little world just like you did mine, and I took it. And I must say, I couldn't be more thrilled about it."

Curtis had no words to speak, so he didn't.

"So, you don't have anything to say?" Tom had asked.

"Just that I had no idea I'd caused you so much pain or that your wife had been killed."

"Yeah, I'm sure you didn't, but at any rate, Reverend Black...you go straight to hell," he'd said and hung up.

Curtis remembered how he'd felt completely numb, how he would have taken back every one of those times he'd slept with Tom's wife if he could. But his numbness had only worsened when his phone had beeped and those five photos had come through. Curtis had been staggered by all of them, but for some reason, the two pictures Tom had taken of him and Charlotte together had hurt him the worst. Even now, Curtis still couldn't shake the images from his mind. In one, she'd been lying on her side with her back to him and with no space in between them; and in the other she'd been cuddled up close, facing him with her head on his chest like she was in love with him. She'd looked as though she'd been sleeping like a baby and had experienced the time of her life, and this had destroyed Curtis's spirit. It had damaged his soul and cut him to the core.

Curtis blinked back more tears, put the gear into Drive, and sped out into the main street. He drove all of two seconds before bright lights blinded him, and another vehicle crashed into the side of his SUV.

Chapter 44

I'm here for my husband," Charlotte said, rushing to the ER reception desk. "Curtis Black."

"Oh, yes, Mrs. Black," the young woman said. "They just brought him in by ambulance not long ago, so I'll get someone to come out and speak to you."

"Is it possible for me to go back there with him?"

"I'm sure you'll be able to eventually, but please just give me a second to get one of our ER folks."

Charlotte looked around the waiting area, then back at the other receptionists, and then down the hallway. This just couldn't be real, not with all that she and Curtis were already dealing with.

"Mrs. Black?" a thirty-something man said.

"Yes," she said and he shook her hand.

"I'm Jason Carthell, one of the physician's assistants on staff, and if you could just step over here, I'll give you an update on your husband."

"Thank you," she said as they walked a few feet away.

"Your husband was in a pretty serious car accident, and right now the doctors are working to get him stabilized. He's suffered a number of injuries, but once we can get a series of tests done, we'll have a lot more details for you."

"Is he going to be okay?"

"As I said, we're working on him right now, and of course, we'll do all we can. I'm sorry I don't have more information, but I promise we'll keep you updated as often as possible."

"Thank you," Charlotte said.

"You're quite welcome." He keyed in a code on the electronic door lock, then reentered the examination room area.

Charlotte went over to a row of chairs, took a seat, and realized she still needed to call Janine. She'd called Matthew as soon as the police had rung the doorbell to tell her the news, but he hadn't answered. She hadn't been shocked, obviously, not with him still not speaking to her, so she'd resorted to sending him a text message instead. Then, during her drive to the hospital, she'd called Alicia and her parents.

Another twenty minutes or so passed. Charlotte signed all the medical consent and insurance authorization forms one of the staff had brought her. Then Matthew and Janine hurried inside together.

"Mom, what happened to Dad?" Matthew said, walking over to her.

"He was in a pretty bad accident."

"How?"

"I don't know. It happened right outside the subdivision entrance and once the police ran his license plate number for his address, they came to inform me."

"Is he okay?"

"I don't know, sweetie," she said, crying. "They're in with him now, and hopefully, we'll know something soon."

Janine sat down next to her best friend and hugged her. "I'm so glad you called me."

"Thank you so much for coming, J."

"Did the police say how the accident occurred?" Janine asked.

"No. They didn't say much of anything at all. Although, it may have been because they knew I needed to get to the hospital."

Surprisingly, Matthew took a seat next to her, and Charlotte put her arm around him. She was worried sick about Curtis but glad Matthew was talking to her. "Your dad is going to be fine, Matt."

"You don't know that, Mom."

"I do know that, and if he were sitting here right now, the first thing he'd say is we need to keep our faith strong. So, that's what we have to do."

Matthew didn't comment, and Charlotte knew he was scared. She was, too, but she tried not to let him see it.

Not long after, in walked Aunt Emma, Anise, and Curtina. Charlotte still hadn't spoken to Aunt Emma in a couple of weeks, so she was sure Matthew had been the one to call them.

Aunt Emma hugged Charlotte. "So what are the doctors saying?"

"We're still waiting to hear something."

"I'm so sorry this has happened," Aunt Emma said.

"I am, too," Anise told her.

"Thank you for being here."

"Of course. We wouldn't be anywhere else at a time like this," Anise added.

Curtina walked in front of Charlotte, smiling. "Mommy."

"Hi, sweetie," she said. "How are you?"

Curtina kept smiling and then moved on to her brother. "Hey, little girl," he said, picking her up.

Finally, a nurse came and directed them into a family consultation room, and two doctors entered only minutes after.

"Mrs. Black," the younger of the two said, shaking her hand, "I'm Dr. Mason, one of the general surgeons, and this is Dr. Rumeister, one of our pulmonary specialists who just so happened to still be here this evening."

"Nice to meet you both."

"And I assume the rest of you are family as well?" he said, looking at the others. All but Janine said yes.

"This is our son, Matthew," Charlotte told him. "And this is my stepdaughter, aunt, cousin, and my best friend."

"Good to meet all of you. Okay, well, we've now had a chance to evaluate things a little better and do some preliminary tests. And what we know so far is that he has a pretty bad concussion, a number of skin lacerations, a slight cervical spine fracture, and a pneumothorax—or, in layman's terms, a collapsed lung."

"Oh my God. Will he need surgery?" Charlotte asked.

"Dr. Rumeister can explain that part for you," Dr. Mason said.

"Not necessarily," Dr. Rumeister said. "But right now, our main concern is his blood pressure, which is way too low, and also his heart rate, which is far too elevated. These conditions are both due to the collapsed lung situation, but we're hoping his lung will correct itself within the next forty-eight to seventy-two hours."

Charlotte didn't like the sound of this. "But what if it doesn't?"

"Then we'll need to go in with a needle to remove air

from his pleural cavity. Then, if that doesn't do the trick, we may have to do surgery and possibly remove damaged or scarred portions of his lung. This will then allow the lung to begin healing the way it should. But again, this is only if it doesn't heal on its own."

"Will his cervical spine fracture affect his ability to walk?" Anise asked.

"No," Dr. Mason said. "It's pretty doubtful, but he may have some neck pain for a while. If the injury had been to his spinal cord, we would have had reason to worry, but fortunately it wasn't. But again, we're going to keep working to get him stabilized and will keep you updated."

"We appreciate that," Charlotte said.

"Do you have any other questions?" Dr. Mason said, scanning the room.

"No," Charlotte said. "I think that's it for now."

"We'll take good care of him, Mrs. Black," Dr. Rumeister assured her.

The entire crew went back out to the waiting area, and Alicia and Phillip stood up. They both hugged everyone, and then Alicia said, "So, how did this happen?"

"We don't know," Charlotte told her, even though she knew Curtis had been highly upset when he'd left out of the driveway and that this was probably the reason he'd caused someone to crash into him.

"What are the doctors saying?" Alicia asked, taking off her leather gloves and wool coat.

Charlotte repeated everything Dr. Mason and Dr. Rumeister had told them a few minutes ago, but looked up when two police officers approached them.

One of them was the officer who had come to her home with news of the accident. "Mrs. Black?" he said.

"Yes?"

"If you don't mind, we'd like to ask you a couple of quick questions for our report."

"Sure. Please go ahead."

"Was your husband ill or upset about something? Or was there maybe some sort of emergency that caused him to leave the house so abruptly? Because not only did he drive onto the street in the midst of traffic, but he didn't have his seat belt on either."

"No," she said, lying. "Not at all."

"Do you know where he was on his way to?"

"To pick up his daughter."

"That's right," Aunt Emma added. "He'd called me this afternoon to say he was going home first and then he would come by to pick her up later."

Charlotte hadn't expected Aunt Emma to say anything, but she was glad she'd helped corroborate her story without even realizing it.

"Was anyone else hurt, Officer?" Charlotte asked. "The other driver?"

"No, amazingly, he only has a slight case of whiplash and is being treated and released."

"Thank God," she said.

"Yes," Aunt Emma said. "Thank God, he's okay."

"That's for sure," Anise added.

"Well, I think that's pretty much it for now," the officer said. "But we'll still need to speak to Pastor Black when he's feeling better."

Charlotte told them that would be fine, deciding she wasn't going to worry about that until she had to. She didn't want to think about the reason this accident had happened, and she was relieved that none of her family members knew about those photos. She was happy they didn't know a thing about her and Curtis's huge blowup or that he'd told her their marriage was over. They had no idea he'd stormed out of the house in a murderous rage.

More minutes passed, and while Matthew was trying his best to be strong, Charlotte could see tears building in his eyes. Alicia must have noticed, too, because she finally stood up and said, "Come on, Matt. Let's go take a walk."

Anise walked over to him. "Here, I'll take Curtina."

Matthew willingly passed his baby sister to his second cousin, but when he got up, his phone vibrated, and he pulled it out of his jacket. Charlotte watched him and wondered why he looked as if he'd just seen a ghost—or something worse. Then, she saw Alicia bugging her eyes, and then looking at her. Now, Matthew gawked at Charlotte, too. That is, until Alicia quickly said, "Matt, let's go," and they left the area.

Charlotte sat there in misery, trying to figure out why Tom had sent those horrid photos to a child.

Chapter 45

*I*t was shortly after midnight. Matthew was slumped down in a chair next to Alicia and Phillip, Aunt Emma had taken Curtina back to her house, and Anise and Janine were sitting near Charlotte. Over the last couple of hours, Charlotte's parents, Elder Jamison, Elder Dixon, Lana, and each of the associate ministers from the church had arrived, and now they were all waiting for another update. They'd even prayed a couple of times as a group and tried laughing and talking about some of Curtis's funnier moments, but there was still this utter gloom hanging in the forefront. Then, to make matters worse, Matthew had stopped speaking to Charlotte again and refused to even look at her.

Charlotte looked inside her purse when she heard her phone vibrating, but when she pulled it out and saw a Chicago area code she didn't recognize, she feared answering it. So far, Tom had always blocked his number whenever calling her, but now that he'd sent photos to both Curtis and Matthew, she worried that maybe he didn't feel the need to do that anymore. So, she let the call go to voice mail as she glanced around the room at other families who were either waiting to hear about sick loved ones or waiting to see a doctor themselves. She sat, trying not to think about Tom and how cruel it was for him to send those photos to Matthew and wondered why he would do such a thing. She tried pushing all of this out of her mind, but she still felt this great need to listen to the message she had a feeling Tom had left for her.

"I'm going to the restroom," she said to no one in particular, and walked down the hallway. When she strolled inside and went into a stall, she closed the door and accessed her message system.

"So, I guess you're still not taking my calls," he said. "Doesn't matter, though, because Reverend Black and I are finally even. You slept with me, and he slept with my wife—yeah, maybe it *was* a long time ago, but he still slept with her and he had no business doing that. Then, the worst part of all was when my son walked in on his mother and the good reverend. So that's why I wanted so badly for your son to walk in on you and me. But since he really didn't get a chance to see as much as my son had to, I figured I'd send him a little photo as a keepsake. At least I didn't send him all five of them, though, so I hope you appreciate that. Actually, I debated sending that photo to your son at all, and that's why I didn't send it until a couple of hours ago. But I finally decided that it had to be done. Anyway, I just wanted to let you know you won't be hearing from me again, and that I hope you have a very nice life. Ciao."

Charlotte pressed Delete and dropped her phone back into her purse. *What are the chances that any woman would go out to a club for the first time in years and then sleep with a stranger who wanted revenge on her husband? Easily one in a million.*

She pondered that whole scenario but decided she just couldn't focus on that now and exited the bathroom. As soon as she did, though, Matthew confronted her.

"Mom, I've been thinking about something," he said coldly. "And I want you to tell me the truth. Did that man send Dad the same photo he just sent me?"

Charlotte stood with a blank stare on her face.

"He did, didn't he?" he said. "And that's why Dad was so upset when he left home. That's why he drove out into the street without looking."

Charlotte's heart raced furiously. All this time when Matthew had insisted he was seventeen and no longer a baby, it wasn't until now that she really believed him—now because he'd figured out this whole mystery she'd been trying to keep a secret.

"Wow, Mom," he continued. "And to think when I told you Mr. Rush had been arrested, one of the first things you said was, 'Not everyone can be trusted. Not even people you should be able to trust no matter what.'"

Charlotte's heart beat even faster. When she didn't say anything, however, Matthew slowly shook his head in a bewildered fashion and backed away from her.

"Matt," she said, calling out to him, but he turned and left.

Charlotte wanted so desperately to break down, but she pulled herself together as best she could and went back to the waiting area. Just as she sat down, though, the doctors came out and this time spoke to them right where they were. Charlotte didn't know if this was because things were looking up or they were so bad, they didn't have time to take them to a closed-door room.

"So far, so good," Dr. Rumeister said, sounding happy

and relieved. "I did go ahead and insert a tube into the side of his chest to let out some of the air surrounding his lung, but his blood pressure is finally back up, his heart rate is a lot closer to normal, and he's even able to breathe on his own. He's still not out of the woods yet, but Dr. Mason and I feel very good about all of this."

"He really is doing as well as can be expected," Dr. Mason added. "Given his situation and the short amount of time that has passed. He's a very strong man."

"Thank you, God," Charlotte said, as did everyone else.

"We're going to monitor him down here for maybe another hour, but we'll be sending him up to the critical care unit right after that. He's still pretty groggy and probably won't be completely awake and alert for a few hours, but you'll still be able to look in on him for a few minutes."

"Thank you so much, Doctor," Charlotte said to Dr. Rumeister and then looked at his partner. "And you, too, Dr. Mason."

"You're very welcome," they both said. Dr. Rumeister added, "I didn't want to say this earlier because it really wasn't the time, but I thought you should know that my wife is probably your husband's biggest fan. She reads all his books as soon as they come out and even buys them as gifts for friends. She's also attended your church a few times in the past."

"That's wonderful, Doctor, and I hope you'll tell her how grateful we are."

"I sure will."

&a &a &a

Curtis was finally settled into his room, and Charlotte and Matthew went in to see him. Charlotte weakened a bit when she saw the bandages taped down his left shoulder and arm and also on the left side of his head, and she didn't like seeing the chest tubing Dr. Rumeister had mentioned earlier. There was also an IV being administered and the usual monitors recording his vitals.

When the CCU nurse assigned to Curtis left the room, Charlotte moved closer to the bed. "Baby, I'm so sorry, and I promise I'm going to make all of this up to you. Things are going to be so different when you get out of here."

Matthew moved closer on the other side and held on to the railing. "You're gonna be fine, Dad. You'll be well in no time."

Charlotte looked at her son, then at Curtis, and then back at her son again. "Matt, sweetie, I need to explain something to you."

Matthew kept his eyes on his dad, acting as though she wasn't standing there.

Finally, he rubbed the top of Curtis's head and said, "I love you, Dad, and I'll be here when you wake up."

Charlotte leaned down and kissed Curtis. "I love you, too, baby."

This time Matthew hurled her a look of disgust and walked out. Charlotte also left the room. She wanted to catch up to him but knew it might make things worse, so she didn't.

After everyone had taken turns looking in on Curtis, Elder Dixon, Elder Jamison, and Janine said they were heading home and would be back tomorrow. Charlotte's parents got her house key from her so they could go take a rest as well, but Alicia and Phillip had decided to stay the night at the hospital with Charlotte and Matthew.

The waiting room was a lot emptier and quieter now, and Charlotte was glad. There was one thing bothering her, however, and that was the noticeably tense vibe she was getting from Alicia, so she knew it was time they chatted.

"Alicia, can I talk to you?"

Alicia didn't say anything one way or the other. Just got up and followed Charlotte in silence.

"I just want to say I'm sorry," Charlotte said, figuring Alicia might sympathize with her since she'd had an extramarital affair before as well. "I'm not sure how much Matthew told you, but I'm really, really sorry about everything. I made a huge mistake, and I'll have to live with that from now on. But I still hope you can forgive me for what I did to your dad."

"Well, let me just say this. I do love you as my stepmother, and I've certainly made a number of mistakes myself, but if Daddy ends up dying or having any serious complications behind this, I'll never speak to you again. And to be honest, I really don't want to discuss this with you right now."

"But—"

"No, don't," Alicia stopped her. "Let's just end this conversation before I say something I'll regret."

Chapter 46

Curtis had made it through the night without any major difficulties, and Charlotte, Matthew, Alicia, and Phillip couldn't have been happier. Actually, he was wide awake and acting as though there had never been an accident. He did cough occasionally and complained about the pain in his chest, but that was pretty much it.

Dr. Rumeister walked in. "So, how's my star patient this morning?"

"Doing fine, Doctor," Curtis said, coughing again.

"You really are a lucky man," Dr. Rumeister said. "You were in a very serious accident, and your injuries definitely could have been a lot more severe."

"This is true, but the Big Man upstairs protected me and kept me in His care."

"I guess He did," the doctor agreed.

"So, when are you letting me out of here, Doc?"

Everyone laughed, including Dr. Rumeister.

"All in good time," he said and Charlotte cringed. Those were the same words Tom had told her on more than one occasion whenever she asked him why he was terrorizing her, and now she hated them. She never wanted to hear that statement ever again.

"But when is that?" Curtis asked him.

"Well, if things keep going as well as they have been, we'll get you moved to a regular room by tomorrow and then maybe home in another couple of days or so. Just depends on your lung and how satisfied I am with your improvement."

"Well, I hope you're satisfied pretty soon," Curtis said, teasing him, but then he held his chest again. It clearly hurt him whenever he breathed too deeply.

"I want *that* to get better, too," Dr. Rumeister said. "And it will once your lung is functioning again the way it should."

Dr. Rumeister studied Curtis's chart and then placed it under his arm. "Well, I guess I'll see you sometime this afternoon, then."

"Thanks a million, Doc," Curtis said.

"You all take care," Dr. Rumeister said to the rest of them and then left.

"Daddy," Alicia said. "It's so good seeing you awake and doing so much better."

"It really is, Curtis," Phillip added. "God is so good."

"That He is," Curtis agreed.

"We were all praying for you, Dad," Matthew said. "And I can't wait for you to come home."

"Neither can I, son. And where's my little Curtina?"

"At Aunt Emma's," Matthew told him.

"Oh. I know she's too young to come inside this part of the hospital, but you make sure you give her a kiss and a big hug for me."

"I will," Matthew said. "I'll go see her later on." Charlotte had wanted to say a few things to Curtis herself. She'd wanted to apologize, embrace him, and tell him she loved him. But she could already tell he didn't want to hear it. She knew because he'd acknowledged and conversed with everyone in the room except her.

"Well, Daddy, you really do need to get your rest. So, Phillip and I are going to head back home to shower and change. We'll be back by early evening, though, if not before."

"You really don't have to do that," he said. "Ninety miles is a long way to travel back and forth when you're doing it more than once a day."

"Now, you know that's not a problem," Phillip assured him.

"Daddy, please," Alicia said, dismissing her father's comment.

"Well, before you go, baby girl, I do want to talk to you about something."

What he really meant, Charlotte thought, was that he wanted to speak to Alicia alone, and Charlotte wished she knew what about. Although, chances were he was going to tell her everything about Tom and Michael. He and Alicia had an exceptional father-daughter bond, so if Curtis was going to confide this kind of personal business to anyone, it would definitely be her. He was going to bare every fiber of his being, and make Charlotte seem like the worst stepmother alive. He would say whatever he wanted, and there wasn't a thing she could do about it.

☙ ☙ ☙

"Close the door," Curtis said when Matthew, Phillip, and Charlotte had gone. "And look in my closet to see if my clothing is in there."

Alicia did what he asked and pulled out a large white plastic bag and looked inside it. "Yeah, your suit and shirt are here, but they must have had to cut it off of you when they brought you in because everything is basically in shreds."

"Is my BlackBerry in there?"

Alicia searched around and found it. "Yep."

"I know this is going to be a little awkward for you, but I need you to pull up five photos of Charlotte and then send them to both your phone and my e-mail address. That way, I'll have copies saved in two other places." Alicia looked at him strangely, and he wondered why. "What's wrong?"

"Well, actually, Daddy, I already know about these. I mean, I didn't know there were five of them, but I did see the one that was sent to Matthew."

"Are you kidding me?"

"No. And he was pretty upset, too. He also told me about his drive over to that motel in Wisconsin."

Curtis closed his eyes, still not able to comprehend what that must have been like for Matthew, but tried to keep his mind on the matter at hand.

"Then, as soon as you leave here," Curtis said, "I want you to call an attorney by the name of Richard Cacciatore. He's located in downtown Chicago, and I just spoke to him not very long ago. Anyway, let him know that I'm in the hospital, and that I need him to draw up both a financial power of attorney document and a health-care one so that I can switch all power of attorney rights over to you. You'll then need to find a local notary who will come here to witness my signature. I also want to change my will and make you executor, but we'll worry about that later."

"But why? Especially, since the doctor has pretty much said you're going to be fine."

"I need you to do this now, so that you'll be able to move all my money over to brand-new accounts within the next day or two. Then, I want you to call Solomon Foley at State Farm to tell him that I need to change the beneficiary designations on all my life insurance policies."

Alicia looked puzzled.

"Sweetheart, I'm sorry for having to involve you in all of this, but I really need you to do this for me."

"So you're not going to leave Charlotte anything?"

"Come on, now. Of course I am. She's a tramp, but she is the mother of my son. I'll leave her enough so she can continue living the exact same way she has been, and then she'll get the rest of what she deserves in the divorce settlement."

Alicia looked confused again. "Are you sure about this, Daddy? I mean, I'm angry with Charlotte, too, but do you really want to divorce her?"

"I do. I won't do it right away because of Matthew, but I am divorcing her."

"Okay, then. I'll do whatever you want."

"I appreciate that," he said, and then something dawned on him. Charlotte was money-hungry, money-minded, and as selfish as they came, so knowing her, she might be thinking of doing the same thing. Cleaning out bank accounts and opening separate everything. Which was the reason he had to stop her cold in her tracks—the reason he told Alicia to tell Charlotte he needed to see her. Now.

Chapter 47

"You asked for me?" Charlotte said, hoping Curtis had decided to give their marriage another chance. Praying he was willing to overlook their dark past and ready to celebrate their upcoming future together.

"I did. Please shut the door."

Charlotte closed it and walked over to the side of the bed. "I have so much to say to you," she started. "So much to apologize for. So much to make up for. But first we have to get you well again and then bring you home."

"Are you finished?" he asked.

Charlotte didn't like the tone of his voice or the detached look on his face. He glared at her like they were lifelong enemies, and she knew this wasn't good.

"Well, are you?" he asked again.

"I guess," she said.

"You know, before all of you came in to see me this morning, I lay here thinking for almost two hours. I thought about our marriage, how rocky it's always been, and how staying together just isn't the right thing for us anymore. It's not good for anyone involved except maybe Matthew, but there are times when I don't think it's all that good for him either. Not when we do so much arguing or end up not speaking to each other for days at a time."

"But we just got beyond all that, Curtis. Things have been great for us this last week, and we've really been happy with each other. We've been happy as a family."

"Yeah, you're right. Until you slept with two men behind my back."

"Yes, and I was very wrong for that. But Curtis, you have to take at least some blame for that whole Tom thing."

"Why?"

"He left me a voice message, saying the reason he blackmailed me and tried to hurt Matthew was because you had an affair with his wife. And that his son caught the two of you together."

"Yeah, but that was at least twelve years ago and way before you and I were even married. What I did to Tom and his son was the worst. I admit that. But your decision to party all night and then go to some motel with a complete stranger was all on you. You did that because you wanted to. And you slept with that other guy for the very same reason."

Charlotte wasn't sure what she should say at this point and could tell she was in a lose-lose situation.

"So, anyway, this is the deal," he continued. "Matthew has a little over a year left in high school, so for his sake, you and I are going to stay married until then and we're going to get along with each other. But after that, once Matt leaves for Harvard, I'm filing for a divorce. And you're moving out."

"Curtis, you don't mean that. Matt will never be okay with us breaking up, even once he leaves for college. It'll kill him. And what about Curtina? Who's going to be a mother to her?"

"Matt will be fine," he said, coughing and grabbing his chest. "And what do you mean, what about Curtina? You've never cared anything about her, anyway."

"That was before I knew how wrong I was. I do care about her. I care about her more than you realize."

"Yeah, right."

"You said yourself that I was now putting forth a lot of effort toward her. You even thanked me for it, Curtis."

"But none of that matters now. What matters is that you don't have a faithful bone in your body, and I'm never going to be enough for you. You've always wanted something more, and I can't deal with that any longer."

"But what about—"

"But what about nothing," he said. "Because I know what you're going to say. That I slept with Tabitha. Yeah, I did, but only after you slept with Aaron. So interestingly enough, this whole string of infidelity originated with you."

"So that's it for us? Our marriage is over?"

"Yes. Oh, and one more thing. Don't even think about withdrawing any large sums of money or closing any of our joint bank accounts. If you do, I'll use those photos in far more ways than Tom ever could. I'll do what I have to to protect my children and their futures."

Now Charlotte knew why he'd wanted to speak with Alicia so privately. She wasn't stupid. He was setting things up so that if something happened to him, his oldest daughter would be in control of everything. He was making sure Charlotte would only have access to what he wanted her to have access to and not a dime more. Her marriage really was finished. And she had no one to blame but herself.

Epilogue

Four Months Later

Charlotte lay in one of the hammocks, not far from the huge wraparound deck, and looked down at Curtina—who was napping peacefully with her body relaxed cozily inside Charlotte's arm and her little head lying on her chest. It was a gorgeous day in June, and as of late, being with Curtina was where Charlotte now found her greatest joy. Actually, Curtina was her only real comfort in life because while four full months had passed since Curtis's accident and they'd recently moved into the new church, he still hadn't changed his mind about divorcing her. He wasn't mean or angry, and he even included her on all the family outings he planned, but he treated her more like a sister than a wife. He'd said he was through, and he'd meant it, and Charlotte still hadn't been able to accept that. Which was the reason she sometimes went to him, asking what she could do to make him love her again. What she could do to guarantee that they did stay together forever, the way they'd promised. But he'd told her there wasn't anything she or anyone else could do to change his feelings about this. He'd insisted that too much betrayal had taken place, too much harm had been done on both their parts, and that he simply didn't trust her.

Charlotte had often wondered if maybe things might have turned out differently had she not slipped and told Curtis about Michael. Maybe if Curtis had never learned that there had been two affairs, he might have been a little more tolerant. Maybe if there had only been one man in the picture—specifically Tom, whom she cared nothing about—Curtis would have been more apt to forgive her. She had completely jumped the gun and told him about an affair he likely wouldn't have discovered. The reason: when Michael had contacted her not more than a month ago, he had admitted the truth—that he'd lied about Sybil knowing about them and that the only reason he'd told her this was so she would do exactly what she'd done. Tell Curtis herself. He'd been hoping she would disclose everything, so that he could be with her. He'd wanted her to leave Curtis and marry him instead.

Charlotte had been outraged and ultimately devastated by the time she'd hung up on him, and she never wanted to hear from him again. He'd claimed he loved her but had manipulated her thinking, caused her to become paranoid, and then sat back waiting for disaster. He'd done what was best for him and hadn't cared a thing about how she would be affected in the end.

Then, there was Matthew, who had gone to a few sessions with a counselor and had totally worked through the whole Mr. Rush dilemma, but he still sometimes looked at her with disappointment. Charlotte's relationship with him was much better than it had been; however, there was still this underlying and very subtle distance between them. She'd been hoping things would eventually get completely back to normal but now she feared that might not happen. But it was her own fault, and the most she could do was be there for him, make sure he knew he was the most important person in her life, and that she would never hurt or let him down again.

Charlotte closed her eyes, enjoying the breeze and warm sunshine. For some strange reason, she thought about Raven, the woman Curtis had been forced to terminate on the spot. Maybe the reason Charlotte thought about her, though, was because she sort of sympathized and could slightly identify with her—identify with the idea of acting selfishly and then having to deal with the consequences.

Sadly for Raven, though, there was going to be jail time involved because Curtis's suspicions had been right. Raven had cleverly embezzled nearly one hundred thousand dollars from the church and had been arrested. Charlotte hadn't been able to fathom something like this, but she guessed Raven's gambling problem had gotten the best of her, and she'd become desperate. She'd done whatever she had to in order to fuel her addiction, and it hadn't been a good thing.

But then who was she to criticize Raven or anyone else, because *she* hadn't made the right choices either. As a matter of fact, she'd made some of the worst decisions in her life and possibly wouldn't recover from them. She would go on and wouldn't give up, but it was certainly a major challenge. It was hard not having the kind of relationship she'd always been used to having with Curtis, and there were many days when all she wanted to do was break down. There were times when she didn't even want to get out of bed. But again, she wouldn't give up. Not on life and not on getting her husband to love and trust her the way he had in the past. She would make this her utmost priority.

Then, if she got him back, she would be faithful until death. She would love, honor, and never betray her husband again.

Reading Group Guide

Discussion Questions

1. If your husband conceived a child with a mistress, would you divorce him? What would be your overall reaction? Do you know someone who has experienced this in real life?

2. As you read *Love, Honor, and Betray*, did you feel that Charlotte had every right not to want Curtina living with them, or was she completely out of line? Please explain your position and opinion.

3. Do you feel that Curtis did all that he could in terms of trying to reason with Charlotte and making things right with her? What could he have done differently?

4. Were you surprised that Charlotte slept with a man she didn't know without giving much thought to it?

5. What did you think when Tom called Charlotte, demanding that she see him again or else? Were you surprised by this?

6. From the beginning of the story until the end, were you expecting Curtis to return to his old ways or continue on the straight and narrow? How did you feel once you learned his decision?

7. How do you think Charlotte's treatment of Curtina as well as her outside affairs will end up affecting Matthew? When he is older, do you think he'll end up with a woman like his mother, or will he end up being unfaithful to the women in his life the same as his father once was?

8. Did you have any idea why Tom was blackmailing Charlotte? If so, at what point did you begin to suspect it had something to do with Curtis?

9. Are you happy that Charlotte has finally accepted Curtina and is now being a loving mother to her? Do you think Charlotte's feelings are genuine? If so, why do you think she's had such a noticeable change of heart?

10. Do you think Curtis truly will divorce Charlotte once Matthew graduates from high school and heads to Harvard? What would you like to see happen with Curtis and Charlotte's marriage?

After dropping out of Harvard to take care of his new baby, Matthew Black discovers that fatherhood isn't what he expected.

Curtis Black has his own fatherhood problem when his long-lost son Dillon returns—and forever changes the Black family.

Please turn this page for a preview of

The Prodigal Son

Chapter 1

Matthew stared at his wife of ten months and shook his head.

Racquel, who was sitting at the opposite end of the chocolate brown leather sofa, looked over at him and frowned. "What?"

Matthew shook his head again. This time, his eyes screamed disappointment. But all Racquel did was purse her lips and turn her attention back to the flat-screen television. It was a noticeably warm Friday evening in May, and though Matthew was a bit tired from his long day at work, he would have loved nothing more than for the two of them to be out somewhere enjoying each other; maybe have a nice dinner and catch whatever new movie was playing. But, as usual, Racquel was contently curled up—like an unconcerned couch potato—doing what she did best: watching some awful, ungodly reality show.

Matthew leaned his head back on the sofa and closed his eyes. Not in his wildest imagination—not in a thousand lifetimes—would he have ever pictured himself being so miserable. But miserable he was, and worse, he now realized that getting married at the young age of nineteen had been a horrible mistake. He'd now turned twenty, but he could kick himself for giving up a full, four-year, academic scholarship to Harvard University, something he'd worked very hard for his entire childhood—and now *this* was all he had to show for it? *This*, a tiny, two-bedroom apartment, a twelve-dollar-an-hour job at a bank, and no love life of any kind to speak of? Not since the day he'd been born had he ever had to struggle financially. Even before he'd met his father, which hadn't happened until he was seven years old, Matthew had lived a pretty good life because his maternal grandparents had always seen to it. Then, of course, when his mom had married his dad, he hadn't gone without anything.

He must have been crazy in love or crazy out of his mind to think he was doing the right thing by getting married. He also couldn't deny how right his mother had been every time she'd warned him about having unprotected sex. He still hadn't spoken to either of his parents in more than a year—not even when they'd mailed him a ten-thousand-dollar check, and he'd torn it up—but his mom had been correct in her thinking. Matthew wasn't sure why he'd been so careless and irresponsible. However, he was proud of the fact that he'd immediately manned up as soon as he'd learned of Racquel's pregnancy and had decided to be there for both her and the baby. Then, as it had turned out, Racquel's parents had also told him that they would take care of little MJ until he and Racquel finished college—since Racquel had been scheduled to attend MIT a few months after the baby was born. So, off to Boston he had gone—and life had been great until that dreadful day in January when Racquel had gone into labor much too early. A huge blowup had ensued between his mother and Vanessa, the two grandmothers-to-be, at

Racquel's baby shower, and Racquel had gotten herself all worked up over it. Next thing anyone had known, her water had broken and she'd been rushed to the hospital.

Matthew remembered how terrified he'd been that Racquel would lose the baby, but thank God, everything had turned out well. Little MJ had been born with a respiratory problem, but he'd ended up being released from the hospital just a few days later. Although, the more Matthew thought about all that had evolved, he was saddened further because none of what had occurred on the day of the baby shower could compare to any of what had happened a few weeks afterward. His mother had concocted the most outlandish scheme, and before long, the Division of Children and Family Services had come knocking at the front door of Racquel's parents', stating that they'd received two phone calls claiming child abuse. Of course, none of this had been true, and although in the end, the truth had been exposed and Charlotte had been arrested, the whole idea of little MJ being snatched away from her had been too much for Racquel to handle. It was the reason she now regularly obsessed over their one-year-old son, and she never felt comfortable leaving him with her own parents, let alone anyone else. She wasn't even okay with Matthew taking MJ to see his sister, Alicia, or his great-aunt Emma because she feared something might happen to him or that he might be kidnapped. That whole DCFS incident had ruined Racquel emotionally, and Matthew had a feeling things would never be normal for them again. As it was, she rarely left the house, and she no longer visited any of her friends when they came home from school for the weekend. She never invited anyone over to the apartment either.

Matthew opened his eyes and turned his head toward Racquel. At first she ignored him, even though he knew she saw him looking at her, but finally, she turned toward him in a huff.

"Why do you keep staring at me?"

Matthew gazed at her. "Because."

"Because what, Matt?"

"Look at you? All that long, beautiful hair. When was the last time you even bothered to comb it? Or put on a little makeup?"

"Excuse me? Well, in case you haven't noticed, I have a baby to take care of. So trying to look beautiful is the very *least* of my worries."

"Maybe. But have you taken a good look at this place?" Matthew scanned the living room and looked toward the kitchen. Her and MJ's dirty clothes were scattered everywhere. He also saw just about every toy MJ owned strewn across the floor. "It's a complete mess, Racquel. We're practically living in filth, and you stroll around here like it's clean as a whistle."

"Like I said, I have a baby to take care of."

"Is that also the reason we don't make love anymore?"

Racquel squinted her eyes. "Is that all you care about?"

"No, but I think it's a cryin' shame that I'm a married man, yet I haven't had sex in over two months. And even when we did it then, I had to nag you for three days about it."

Racquel rolled her eyes and turned back to the television.

Matthew snatched the remote control from the sofa and turned it off.

Racquel stood up. "Are you crazy? What's wrong with you?"

"Everything, Racquel! I'm sick of this. All you do is watch those mindless reality shows, eat a ton of junk food, and then you watch *more* stupid reality shows. And I'm not sure how much more I can take."

"Oh really? Well, why don't you leave then? Why don't you just file for a divorce, because nobody's forcing you to be here."

Matthew swallowed hard. He'd known for a while that they had major marital problems, but he hadn't expected her to suggest a breakup so quickly. "Wow. So that's how you feel about me?"

"You're the one complaining, Matt, so if you want out I won't try to stop you. If you're that miserable and unhappy, then what's the point?"

"Are you saying you don't love me anymore?"

"I'm not saying that at all, but your mother ruined everything for us. She had my child taken from me, Matt. She made false accusations about me and my mom, even though neither of us would ever do anything to hurt little MJ. I nearly had a nervous breakdown over that nonsense."

"I understand that, baby, but my mother hasn't been in the picture for a while. I cut her off because of what she did, and then I married you. I stuck by you, because I love you."

Racquel didn't respond and walked into the kitchen. Matthew wasn't sure whether to follow her or not. He knew she'd been traumatized, but he also didn't think it was fair for her to blame him for his mother's actions. He hadn't done anything to cause her pain, and actually, all he'd done was try to love her and be there for her. He'd given up Harvard, a close relationship with his parents, and a comfortable way of living—all of which he hadn't minded doing as long as he had his wife and son.

Racquel walked back into the living room with a can of orange soda and a package of cookies in her hands and dropped back down on the sofa. She sat as close to the arm of the couch as she could and as far away from Matthew as possible.

"Maybe we should see a counselor," he said.

Racquel picked up the selector and turned the TV back on, but she never looked at him. "I don't think so."

"Why?"

"Because there's nothing wrong with me."

"Maybe not, baby, but you just said yourself that you nearly had a nervous breakdown."

"That was then, but I'm fine now. I'm good."

"No, you're not, and neither are we as a couple."

Racquel sighed loudly and pulled her legs under her behind. She flipped through a few channels and finally settled on ... another reality show.

Matthew wanted to protest—wanted to shut the TV off again—but instead, he got up and went into their bedroom. He dove face-first onto the bed and took a deep breath. A ton of thoughts gyrated through his mind but there was one thought that troubled him a great deal: he regretted ever marrying Racquel. He did still love her, he guessed, but he was starting not to like her very much and that wasn't good. As a matter of fact, to him, not liking the person you were married to was a lot worse than not being in love with them. If you didn't like someone, you almost hated having to be around them. Then, you eventually got to a point where you avoided them completely, and there was usually no turning back from that. Matthew hated the way he was feeling because something told him that his once happy marriage was only going to crumble even further—not just slightly but to the extreme.

Chapter 2

*D*illon smiled at his stepmother, but silently he hated her. Charlotte was a real piece of work, one of the wickedest women he'd ever met, and he couldn't stand her. The only reason he pretended that he was genuinely fond of her was for his father's sake, because he could tell that this *relationship* between Dillon—his new son—and the wife he loved so much made Curtis happy. Dillon lived for the day when he would no longer have to deal with Charlotte, but for now he tolerated her. He did whatever was necessary to remain in his father's good graces.

Take this evening, for instance; he would have much rather been spending some one-on-one time with his father, but instead, he sat there laughing and chatting with that witch, Charlotte, his bratty baby sister, Curtina, his spoiled twenty-seven-year-old sister, Alicia, and her ex-husband, Phillip. Of course, his fiancée, Melissa, had also accompanied him to his dad's house, but to be honest, he didn't want her there either. Last year, when they'd first moved to Illinois—before Curtis had learned that Dillon was his son—Melissa had sneakily helped him get close to his dad. However, as far as Dillon was concerned, she had served her purpose and he no longer needed her.

He had in fact given her an engagement ring, but that had only been so he could convince his father that they were about to be married and that they needed premarital counseling sessions with him. But Dillon certainly didn't love her—not even as tall and beautiful as she was. Still, Melissa wouldn't leave and move back to Atlanta the way he'd tried to persuade her. He'd even offered her a few thousand dollars as a way of saying "thank you"— something he could definitely afford since his father had gifted him with such a large chunk of money a year ago— a half million dollars to be exact. But Melissa had turned it down and then made it clear that all she wanted was to love him and be with him. Right now, though, his only priority was building the best father-son relationship he could with his dad, so for the most part he didn't have much time for Melissa. She was good to have around for sexual purposes and she took care of their condo pretty well, but she would never be his wife.

Dillon watched and listened as his father played with little Curtina, and for a moment a tinge of rage and resentment overtook him. Curtina had just turned six last month, and she was having the time of her life. She was by far one of the happiest children Dillon had ever seen, but what angered him was the fact that *he* was Curtis's child, too—his firstborn—yet Dillon hadn't been given the same opportunity to grow up in a loving environment the way his baby sister was. His dad had slept with Dillon's mom, denied that he was Dillon's father, and then he'd blackmailed Dillon's mom in such a cruel way that she'd taken her own life. Dillon had only been a newborn at the time, but fortunately, his aunt had been kind enough to take him in and raise him. Still, he hadn't lived the kind of life Curtina was living, because his aunt worked a lot of hours and had been forced to leave him with a lot of different babysitters; not to mention that most weeks she'd barely been able to make ends meet.

Which was the reason that even today there were times when Dillon felt like an abandoned orphan. He felt as though he were alone in this world, and that he would never fully know what it felt like to truly be loved by someone. He wasn't looking for the kind of love Melissa and other women had tried to offer him; no, what he wanted was unconditional love from a parent. Love from his biological father. Love from the man who was sitting a few feet away—the man whom everyone said Dillon looked like. Love from a father who was having a joyous time with the baby of the family and not paying much attention at all to his son. More than anything, what Dillon wanted to know was when it would be his turn. In the beginning, his father had seemingly gone out of his way trying to welcome him to the family and, yes, he'd also included Dillon in all their gatherings, but every time they seemed to be getting closer, Alicia or Curtina always interrupted them. Two months ago, when Curtis and Dillon had planned a trip to downtown Chicago to see the car show, Charlotte and Curtina had decided at the last minute to join them. Then there was the time when Curtis had invited Dillon to drive up to a church in Milwaukee where he was scheduled to be the guest speaker, but Alicia and Phillip had met them there as well. Or like tonight, when they'd originally planned on ordering Mexican food for dinner—because Mexican was one of Dillon's favorites—they'd decided against it because Queen Curtina had wanted pizza. So, needless to say, Dillon was starting to realize that Curtina would always get what she wanted and that she would always be more special to Curtis than he was. Everything was always about Dillon's two sisters, and had his brother, Matthew, not ended his relationship with his parents, Dillon was sure he'd have to compete with him, too. So again, every time Dillon looked forward to spending good quality time alone with his father, someone always went out of their way to ruin it—and Dillon was becoming a little tired of it.

But then, maybe if he hadn't gone public on television about what his father had done to his mother, his father might work a bit harder at making him a priority. Dillon hadn't wanted to go that far, anyway, placing his father on blast on live television, but that was a whole other story, and now he had to live with his decision. Although, actually, what he'd done hadn't seemed to bother his father so much at the time, and to prove it Curtis had apologized profusely to Dillon for disowning him for so many years and he'd given Dillon that huge windfall. So now Dillon didn't know what to think or what he needed to do to become his father's most beloved child—the child he cared about more than he did any of the others.

"It's getting real close to your bedtime, little girl," Charlotte said to her daughter.

Curtina was still playing with her dad but said, "Can't I stay up just a little while longer, Mommy? I don't even have school tomorrow."

"I know, but around here curfews don't change just because it's the weekend. Little girls need all the sleep they can get."

Alicia got up, walked over, and tickled her baby sister out of the blue, and Curtina squealed with laughter.

"Stop it, Licia!"

Alicia tickled her more, and Curtina squealed louder. Curtis, Charlotte, Phillip, and Melissa laughed out loud, but Dillon wanted to slap that little brat. Once again, Curtina had stolen the show, and Dillon just sat there like a stranger.

Thankfully, Charlotte told Curtina again that it was time to head up to bed.

"We'll be up to kiss you good night," Curtis told her, and she ran on her way.

"Oh well," Charlotte said, scooting to the edge of the grained-leather loveseat that she and Curtis were sitting on. "I think I'll turn in myself. I have to be up pretty early for the women's breakfast."

"Me, too," Alicia said, "so I'll be right behind you."

"I'm so glad you're going," Charlotte said. "It's gonna be a great time."

"I'm glad you invited me."

Wait a minute. Was Alicia spending the night here? Dillon knew she still had her own bedroom there, but all this time he'd been sure she and Phillip were only visiting and that they would be heading back to Chicago tonight. But apparently not. Even more so, where was Phillip staying? His dad's house was nearly a mansion, but clearly Phillip wouldn't be shacking up in the same room with Alicia, because it wasn't like they were still married. Dillon shacked up with Melissa every night, but he would never do something like that in his father's house. He had better respect for him than that.

Charlotte looked over at her former son-in-law, and it was almost as if she'd been reading Dillon's mind. "Agnes freshened up one of the guest rooms for you, Phillip. The one toward the end of the hall and around the corner."

"I really appreciate that," he said. "Especially since your *husband* and I will be getting up much earlier than you and Alicia."

"Isn't that the truth," Curtis said, laughing. "I can't believe I let you talk me into goin' fishin' at the crack of dawn."

"Best time to go," Phillip said, chuckling.

Dillon looked at his father and Phillip, as they laughed together like father and son, and his heart dropped. A part of him wanted to burst into tears, but he would never give any of them the satisfaction of seeing how hurt he was. Not only were his sisters sucking up all his father's time, but now some ex-son-in-law was going to spend an entire Saturday with him? This was dead wrong on so many levels, and Dillon could barely think straight.

"It was good seeing you again, Melissa," Charlotte said, hugging her and staring coldly at Dillon. Charlotte was so slick with her dirty ways, and Dillon knew no one else had seen the way she'd looked at him. She did this all the time, even at church on Sunday mornings, and she always got away with it.

"Thanks for having us over," Melissa said, smiling.

Alicia hugged Melissa, too. "Maybe one day my brother will step up and make you my sister-in-law . . . isn't that right, Dillon?"

What? Alicia couldn't have been serious? And what gave her the right to meddle in Dillon's affairs, anyway? She had better be glad they were at their father's because what he wanted to tell her was, "I'll marry Melissa just as soon as Phillip makes the stupid decision to marry you again." But Dillon kept his mouth shut. Instead, he sat for a few seconds thinking about how badly Alicia wanted to remarry Phillip, even though she'd messed around on him with a drug dealer. That was how she'd lost Phillip in the first place. The reason Dillon knew this was because she'd shared that pathetic story with Melissa, and Melissa had told him everything. For some reason, Alicia had taken a liking to Melissa, so maybe she hadn't seen anything wrong with fessing up about her indiscretions. Alicia had talked a lot about how even though she'd messed up her marriage, the important thing now was that she'd learned her lesson and that she was a changed woman. She'd claimed she would never hurt Phillip again, no matter what. That sort of sentiment was all fine and well, but from where Dillon was sitting all he could think about was one thing: once a slutty whore, always one. This was especially true of ridiculously spoiled women like Alicia who'd been given the best of everything since the day they were born. It was also women like Alicia who never learned from their mistakes and who always ended up doing whatever they wanted, regardless of whom they hurt in the process. Phillip would be a fool to marry that woman again.

But instead of airing such sinister thoughts verbally, Dillon finally said, "I don't know. Maybe sometime soon."

"I hope that's true," Alicia said. "She's a really good woman, Dillon."

Melissa smiled but didn't say anything.

Of course, Charlotte just couldn't help dipping in her two cents either. "She really is a wonderful person, and any man would be lucky to have her. Any man at all."

It was at moments like these when Dillon wished his father would divorce this tramp. Charlotte had made it known very early on that she didn't care for Dillon and that she would never accept him, so Dillon knew she'd only made that comment as a way to annoy him. She was indirectly taunting at him, making it known that Melissa would be much better off with someone else, and it took everything in Dillon not to physically hurt her. Sometimes he even dreamed about hurting her, and he'd be lying if he'd said those dreams didn't give him great satisfaction. Charlotte was such a hypocrite and from what Dillon had heard, she'd done a lot of whoring around herself, the same as Alicia. So, no matter how much his father loved his wife and had forgiven her, Dillon knew who Charlotte was. He knew how deceptive she could be and that he had to watch out for her. He needed to be ready for any tricks she might toss his way, and he would be. That was a guarantee.

For information on GCP African
American titles, please visit our website at
www.gcpafricanamericancatalogue.com/